Praise for Karen Kincy's
Other

"*Other* has it all: love, shifters, pookas,
and nail-biting action. What's even better,
Kincy's characters are vibrant, real and lovable.
This is a debut that leaves you aching for more."

—Carrie Jones, *New York Times* bestselling
author of *Need* and *Girl, Hero*

"This who-done-it is an unusual blend of mystery
and fantasy, starring original characters not often
featured in modern urban fantasy for teens.
I really enjoyed it."

—Annette Curtis Klause,
author of *Blood and Chocolate*

Other

Other

karen kincy

Woodbury, Minnesota

First Edition
First Printing, 2010

Cover design by Lisa Novak
Cover image © Ebby May/Digital Vision/PunchStock

Flux, an imprint of Llewellyn Worldwide Ltd.

Library of Congress Cataloging-in-Publication Data
Kincy, Karen, 1986–
  Other / Karen Kincy.—1st ed.
    p. cm.
  Summary: Gwen Williams is like any seventeen-year-old except that she is a shapeshifter living in Klikamuks, Washington, where not everyone tolerates "Others" like Gwen, but when someone begins killing Others she must try to embrace her true self and find the killer before she becomes the next victim.
  ISBN 978-0-7387-1919-1
  1. Youths' writings. [1. Shapeshifting—Fiction. 2. Supernatural—Fiction. 3. Serial murderers—Fiction. 4. Murder—Fiction. 5. Self-acceptance—Fiction. 6. Washington (State)—Fiction. 7. Youths' writings.] I. Title.
PZ7.K5656Oth 2010
  [Fic]—dc22

                                                    2010005297

Flux
Llewellyn Worldwide Ltd.
2143 Wooddale Drive
Woodbury, MN 55125-2989, U.S.A.
www.fluxnow.com

Printed in the United States of America

To my mom,
for all her fabulous help and infectious love of reading

one

I can't last much longer. It's been one week, three days, and I forget how many hours.

My belly cramps, and I curl on my bed, staring out at the stars. A delicious breeze glides through my window and cools my sweaty forehead. The air smells of summer— mowed grass, recent rain, lingering barbecue—and tempts me more than I want to admit. Shards of moonlight and shadow shift on the wall. I clench my teeth and toes and try to ride out the pain. My bedroom drifts counterclock- wise, and I shut my eyes.

It can't be good for me, not shapeshifting.

All the *don't*s I've heard circle through my mind like vultures preying on my doubts. Don't worry about what people think of Others, Gwen, they don't understand. Don't worry, Gwen, we love you just the way you are, but don't tell anyone outside the family. If they don't know you're

Other, it won't hurt anyone. And don't ever let anyone see you shapeshift, especially not the neighbors. Don't.

I shouldn't. It's stupid, dangerous, unnecessary—no, it's very necessary. Just taboo.

I kick off my blankets, slide out of bed, and lock my door. My heartbeat quickens. My breathing sounds too loud. I glimpse a pair of golden lights reflected in the mirror above my bookcase: my eyes, betraying their true nature. Most of the time I pass them off as pale hazel. Maybe my body's telling me I should be human only 50 percent of the time, because that's what I am. Half-human. The rest: a guilty pleasure, a shameful secret.

Screw it. I'm going to. I *have* to—it's as urgent as breathing.

I don't look at my reflection as I peel off my T-shirt, pants, underwear. Embarrassing sometimes, but I have to be naked. A shudder both painful and pleasurable ripples down my spine. Tingles build in the pit of my stomach. I tighten my abs, trying to hold it back. Can I get outside before it happens? I don't think so.

My skin prickles as if I ran naked through a field of nettles. It becomes almost unbearable. I hug myself tight, then gasp as magic floods my veins. My mind blanks, and it happens between heartbeats.

When I open my eyes, I'm on all fours, carpet beneath my hooves. The floor groans, and I wince. Hopefully it won't come crashing down under my half-ton weight. I see myself in the mirror. A pure black horse. I arch my neck and toss my mane, then sidestep from my reflection. My

2

hoof clunks on a bedpost. I didn't choose this big awkward animal, trust me—it's what comes most naturally to me. My nostrils flare at the sweet scent of grass, and I stick my head out the window to ogle the lawn.

Whoa there, Gwen, I tell myself.

My legs itch with unspent energy. I want to go outside, even as guilt wriggles in my gut. I hate having to sneak around like a pervert. Well, if the neighbors saw me, what would they do? Probably they'd freak and break out the pitchforks. In a backwoods town like Klikamuks, Washington, laws can be conveniently forgotten, and nice politically correct terms like "person with paranormal identity" disappear.

Whatever. I've earned this. I'll be careful. I've been a good little girl for long enough. It's easy to transform again, I'm so giddy with the lingering magic. Back to girl I go. I climb through the window and onto the roof. Naked, I curl my bare toes around shingles and grin nervously in the moonlight. I hope nobody's awake.

Wind tosses my curls. I clench my hands and stir the magic inside me. Power boils through my veins, dizzying me. Concentrate. The night snaps into sharper focus. I jump. My arms, my wings, strain upward. Feathers unfurl from my skin. My plummet curves into a swoop, and I tuck my talons beneath my body.

From girl to great horned owl in about a second. Pretty good, huh?

Flapping hard, I climb skyward in a tight spiral, then fan my wings and coast on the wind. My moldy old white farmhouse of a home looks almost quaint so far below. With my fantastic eyesight, I can count the morning glories clambering over the rusty swing set in our yard. Rodents scritch and nibble in the tall grass, and my stomach aches. No. Bad owl. Shapeshifting always makes me hungry.

Unfortunately, I know what mice taste like. To avoid temptation, I gain altitude. A somber amethyst glow colors the clouds to the west—the lights of Klikamuks. To the east, toward the Cascades, lies truly dark sky. I fly into the darkness. A sea of trees sighs beneath me. Nearly 50,000 acres of old-growth forest lies beyond our backyard—the Boulder River Wilderness Area, part of the much larger Mount Baker-Snoqualmie National Forest. A perfect hide-out for Others like me.

I stretch my wings, a sweet ache in my muscles, and ride a breeze. I always forget how boring my normal life is, until I fly. A weight in my stomach tells me this is wrong, that I shouldn't be sneaking out and unleashing my Otherness. I focus too hard on enjoying the sensation of soaring, and the pleasure fades.

Howls chorus in the distance. Adrenaline spikes my blood. Please don't it let it be what I'm thinking. Coyotes sound a lot more yippy, dogs don't run in packs around here, and there are no real wolves left in Washington.

Werewolves. Great. Just what I need.

The moon glows like a Cheshire cat's grin. It's a myth that werewolves can change only on the night of a full moon. They're forced to, those nights, but if they're strong enough, they can transform whenever they want. Apparently, I'm not the only Other sneaking out for a midnight shapeshifting snack. Did these werewolves come down from Canada? I heard about a pack up there, the bane of farmers and ranchers.

Hooves drum a panicked beat on the dirt below me. I swivel my head to pinpoint the sound, and dive. A stag bounds over a log and crashes through bushes. I swoop so low I can see the fearful gleaming whites of his eyes. Then the stag disappears in the darkness.

I want to go to bed.

Flying home feels like a chore. I swoop through my open window, banging my wing on the frame, and curse silently. I have to stop doing this. Starving myself, then doing binge transformations. But I can't keep my Otherness bridled 24/7, even if my parents and the whole wide world think I should. I return to my girl body and exhale.

My stomach grumbles loudly enough to resemble seismic activity. I sigh, tug on my clothes, and sneak downstairs to refuel on food. After eating a bagel sandwich, I climb back into my bed, my cocoon.

My stomach is full, but I still feel hungry. Sleep refuses to come.

Only werewolves would be stupid enough to hunt so close to a town and risk terrifying humans. You know, werewolves, vampires, and the rest of the bloodborn Others really piss me off sometimes. They just can't resist biting a lot of people and making new Others, like themselves, who don't play by the rules. There are laws for a reason. People won't give a damn about the rights of Others if rogue werewolves insist it's their birthright to hunt without permits and claim territory already owned by the government.

I wasn't bitten. I was born this way. My dad—my real dad—was a pooka, a shapeshifting spirit from Wales. You probably haven't heard of them. No, they're not something cute and cuddly, and please don't ever call me pookie. A few surviving pookas hide in scraps of British wilderness. I don't know about any other half-breeds like me. Maybe they're also under the bed, as they say. Monsters that haven't come out yet.

Everybody's read the stories, but nobody should believe them. Not even that stuff in Paranormal Studies textbooks. They say pookas show up as a dark horse with glowing golden eyes, stalking travelers on murky nights, inviting them on wild rides, throwing them into bogs, over cliffs, trampling them…

I've never done that. It's just human propaganda against Others. Pookas are also accused of destroying crops and breaking down fences. Blame the livestock, I say. Okay, so I did try making crop circles with a friend. Once.

But why do I want to shapeshift so often? Is it normal? Ha, as if I can call myself normal. Is something wrong with me? This isn't the first night I've lain awake in bed, the urge to shapeshift boiling over. It seems to be getting worse as I get older. I can't remember this ever happening when I was a kid.

Maybe it's natural, nothing to worry about. I wish I could ask my pooka dad, but I've never met him. I'd ask my parents if they ever might possibly be able to help me, but the likelihood of that is a big fat no. They're humans—I'm not.

When I wake up, everything's pleasant—until I move and my muscles ache. Then I remember the new werewolves in town.

"Bollocks," I mutter, a choice word I picked up from my mother.

Deep breaths. I count the stitches in one of the mushroom yarn paintings I thrifted. Some people use labyrinths or mandalas to calm down. I prefer anything gloriously tacky. When my heart stops pounding in my ears, I get out of bed and inspect my room. Hoof prints emboss my carpet. I rub my foot over them to smooth them out. A tawny owl feather rests on the windowsill. I slide open my window.

"Breakfast!" my dad bellows from the bottom of the stairs. Stepdad, to be exact.

I jump and toss out the feather. It seesaws down and lands on the lawn. Maybe they'll think it belongs to a normal owl. When I open my bedroom door, the heavenly aroma of pancakes lures me downstairs.

My family's already there. I glance at their faces, but nobody seems worried.

In the corner of the kitchen, Mum perches on the window seat and cradles a mug of coffee. Her auburn ponytail clings to her staticky sweater. Gazing at the gray blanket of clouds outside, she takes a pensive sip.

She sighs. "Reminds me of Wales." You would think she's about to rhapsodize, but she adds, "It was just as bloody rainy there."

I wonder if Mum misses Wales. She left soon after she had a fling with a pooka and discovered she was pregnant. She was more than a wee bit embarrassed—that stuff doesn't happen in stories. I have to give her credit, though. Her family wanted her to give me up for adoption, or worse. Said I was faerie spawn. Hey, they were right, but luckily Mum doesn't believe faerie babies are little bundles of evil. Okay, so I'm not sure my grandparents actually said that when I was born, but let's just say reunions with the Welsh side of the family have ranged from nonexistent to nightmarish.

Dad pokes at a pancake in a frying pan. "Who wants some flapjacks?" He always calls them that. He sort of looks like a storybook lumberjack, big and shaggy, though he owns a hardware store in Klikamuks.

"Me!" Megan says, scrambling off the couch.

I refrain from saying "Me too!" because I hate echoing her.

Megan drags a textbook to the table. I roll my eyes at my half-sister. She's all human, unlike me. I'll spare you the details of her virtuoso cello playing and mathematical prowess, but Megan's the "gifted" one in the family, while I'm the black sheep. Or should I say, black horse? Okay, not funny.

I decide it's time to break the news. "There are werewolves in the forest."

"Oh?" Mum says.

Dad concentrates on scraping a pancake from the pan. "Huh."

"What, like that guy at the gas station you thought was an imp?" Megan asks.

I blush. "That was, like, four years ago. I was a kid."

"You were thirteen. And what about the Johanssons last year? The 'elves'?" Megan waggles her fingers in air quotes.

"This is serious," I say. "Didn't you hear the howls?"

"Nope," Megan says blithely.

I glower at her. "Mum? Dad?"

"Maybe you were dreaming," Dad says.

"Right," I mutter.

I shut up and eat my pancakes. No use mentioning why I was up so late, or that I just happened to be flying over the forest.

After breakfast, I head upstairs. Megan's bedroom door, opposite mine, is closed. I'm sure she's studying again. Megan and I are homeschooled, so Mom can keep my powers hidden while cultivating Megan's talents. But even homeschoolers get summer vacation. Try telling that to Megan, though. She's quite possibly the nerdiest, stodgiest fourteen-year-old I've ever met. It annoys me when people think she's older than me. I hope it's just her height (she's three inches taller), but I suspect it's her behavior.

I check my blog, "Premeditated Snarkiness," for new comments. I stay anonymous behind the username "black-magic" so I can rant about everything from sloppy online grammar to prejudices against Others.

Yesterday, I posted about the ridiculous portrayal of vampires on TV. People seem to think they're either elegantly angsty immortals or vile bloodsucking criminals. Correct answer: depends entirely on the vampire. Granted, I don't know any personally, but they do have a midnight Vampire Pride Parade every year in Seattle. You see everybody from white-haired old ladies to nerdy teen guys there.

Sometimes I wish we lived in Seattle, not Klikamuks. It's way more liberal there, and it seems to have a lot more Others. Of course, people always think there are more Others than there actually are. We're definitely in the minority. It's just that the Others who come out are so … visible. How could you not miss a Sasquatch running for mayor of Seattle? Who cares if he didn't even get close to winning.

I got a few sympathetic comments about my post from my friends—most are of the online variety—and another from an anonymous poster. Anonymous said,

> i think my ex girlfriend gave me that werewolf
> disease. i'm starting to feel really screwed up around
> the full moon. i'm scared. can you help me?

Lycanthropy can be transmitted via bites, and it's also an STD. Same with vampirism and all the other blood-born ways of becoming Other. The first transformations can be brutal on the mind and body. Is some poor clueless guy really asking me for help? I type a quick reply.

> Are you sure it's lycanthropy? You should check out
> WereRecovery.com. They have a lot of info. Hope

this helps. I know lycanthropy can be hard to deal
with sometimes.

Within a minute, the guy replies.

so your a werewolf? knew your a bitch. you and your
fucked up faerie friends disgust me.

My face flames, then goes cold. I see a faint golden glow
reflected on my monitor—my eyes, burning with anger. My
fingers rattle the keys.

If you don't like my blog, don't read it. And for your
information, I am not a werewolf. Though I'm sure
you are a pathetic little parasite infecting the Internet.
Crawl back up whatever asshole you came from.

I almost post the comment, then hesitate. Do I really
want this marring my blog? With a sigh, I delete all the comments by Anonymous.

A new comment pops up. I hope it isn't Anonymous,
back for a flame war. But it's Takehiko, one of my online
friends. He's a talented artist who draws manga. Like, car-
toons of these Japanese fox spirits.

Allow me to sic many rabid foxes on Mr. Anonymous
Moron.

I reply, relieved.

Don't worry. I've banished the comments to oblivion
via the delete button.

Good riddance.

Takehiko doesn't write more. Alas.

He posted a cute photo of himself on his blog awhile ago, then deleted it, probably out of shyness. With his high cheekbones and dark eyes shaded by tousled, spiky hair, he almost looks like a Japanese version of Johnny Depp. Yes, I'll admit I have a mild and purely fanciful e-crush. Though I already have a boyfriend.

Oh, look. An email from my aforementioned boyfriend. My heart does a little skip.

> From: Zack
> Subject: How art thou today, milady?

I'm already smirking. Zack has a wicked sense of humor. He's also really into medieval history, so we've had this fake courtly speech thing going on.

> Good morrow, Lady Gwenhwyfar.

I blush. I've told him not to call me that, multiple times. Leave it to my mother to bestow upon me a ridiculously convoluted Welsh name. I'm amazed anyone can even spell it. Hey, I couldn't until second grade.

> Fair Gwen, I am not skilled at expressing mine feelings well. For I am but a humble knight, and no sweet-tongued troubadour. But for you, I shall try. It hath been far too long since I gazed upon thy scarlet locks and comely face. Mine fellow knights thinketh me moonstruck with love. But you knoweth these art mine heart's true wishes. 'Tis a fine day, as both dragons have left the castle unguarded. Wilt thou be at the gates today? Mayhap we shall stroll through

the park on this fine day. I shall look for you and
hope.

Your faithful knight,
Sir Zachary the Smitten

I grin. "Dragons" is code for Zack's parents, "castle" for
his house. His parents forbid him to have girls in his bedroom, so of course he invites me over every chance he gets.

Humming, I trade my pajamas for a strawberry print
tank top and black leggings. I try to tame my wild red curls,
then grab the Bean—my purse, the exact shape and color of
a kidney bean—and head for the door.

"I'm going to Zack's!" I call, before my parents can
detain me.

"Be safe!" Mum calls from her office, clacking away
on her keyboard. She works as a programmer for a little
software company. They make computer games, mostly
science fiction role-playing ones. They used to do fantasy
RPGs, where you chop up trolls and werewolves, but that
stuff isn't politically correct anymore. Besides, mainstream
America seems wary of anything magical. I ponder public
opinion about Others as I ride the bus, but come to no
great revelations.

Zack's family lives in a neighborhood of posh house-
clones. Manicured shrubbery, three-car garages, a fountain
across the street. His house has an imposing arch over the
door, as if the building has a huge ego. The designer deco-
rations change like clockwork with the seasons, from artifi-
cial evergreens to pastel eggs in sterile nests.

I ring their doorbell and hear a cheery chiming version of "When the Saints Go Marching In." I'll admit I freaked out when I first learned just how religious Zack's parents are, since Christians and Others have been enemies since biblical times. But they seem like such genuinely nice people.

Of course, they don't know what I am. Neither does Zack.

The door sweeps open. As usual, I'm dazzled by his smile. "Hey, Zack."

"Greetings, Lady Gwenhwyfar."

I roll my eyes and start to say something, but Zack bends down—he's quite tall—and silences me with a kiss. His hand curves around my waist as if it's meant to fit there. His touch kindles a warm glow inside me. I still can't believe this guy is my boyfriend and has been for over a year. A knot of guilt tightens in my stomach. Why haven't I told him I'm Other, even after all this time, all these opportunities?

I pull back, face flushed, and attempt not to look giddy. "How's it going?"

"Great."

I close the door behind me. The soft click of the lock makes my heart beat a little faster.

Zack pulls a rubber band off his ponytail. He shakes out his long blond hair, smooths it with his hands, then twists the rubber band around it again. I can't help staring. He's just so ... handsome. Once, when we went to a medieval fair, I rented an ill-fitting wench dress and he got fake chain mail. I looked hilariously sluttish, but he looked like a real knight. A crusader, with the cross necklace he always wears.

"Come on up," he says, climbing the stairs to his bedroom.

Zack's room has a faintly dusty, boyish smell to it. Hard to describe. Like a mixture of his sweat, laundry detergent, and an overall lived-in smell. I like it, and always breathe deep when I step inside. He has a tapestry of King Arthur above the headboard of his bed, a replica broadsword mounted on the wall, and shelves burdened with books. Like I said, he's really into medieval stuff. I spot new knight figurines on his desk.

"Cool," I say, reaching for one.

He catches my wrist. "Caution: wet paint. I was just working on them."

I nod and crouch to look closer. The detail's fantastic: feathers on their helmets, tiny dragons and unicorns—Others—on their shields. That is, Others hunted to extinction back in ye good olde medieval times, when killing dragons filled people with religious zeal, and the healing powers of unicorn horn filled them with greed.

I wonder what Zack's parents think of Others. What he thinks.

"So, did you want to go out? Maybe to Wilding Park?" I ask.

"Sure." He smiles. "We can spend a little time here first."

Zack strokes aside my hair and kisses the four-leaf clover tattoo at the nape of my neck. For luck, he always says.

And it always liquefies my knees. I sink onto the chair at his desk, trying to look as if I planned on it. He spins me to face him. I stare into his eyes, blue as the hottest flame. Shivers race down my spine.

I hook my fingers behind his neck and drag him into a kiss. His soft moan urges me on. I tug him to his knees and dig my nails into his shoulders as if marking him as mine. His arms tighten around my waist. I nip his ear and he seems to like it, so I test my teeth on his shoulder. When I bite his neck, he yanks back.

"Ouch!" He touches the teeth marks, and his fingers come away red with blood.

I'm breathing hard, my eyes stinging. Glowing. I turn away and shut them fast. Oh crap. I run my tongue over my teeth and found they've sharpened into feline fangs. What happened? I've never lost control before.

two

Ikeep my eyes shut—I can't bear to look at Zack. Any second now, he's going to say something horrible, be horrified of me. My muscles tighten, but I'm not sure why. An instinct to brace myself, perhaps, or run away.

"Gwen?" he says. "Are you okay?"

When I'm sure my eyes are normal, I open them. Instead of disgust and shock on Zack's face, he looks surprised, bemused. I look at his neck and wince, though the bite isn't as nasty as I thought. I grit my teeth until they return to human bluntness.

"Sorry," I say. "I ... I got a little carried away."

Zack arches an eyebrow. "A little?"

Scalding blood rushes to my cheeks. I look away from him, my hair curtaining my face.

"Hey." He tucks my hair behind my ear. "Don't be embarrassed. I like seeing a little of your wild side."

I laugh feebly. "Yeah." If only he knew just how wild.

Zack touches the bite again. "Let me clean it up."

He heads for the bathroom, and I slump in the chair. Bollocks. Why do I feel so turned on? And why is that waking up my Otherness? I shouldn't have shapeshifted last night. I must have really riled up my pooka side.

Zack returns, holding a tissue to his neck. He brings it to his face. "I think it's clotting."

Clotting. How romantic. "I'm so sorry," I say.

He stares at me. "You, uh, have some on your mouth."

I lick my lips and taste blood. My stomach squirms. He hands me another tissue, and I wipe it off.

The corner of Zack's mouth curves upward. "Blood-sucker."

I try to laugh, but my face burns. "Ugh. Vampires are disgusting."

"I don't know." His smile widens. "They're kind of sexy."

If only he knew what I'd just blogged about. I wish he'd stop joking around and say what he actually thinks of Others, bloodborn or natural born.

I wrinkle my nose. "I don't think so."

He nods. "My parents say they're soulless. Children of Lilith and all that."

My heartbeat stumbles, then comes back, pounding harder than ever. Some Christians interpret the Bible to mean that Lilith's demonspawn offspring are what we now call Others. Does Zack actually believe this?

"Oh?" I try to sound flippant. "What do you think?"

He shrugs. "Probably just stories to spice up the Bible."

"You do know that vampirism is nothing more than a glorified disease. They shouldn't even be called Others, probably. Not the same at all."

"Same as what?"

My heart thumps against my ribs. "Others who are natural born. You know. Not bitten."

"Close enough," he says.

I really, really wish I could set him straight.

"Anyway..." Zack slides his hand up my back.

I exhale. The taste of blood lingers on my tongue. My fingers brush the bite on his neck. He flinches, but lets me touch it.

"That's one heck of a hickey," he says.

I groan. "Heck of a hickey? Lame, Zack, lame." But I'm smiling.

"I tried," he says, leaning in for a kiss that I dodge.

I glance at the clock. "We should get going if we want to catch the bus to Wilding Park."

"All right," Zack says, and I can't read his voice.

As we sit together on the bus, he puts his arm over my shoulders and stares out the window, his eyes cool. I never thought we would be together so long—or get so intimate. I still haven't told him I'm a virgin. Or that I'm Other.

I can't keep lying to him. He doesn't deserve it. I don't.

Zack and I walk through Klikamuks, hand-in-hand. Wilding Park is in the middle of town, on the Stillaguamish River. Dollops of lemon meringue cloud float high in the sky. Balsam poplars rustle by the river and scent the air with their honey-spice resin. Kids scamper around, shrieking, and a guy does tricks with a kite.

We lounge on a lawn spangled with dandelions and I inhale the clover-sweet hay-smell of grass. I want to shapeshift into a cat, curl up, and snooze. Cats can get away with that. I sigh and shut my eyes. Maybe the rest of today will be peaceful.

"Your hair," Zack says.

"What about it?"

"It looks like a halo." He fingers one of my curls.

I smile, keep my eyes shut, and let myself relax. Zack's sweat has a subtle musky aroma, sweet as rain and earthy as truffles—intoxicating. Warm breath fans across my face. My eyelids snap open. Zack is leaning over me, a hairsbreadth away from kissing me. He touches my cheek, strokes my neck, and lets his fingers linger on the pulse leaping there. The cross dangles from his neck, winking in the sun. I can't look away.

"Where did you get that from, anyway?" I say, to distract both him and myself.

He frowns. "Get what?"

I catch the cross between two fingers. "This."

"My grandmother gave it to me before she passed away."

"Oh."

Zack leans closer to me. The scattering of blond stubble on his jaw glints.

"All these people are watching," I say.

His mouth twitches. With amusement or annoyance? "You never cared before."

Before I can speak again, he knots his hands in my hair and kisses me without restraint. I clench fistfuls of grass.

I remember my first kiss with Zack (my first kiss with a guy, if you discount a kindergarten birthday party). We met when we were both volunteering at the Klikamuks Public Library. One evening, the power went out. Pitch black. We blundered into each other, whispering, laughing. Zack found a flashlight and turned it on—but it dropped from his hand and rolled onto the ground when our lips met.

When he withdraws, he frowns. "What's wrong?"

"Nothing," I say, somewhat breathlessly. Though of course it's a lie.

"You seem tense. You're not still worried about the bite thing, are you?"

I shrug, awkwardly with him leaning against me like that. I've got to tell him. It's no use trying to keep pretending I'm fine.

"Don't worry about it," he says. He runs his hands through my hair. I wish he wouldn't—it's making this harder.

"I want to ask you something," I say.

"Go ahead."

I force myself to meet his gaze. He lifts one eyebrow.

"You don't know everything about me," I say. The words sound staccato, squeezed by the tightness in my throat.

He nods. "That's okay. I want to get to know you better."

"Yeah," I say lamely.

Zack plucks a dandelion and starts tearing off petals. A brutal version of she loves me, she loves me not.

"Let's go walk by the river," I say. "Find someplace more private."

His eyes brighten, and I regret my choice of words. I want to talk, not make out.

We zigzag down a paved trail to a beach along the Stillaguamish River. Egg-sized pebbles clatter underfoot. The river always smells like green, sun-warmed water. It usually tastes good, too: lukewarm, a little cloudy, and sweet. But when I cup my hands and bring river water to my lips, a sour smell stops me. I hear the faraway drone of an airplane and faint conversation, but no birdsong, no peeping frogs.

"So quiet today," Zack says.

I nod and twist my toes inside my sneakers. I let him lead me to a bench nestled in salmonberry bushes.

"Zack?" I say.

"What?"

As lame as this sounds, I don't—can't—say anything.

"Maybe we've both been trying to say the same thing." He clasps my hand and rubs his thumb over my knuckles.

"Um…" I laugh nervously. "Have we?"

"It's okay." Zack circles his arm around me. "I totally understand."

"You do?"

"It has to be the right time. I believe sex should be special." He flushes slightly.

"Oh. Yes. Of course." I blink several times and withdraw. "I'm glad you think so."

He nuzzles the hollow of my neck, sending a stab of desire through me.

"Let's walk." I'm amazed how lighthearted I sound.

Zack tries to hold my hand, but I pretend not to notice. I reach for a pebble glinting with mica. Then I freeze. Right beside my foot, a dead brown bird lies spread-winged, still as a stone, its beak open piteously.

"Oh." The word escapes me as a puff of air. "Poor thing."

"Don't touch it," Zack says. "It could've died of disease."

I frown at the bird and keep walking. Beneath the fallen leaves of a bush, I find a dead tree frog. Then another, nearby.

My frown deepens. "Maybe some pesticide got into the river."

"Probably," Zack says.

We find two more frogs by the riverbank. They lie with their legs splayed and pale bellies bared. They look pitiful.

"It's got to be poison," I say. "Maybe we should stay away from the water."

Zack nods.

I walk away from the Stillaguamish and climb a pebbly slope. On the other side lies a backwater pool. And—

"Holy crap." I suck in my breath. "Zack!"

He jogs up the slope and stops beside me. "What…?"

Two bodies float in the pool. A man, facedown, duckweed clinging to his shirt. A woman, staring heavenward. Her long, dark tangle of hair drifts over her marble-pale arms. Waves lap her pregnant belly.

Zack presses his hand to his mouth, even though I don't smell anything. They must have just died. I slide one foot forward, then the other. I see myself reflected in her unseeing blue eyes. She was—still is—beautiful. A mosquito larva swims between her cupid's bow lips and rests on her pearly teeth. Her skin looks silvery, though that might be the water. I squint at her hands, at a translucence between her fingers…

"Gwen." Zack sounds hoarse. "Let's go. We need to get help."

"They're already dead," I say flatly.

"We need to tell someone."

I nod, but don't move when he tugs on my arm. I can't stop staring.

"It's okay," Zack says. "Come on. It's okay." He seems to be saying it to himself.

When I at last look away, I realize what I saw. Webbing between her fingers. "Water sprites," I whisper.

Zack doesn't say anything. I hope he didn't hear me. After he calls 911, we clasp hands and walk away from the pair of bodies. I can't stop shivering, even in the sun. We huddle together on a log until the police come.

The police head for the bodies and check futilely for signs of life. A woman with steel-wool hair introduces herself as Officer Sharpe from the sheriff's office. She asks for ID. Zack digs out a driver's license and I show my learner's permit. Officer Sharpe inspects them. Another officer starts questioning Zack.

Officer Sharpe asks me why we were here and how we found the bodies. I try not to wilt under her stern stare. My voice quavers as I answer, and sweat wets my armpits. Please don't ask me if I'm Other. Not in front of Zack.

The CSI unit arrives and ropes off the pond with yellow tape. Surely they'll uncover the truth about the water sprites.

"Gwen?" Officer Sharpe snaps me out of it. "Did you?"

"Sorry. What did you say?"

"Did you know these people?"

I shake my head hard. Too vigorously, maybe, because Officer Sharpe frowns and scribbles something on her notepad.

"Did they drown?" I ask, playing dumb. Water sprites breathe water just as well as air.

"We won't know until we run some tests." She scribbles some more. "You're free to go. We might follow up with a detective."

"A detective?" My voice sounds squeaky.

"Don't worry," Officer Sharpe says briskly. "Standard procedure."

I exhale and move into Zack's arms. "I want to go home."

He hugs me. "Let's go."

We're silent all the way back to the bus stop, until we sit on the bus stop bench.

"Poor people," Zack says softly. "I wonder how they drowned."

I say nothing.

That night, I dream of cold white flesh and death-clouded eyes. My toes touch the shore of a black pool. Water sprites reach for me, pondweed clinging to their arms.

"Help us," they whisper.

"I can't," I say, my gut twisting. "You're dead."

They stroke my ankles with icy fingers. "You are one of us."

I run away and let them die.

On the morning news, I learn their names: Nadia and Douglas Nix. They lived in a suburban area on the outskirts of Klikamuks. I didn't even know they existed. How many of us are out there, too scared to even admit our Otherness? And they died before I could ever meet them ... all because of pesticide in the river.

Pesticide. Wouldn't it take a *lot* to kill two people? And the nearest field is maybe ten miles from Wilding Park. If some farmer really did dump a lot of horrible chemicals into the river, there would be dead fish all over the place, not a few animals by one backwater pool. Unless, of course, somebody poisoned it on purpose.

Were the water sprites murdered?

When I tell my parents my theory, they both sit at the kitchen table and stare at me.

"Gwen," Mum says, her face tight. "What you saw must have been...shocking. But there's no proof of poison."

"It was an accident," Dad says. "Let the police handle this."

"It wasn't," I say. "Water sprites *can't* drown."

Dad scratches his beard. "How are you sure they're water sprites?"

"They had webbing between their fingers."

Mum shakes her head. "That's a medical condition, you know. In humans."

"How common is it?" I say.

"I'm not sure," she says. "But Gwen...I wouldn't worry."

"On the Internet," I say, "it says water sprites have thin skin, like frogs. The poison must have killed them that way."

"You can't believe everything on the Internet," Dad says.

"Whatever!" I throw up my hands. "I know what I saw."

My parents share a long-suffering look that irritates the crap out of me. I stalk upstairs and shut—okay, slam—my bedroom door. I hate how they think they know everything about every Other on the planet just because I'm half pooka.

I grab my cell phone and call my number one confidant. Drat, voicemail. Oh well, I'll leave a message and then go to her place. "Hey, Chloe, it's Gwen. I'm going to head over to the B&B and see if you're there. I need somebody to commiserate with. Life sucks, as usual. Not to sound emo or anything. Okay, see you later. Bye."

I jog to the bus stop, my throat tight. I neglect the bench and kick pinecones into the ditch until the bus comes. I need to talk to somebody. On the ride to Klikamuks, the heat of my anger cools and my skin feels clammy. The bus rumbles over a bridge and crawls along Main Street. Tourists prowl the sidewalks, lured by antique stores with silly things like amethyst cut-glass vases, Victorian ladies' gloves and boots, and porcelain cat figurines. I get off and walk past cottages with gingerbread trim, then stop outside a sunny yellow B&B called Bramble Cottage.

It looks oh-so-quaint, a perfect tourist trap. Postcard-worthy roses clamber over the walls. Almost all are abloom, and perfume drifts across the street. The owner, Chloe Amabilis, happens to be a garden addict—and a dryad.

I hadn't even met Chloe until two years ago, when I got lost in the forest and she saw me shapeshifting. I almost panicked, but after a tense standoff, she revealed she was also Other. I was totally flabbergasted to discover a dryad. They're an endangered species—only a handful remain after centuries of logging. Dryads used to be worshipped in Greece as the guardian spirits of trees, but now a lot of people see them as squatters on valuable land. Chloe emigrated to America in search of friendlier forests.

I hear hammering inside Bramble Cottage. When I open the door, I see a guy on a ladder tacking up wooden trim in the foyer. His paint-flecked jeans droop low, weighted by the tools on his belt. I try not to stare at his butt.

This has to be the new guy Chloe's been going on and on about. Chiseled, rugged, stubbly. Just her type. When he sees me, he pulls off his headphones. I hear classical music. Huh. For some reason, I expected heavy metal.

"Are you Randall Lowell?" I ask.

"Yeah." He has a low, husky voice. "How'd you know?"

"Chloe mentioned you."

"Ah." Randall brushes his hair—shaggy dark brown, with a streak of silver—from his eyes. "She's upstairs."

"Thanks."

I climb the creaky narrow staircase, gripping the banister. I don't know why more Victorians didn't break their necks. Upstairs, sunbeams stripe the faded pink carpet and the botanical prints of magical herbs. On the wallpaper, faeries are darting through vines. Not the fluttery Tinkerbell kind, which is a stereotype started by faeries to befuddle humans, but exquisitely elegant winged people with fire in their eyes.

"Chloe?" I call.

"In here," she says, behind a half-open bedroom door.

I step inside. A cabbage-rose rug covers most of the floor. Chloe is dusting a collection of rose-shaped chamber pots. A sunbeam slants through the dormer window and glimmers on the corn-silk hair swaying at her slender waist. She wears a dress of unbleached, 100 percent organic cotton, being a true tree-hugger. I clear my throat, and Chloe glances back at me, her eyes the serene green of a woodland glade.

"Gwen." She touches my arm, and I catch a whiff of her sweet scent. Sometimes it reminds me of an orchard of ripening pears; other times, of hay drying in the sun. "Is everything all right? You look a little pale."

"Except for discovering two dead bodies, I'm okay."

"What?" Chloe's eyes widen. "You aren't joking, are you?"

I shake my head.

"Let's go upstairs to my room," she says. "I don't want any guests interrupting us."

"Definitely," I say, with a crappy attempt at a laugh.

I follow Chloe upstairs to her attic bedroom. There's a prim little bed in the corner, though she prefers slumbering in trees as often as possible.

She sits at the foot of her bed and pats the quilt beside her. "Now tell me everything."

three

As I talk to Chloe, I twist a strand of hair around my finger, tighter and tighter.

"Randall mentioned rumors about water sprites," she murmurs, "but I didn't believe him."

"Well, I'm pretty certain. Considering how I actually saw them and everything." My sarcasm doesn't quite mask the wobble in my voice. "And the more I think about it, the more I think it couldn't have been an accident."

"Murder?"

"Yes. My parents don't believe me at all, which I find absolutely insane."

Chloe purses her lips. "I didn't see the bodies, so I can't be sure."

"I just can't believe they lived right here in Klikamuks! How many Others are there?" I laugh bitterly. "Why can't I meet any live ones?"

She gives me a serious stare. "Others have good reason to be secretive. You know that."

"Of course," I sigh.

Chloe told me how there used to be more Others in the area, ages ago, back before Washington was even a state. She would dance by moonlight with wood wives, sprites who emigrated from the forests of Germany in search of virgin trees. The native Others, whose names Chloe can't pronounce, would join them on occasion with drumming and dancing of their own. But those days are gone.

The more humans there are, the fewer Others. A pretty reliable ratio, wherever you are. Though some of the more communal Others have adapted to the urban life—I hear there's a big population of faeries in New York (you can spot them at operas and posh parties), and gnomes scurry in the subway tunnels. And, of course, vampires always live where there are plenty of humans, their preferred prey.

"Perhaps your parents are right," Chloe says softly.

"What do you mean?"

"Someone may have dumped a hazardous liquid into the pool rather than disposing of it properly. Death by carelessness."

"Maybe." I growl and rake my fingers through my hair, then wince as they snag a snarl.

"Gwen. I know you're upset by this, but there's no need for excessive stress." She lays her hand on my knee. "You need to hang loose."

Sometimes Chloe gets her decades of slang mixed up. I laugh. "Hang loose?"

"Archaic already?" she says, sounding faintly surprised.

"Oh yeah," I say.

"By the way…" Chloe lowers her voice. "Did you hear them last night?"

"What?" I say, my train of thought derailed.

"I was sleeping in my favorite bigleaf maple when I heard howls."

"Oh! Right." I mime smacking my forehead. "Werewolves?"

"Perhaps," Chloe says, her eyes guarded.

"I wish they hadn't come here."

"You mean that?"

"Yes," I say, even though I know she doesn't want me to. Chloe frowns out the window.

"Well," I say, "they're going to stir up a lot of trouble."

She purses her lips. "Can you be sure of that?"

"No, but they're not exactly a poster child for Others."

"Gwen," Chloe says, "it's not as if all werewolves are inherently evil."

I sigh dramatically. "A bunch of them are criminals who bit other criminals on purpose."

"And even more of them are innocent people trying to live as normally as they can with an ostracized, contagious disease."

"That's what all the bloodborn Others are," I say. "Diseased."

"And if you had a disease, would you want people to treat you differently?"

"Why are you always the voice of maturity?" I mutter. "It's no fun."

Chloe looks twenty-one, but being about two centuries old, she has plenty of words of wisdom. And she's not afraid to share them.

"Gwen," she says. "Just leave the werewolves alone."

"So long as they leave me alone."

She stares at me. I hate how she can make me squirm. An awkward silence stretches out, like bubblegum between sidewalk and shoe.

Finally, I say, "You know Zack and me?"

"Yes."

"I still haven't told him. About me."

"You really should."

"I know." My face warms. "This morning…we got kind of carried away…"

"Carried away how?"

The heat in my face intensifies. "It's not what you're thinking. I bit him."

Chloe's mouth wavers between a frown and a smile. "Some people like that."

"I mean I *bit* him. Drew blood." I lower my voice. "I shouldn't have shapeshifted last night. It really stirred up my pooka side."

"Has this happened before?"

I shake my head.

Chloe sighs, her forehead furrowed. "Gwen, if you're not ready to tell him the truth, you're not ready to sleep with him."

"I know!" My voice sounds shrill. I glower at myself.

Chloe looks me in the eye. "Promise you'll tell him soon. Okay?"

"Okay. Sheesh. It's like I have two mothers."

"It's for your own benefit." Chloe smiles. "It's a lovely day outside. You should be out frolicking or something."

I punch her lightly on the arm. She laughs, then heads downstairs. I follow.

Randall hops off the ladder. "Hey, boss. I finished the trim. What next?"

"Boss?" Chloe sniffs. "I thought I told you not to call me that."

He grins. "Okay, but you are my boss. Right?"

I waggle my eyebrows suggestively at Chloe. She steps on my toes as she passes.

"Come out in the garden," she tells Randall. "I need help with some trellises."

"Yes, ma'am."

"And don't call me ma'am, either."

"Yes, ma—"

She stops him with a glare, though she's smiling.

Randall looks at her with puppy-dog eyes. "What am I supposed to call you?"

"Chloe," she says. "Just Chloe."

I hum a James Bond theme song and stroll outside, feeling much better.

"Gwen!" Mum calls. "Come see the news!"

I close all webpages and jog downstairs.

On the TV, an unblinking woman with fakey blonde hair delivers the eleven o'clock news. "… Family on the outskirts of Klikamuks saw two near their home."

"Two what?" I say.

Megan sits on the couch, her wide eyes full of reflected light. "Werewolves!"

She says it like it's something exciting, straight out of a movie, and I can't pretend that a thrill didn't just skitter down my spine. Sure, there might be a lot of bloodborn in the world, but that doesn't mean you see them too often.

"I *knew* it," I mutter.

It switches to a shot of a family standing in the rain. The pasty-faced dad points to a forest behind a chain-link fence. "They were right there, behind the fence. God, I hope it's tall enough to keep them out."

"It used to be so safe around here," the mom says.

A little girl with white-blonde pigtails pipes up. "I saw them. They were huge. The boy one pee-peed on the fence."

The dad nods. "Do you think they're claiming this as their territory?"

We never get to hear an answer, because it cuts back to the newswoman. "Sheriff Royle has some comments as well."

Sheriff Royle leans against the door of his police cruiser. He hooks his fingers in his belt and stares into the camera with half-closed eyes. "Local law enforcement is well aware of the threat. We're doing everything we can to keep the people of Snohomish County safe."

"And have werewolves perpetrated any crimes?" asks a newsman.

Sheriff Royle squints. "Why, of course. Killing game outside of hunting season. We can't prove anything else till we catch them, though there's been a surge in vandalism. And a masked man robbed an espresso stand two weeks ago, remember?"

"An espresso stand?" Dad says. "I didn't know werewolves like coffee."

"Nicholas," Mum says. "This is serious."

"Wonder if they crave caffeine on the full moon?"

"Dad," I groan. I can't believe my own parents sometimes.

"Wait, what's this?" Megan says, turning back to the TV.

The fakey blonde newswoman returns. "Late last night, a clerk discovered the body of a female vampire in the alley behind the 7-Eleven in Klikamuks. Her wounds were most likely inflicted by an iron stake, and her fangs had been removed. Police are working to identify the body." She speaks so calmly that I shiver.

"Vampire?" Dad says. "Sounds like clan rivalry."

Mum frowns. "I didn't think there were any vampire clans in the area."

Dad shrugs. "Vampires roam."

I stare at my parents. I can't believe how calmly *they're* talking.

"Vampires and werewolves are mortal enemies, right?" Megan says.

I snort. "That's Hollywood for you."

Megan sighs and shakes her head, as if she's so much more mature than me.

I stalk upstairs. My collection of fish toys stares at me from a big glass fishbowl on my nightstand. I hug a ratty old shark to my chest, feeling small and childish. I slide open my window and lean into the darkness rushing past like a river. The rich smell of rain-soaked earth fills my nostrils.

Werewolves. I hope they aren't as dangerous as some of the stories make them sound. As I told Chloe, I've heard that a bunch of them were criminals who got bitten and hid out in the woods, away from law enforcement, occasionally skulking into town to steal and rough up anybody who got in their way. Nothing more than thuggish brutes. How big is the pack? Why did they come here? Would they be friend or foe to an Other like me?

My legs tense, seized by a sudden urge to run. Not away from the werewolves, but toward them.

Wait a minute. Reality check, Gwen. Just because the werewolves and I are both Other doesn't mean we'll hold hands and skip in a circle together, best friends forever. They're probably just as bloodthirsty and beastly as everyone thinks. Not that I've ever gotten close enough to a werewolf to interview one. That might be interesting … though I doubt we'd have anything in common at all. I inhale slowly and shut the window.

The morning dawns overcast, with a mizzle drifting down from the blank white sky. That's a cross between mist and drizzle, for those who are rain challenged. Dad bursts into my bedroom just as I'm getting dressed.

"Daaad!" I wail.

He shuts the door. "Sorry, Gwen!" he says cheerfully. "Feel like driving today?"

"Driving where?" I ask, somewhat suspicious.

"Into town. So you can practice for your license. Oh, and I want to buy cashews at Safeway. Your mother forgot to get some."

I knew it. Dad needs to satisfy his cashew craving. "Okay," I say. "But let me eat breakfast first."

"You're the last one down," Dad says.

I grunt neutrally and try to tame my hair.

The drive to Klikamuks is uneventful—except for the old lady in a slow Buick who I get stuck behind and don't have the guts to pass, and the driver who honks at me because I don't screech into a roundabout without yielding to traffic, and the panic stop I do for the stupid bike rider who materializes out of nowhere. When I finally park outside the Safeway, the car still intact, I peel my sweaty hands from the wheel.

I always find grocery stores surreal. Fluorescent lights buzzing overhead, wide aisles tempting me to run, vivid ads tugging my gaze this way and that. It seems so far removed from actually eating. Sometimes I have a strange impulse to climb shelves or rip open packaging and taste everything. But I mustn't succumb to pooka mischief.

I follow Dad to the Promised Aisle that contains cashews. He really is addicted.

We pass various products inspired by Others. There's unicorn horn soap (they stopped adding horn ages ago, ever since unicorns died out, but still claim it has "added purity"). Vampire toothpaste (which really should be fang-paste) promises to bleach bloodstains. A lot of seafood is supposedly caught in mermaid-safe nets. Marketers prefer "good" Others like mermaids and unicorns.

A bay centaur noses around the produce, his hooves clicking on the floor. Grocery store employees stare, slack-jacked, and moms tug their kids away. I can't help staring, too. He's not wearing anything and has killer abs. I've never seen a real centaur before. I had no idea any of them lived outside rural Greece nowadays.

"Do you see that?" Dad whispers.

That. As if the centaur isn't a person.

"Of course I see *him*," I whisper back. "He must be foreign." Definitely Greek, judging by his dark curly hair.

The centaur sniffs an apple, then drops it into the basket hooked over his arm. Everyone watches as he ambles to the cabbages, his black tail swishing.

"Damn," Dad mutters. "I wish I brought my camera."

My face burns. "Dad." I tug on his arm. "We'd better not stare."

"I do not mind," says the centaur, without glancing at

his audience. "I am sure you Americans do not see a centaur every day."

My face burns even hotter. I steer my dad from the produce section. Dad rubbernecks on the way out.

I sigh. "Come on. Cashews."

At the checkout, we see the centaur again. He sets his basket on the conveyer belt as a line of gawking shoppers forms behind him. I politely avert my eyes, and my gaze falls upon three strangers at the next checkout.

Two stubble-jawed guys, maybe brothers, with tousled brown hair. A Native American woman with obsidian hair that falls to her waist. She rubs the inside of her elbow and I glimpse red scratches. They all look scroungy, with moss in their hair, like they've been camping. Even from here I can smell woodsmoke.

The woman wheels their cart through the checkout, and all of them work together to pile food on the conveyer belt. Ground beef, hot dogs, canned stew, and a huge bag of dog kibble. One of the guys hefts the kibble so the checkout lady can scan the bar code. Muscles bulge in his arms and shoulders.

"What's its name?" asks the checkout lady.

"Huh?" says the guy.

"Your dog. It must be a big breed."

"Something like that," he mumbles, his voice husky.

The checkout lady's gaze drifts to the centaur. I keep staring at the three strangers.

They wheel their cart toward the doors. The Native American woman squints at a paper tacked on the bulletin board. Her eyes—her amber eyes—narrow to hateful slits. She rips the paper down, crumples it into a tight ball, and chucks it into a trash can. The automatic doors swish open. They all stalk out.

My palms start sweating. As Dad rummages in his wallet, I jog ahead to the doors.

The three strangers are loading their groceries into the back of a rusty baby-blue pickup. I see a tarp, a cooler, and a tattered tent. They have a Canadian license plate. I turn to the trash can and pluck out the crumpled paper.

It has a crude clip-art drawing of a wolf. *WANTED: WOLF PELTS*, it proclaims in bold red letters. *$300 reward for an adult. $150 reward for a juvenile. All pelts must meet special paranormal requirements.*

Special paranormal requirements. Werewolf pelts. Remind me not to shapeshift into a wolf anytime soon.

The baby-blue truck drives away. The sheriff passes them and drives cluelessly on.

"Ready, Gwen?" Dad stands behind me in the doorway, grocery bags in hand.

I nod and try to look just as clueless, then follow him to our car. As I pull out of the parking lot, Dad pries open his bulk tin of cashews and starts crunching. He doesn't say anything, so I don't either. I drive west, away from the mountains, away from the road the werewolves took. Rain drums on the windshield like the impatient tapping of fingernails. I shiver, but tell myself it's from the clouds curdling above.

four

The next day, we have abnormally sunny weather. Abnormal for Washington, anyway. Cobalt blue skies, sunshine so thick it's like syrup pouring down, lawns exhaling old rain in clouds of mist. Outside Bramble Cottage, Chloe waters the roses. Randall pushes a lawn mower across the backyard, sweat glistening on his bare chest. Chloe seems blasé, but my gaze lingers on his muscles before I look away.

I walk up to her. "Hey, Chloe."

"Gwen." She smiles. "What brings you over here?"

I smooth my hair—or try to, anyway—and sigh. "I was hoping we could talk. Maybe over lunch, if you're not too busy."

"Certainly." She turns off the water and coils up the hose. "Let's go to the Olivescent."

"Great. I'm starving."

She sighs. "You're always starving."

"I can no longer suffer in silence."

Chloe laughs. "Randall!" she calls.

He kills the lawn mower and strides over. "What?"

"We're going out for lunch. Can you watch the B&B for us?"

"Sure." Randall gives me a polite smile. It deepens into something genuine when he looks at Chloe. "See you later."

As soon as we walk out of his earshot, I whistle low under my breath.

Chloe arches her eyebrows. "What?"

"He likes you," I singsong.

"Poor guy. He's always giving me lovesick glances. If only he knew I'm old enough to be his great-great-great-grandmother."

I smirk. "What, not into cradle robbing?"

Chloe shakes her head, her bigleaf-maple-blossom earrings tinkling. "The thought of a boy toy does have some appeal."

I roll my eyes, then notice that her hair looks greenish at the roots. "Uh, Chloe?"

"What?"

"When's the last time you dyed your hair?"

She frowns and digs a compact mirror from her little crocheted purse. "Oh."

I bite back a smile. Chloe actually has startlingly verdant hair, the same color as her eyes, but she bleaches it.

"It's not too bad, is it?" she asks.

I shake my head. "Makes you look sort of punk."

Chloe wrinkles her nose.

I laugh. "Pretend you've been swimming. Chlorine makes hair green."

She sighs. "I suppose."

We stroll down the sidewalk to the Olivescent, the best pizzeria in Klikamuks. Tantalizing aromas waft from its steamy windows. Locals and tourists alike cluster around the Olivescent, their noses tilted skyward. We order the usual: a slice of vegan pizza topped with sun-dried tomatoes, roasted garlic, and veggie pepperoni for Chloe, and two slices oozing cheese and mushrooms for me. And some cinnamon bread-sticks. And some calzones. All for me. Hey, I'm hungry. I seem to have a really fast metabolism.

We carry our plates outside to the patio. A froth of baby's breath and petunias overflows from hanging plant-ers. Bumblebees buzz through the perfumed air. A guy in a Safeway uniform drags a hose through flowers for sale outside the store. Water spatters on the hot pavement and steam curlicues toward the wispy clouds.

Chloe sits and daintily crosses her legs. "Nice day, isn't it?"

"Yeah." I drag my chair closer, wincing as it grates on the concrete. "I think I saw some werewolves the other day."

"Oh?"

"At the Safeway. Two guys and a woman. They looked all rugged and outdoorsy, and bought a ton of kibble and meat."

"Kibble?" Chloe smiles. "They could just be camping with dogs."

"But the woman had amber eyes. And I saw her rip down a werewolf bounty poster."

Chloe's smile fades. "Bounty poster?"

"Yeah. It sucks. The werewolves give the people of Klikamuks a reason to hate Others."

"Do they?"

I shrug, my face hot. "You know what I mean."

Chloe frowns into her glass of lemonade. She swirls it so the ice clinks together, then gazes across the street, her face clouded.

"Hey, look," I say. "There's a sale at Slightly Foxed Books."

"Oh?" Chloe's face clears. "Let's check it out."

We finish our pizza and head over to the quaint used bookstore wedged between a coffee shop and an antiques mall. Gilt calligraphy flakes above the windows: *Slightly Foxed Books: Rare and Gently Used Literature*. Weird name, but apparently it has something to do with the reddish-brown spots on pages.

A bell jingles when I push open the door. I inhale the familiar musty scent—which I always think smells like secrets, if secrets have a smell. Rainbow ranks of books crowd the shelves. A ginger cat lounges in a square of sunlight.

"Hello, kitty," I say in a high voice.

The cat flicks its ear, cracks open its yellow eyes, then goes back to sleep.

"Don't you look like that as a cat?" Chloe asks.

I nod.

"Just as lazy, too," she says.

I poke her in the ribs. She smirks.

The labyrinthine shelves beckon. You never know what you're going to find. I like reading old books of fairy tales and folklore. They often say wildly inaccurate things about Others, but that's part of the fun. I spot a reprint of *Faerie Folk of Britain* by Alastair Finch, first published in 1841. Prime snarking material. In the nineteenth century, humans were starting to look rationally at Others, rather than always considering them monsters and running screaming in the opposite direction. Ahem. I may be exaggerating a bit.

"Pooka, pooka," I mutter. The word sounds silly—couldn't we have a cooler name?

Aha, here's the entry. I spread the dog-eared pages flat.

Pooka: A shapeshifting spirit of the faerie family; a malevolent trickster. Indigenous to Ireland and Wales. Most commonly appears in the form of a black horse with nary a white hair upon its body. Can also assume the shape of a goat, a dog, an eagle, or presumably any animal. Whatever form the pooka chooses, it can always be detected by its sulfurous yellow eyes. In the form of a horse, a pooka uses persuasive magic to entice travelers on a wild nighttime ride. This ride invariably ends when the pooka throws the rider into brambles or bog, usually not fatally, though some pookas favor precipices. The Celts once revered pookas. On the night of Samhain, the first of November, they would consult a pooka for prophetic answers. This heathen practice must be discouraged, as pookas are dangerous beasts with little affinity for humans.

Yeah, sure. Pookas are the bad guys in all the bedtime stories, but I've never noticed any persuasive magic at my disposal. If I had it, you'd think I'd know. And where are those Celts who want to revere me? Ridiculous. I'm tempted to chuck *Faerie Folk,* but I slide it back onto the shelf in case any employees are watching.

Chloe is drifting toward some folios of botanical prints. I peek around a corner.

A short Asian guy, maybe about my age, stands on his toes and tries to slide a thick book onto a shelf that's too high for him. With a growling sigh, he wheels a ladder over and climbs up. I stifle a laugh.

He glances down at me. "Can I help you?"

Something about his face, his almond eyes, looks familiar. I size up his clothes—vintage-looking jeans, a black-and-white polo, a silvery aviator watch. Probably has well-off parents who want him to work anyway.

"Oh," I say, "I'm just browsing." I hesitate, my heart doing a little loopty-loop inside my ribs. "Do I know you?"

He tilts his head. "I don't think so."

Aha! At that angle, I recognize him. "Do you blog?"

"Yeah," he says, his gaze on the books again. "Why?"

My heart's really doing acrobatics now. "Are you Take-hiko?"

His gaze snaps to me. "How did you know?"

"You posted a photo of yourself."

He blushes. "Ah, yes. Then deleted it in a fit of sanity."

Now I blush. "I saved it." Why did I say that? Crap, I sound like an Internet pervert.

"Oh," he says. "Uh … Takehiko's just my username. I'm actually Tavian."

"This is so weird," I say. "It's like we've already met, online."

Tavian shrugs with a half-hearted smile. "Do you blog?"

"Yeah." Wait. I can't compromise my blog's anonymity. "I mean, I read blogs. But I haven't started one yet."

"You should. It's fun." Tavian hops off the stepladder.

I smile. I'm five foot seven. He looks maybe five four. "You're shorter than I expected."

Tavian snorts. "Can I help it if you're a giantess?" He turns his back on me. "If you need anything, let me know."

"Okay," I say.

Arrrgh. I want to beat myself over the head with a dictionary. I settle for knocking my forehead against a bookshelf. Why did I say such dumb things? I probably offended him. I'm so tactless.

I watch Tavian walk deeper into the bookstore. He passes a window, and the sunlight throws his shadow on the wall. I blink. For a second, I think his shadow has a *tail*. Then it's gone. Okay, maybe I shouldn't have beat myself over the head.

"Did you see that?" I ask Chloe.

"Hmmm?" Totally engrossed, she doesn't look up from her book of botanical prints.

"That cute Asian guy," I whisper.

She sighs, still not looking up from the page. "One word: boyfriend."

"I'm not letting good eye-candy go to waste. And do you who know he is?"

"No," she says. "But I believe you're going to enlighten me."

"He's Takehiko, that blogging anime artist I told you about. His real name is Tavian."

"Interesting." Chloe closes the book with a thump. "I'm going to buy this."

She lugs the heavy folio to the front of the bookstore. Behind the counter stands Tavian. I bury my nose in an old romance novel and pretend to read. *He unlaced her bodice, his hands calloused yet gentle. Her bosom heaved, two creamy mounds tipped with carmine, and she quivered with anticipation.*

Urk. Hideously flowery, yet strangely intriguing.

"Excuse me?" Tavian says. "Are you going to buy that?" It sounds like he already asked me at least once.

I slam the book shut. "Uh, no." I stare at the brawny kilted man and half-naked woman locked in a kiss on the cover. "Definitely not."

"Sure?" Tavian says, a hint of amusement in his voice. "The cover's nice eye-candy."

My face goes so hot I think I'll burn to a cinder of

embarrassment. I glance sideways at him. He looks innocent enough for a halo.

"Definitely not." I sniff and chuck the romance novel back into a bin.

Tavian raises his eyebrows. "Were you looking for anything in particular?"

"Nope." I head for the door. "Bye."

"Bye—what was your name again?"

I don't even look back. "Gwen."

I stride outside, Chloe at my heels.

"Gwen!" she whispers, smiling slyly. "What went on between the two of you?"

I roll my eyes. "Nothing."

I glance over my shoulder, through the windows of the bookstore. Tavian smiles to himself as he polishes the counter with a rag. He looks even cuter smiling, but I'm not going to admit that out loud.

"Hey," I say, "did you notice anything unusual about his shadow?"

"No. Why?"

"I thought it had a tail."

Chloe's eyes round. "You think he's Other?"

"Maybe." My heart thumps faster. Could a closet Other be living in my town? A cute closet Other? Wait. Mustn't think that. I have a boyfriend.

I glance at Chloe. "How come I never met Tavian before?"

"He must have just started working there."

"Yeah." I sigh blissfully. "What's with the sudden influx of good-looking guys?"

"An influx? Who else?"

"Oh, come on." I smirk. "You think Randall's hot."

Chloe puts on an aloof expression, but then she bites her lower lip.

"Come on," I say. "I know you're not telling me something."

She shakes her head. "I'm not even sure myself."

"How can you be unsure of Randall's hotness?"

"Gwen. I'm not referring to that. Doesn't he strike you as a little … extraordinary?"

"In what way?"

Chloe absently strokes a tree growing by the sidewalk. "It's not often that I feel this … familiarity with someone."

"Ooo," I tease. "Is it looove?"

"Gwen," she sighs, sounding very I'm-more-mature-than-thou. "Use your head. I'm sure you can draw your own conclusions."

I smirk, though in my head I'm quite conclusion-less.

Chloe glances at the height of the sun. "I should head back. I enjoyed lunch."

"Yeah. We should do it again sometime. And I'll try to talk less about doom and gloom."

A corner of her mouth curves upward. "Goodbye, Gwen."

I head for the nearest bus stop. Outside a white clapboard church, people cluster around tables laden with stuff. It looks like a rummage sale, until I see what they're buying:

crucifixes, candles, salt, iron jewelry, and bottles of what looks suspiciously like holy water. Nearly all of it useless. I spot Zack standing half-hidden behind a tree. His loose hair, pale gold in the sun, swings in front of his face as he bends over the crosses.

"Hey, Zack!" I call.

He breaks into a smile. "Hey, Gwen."

Zack bends to kiss me, but I peck him on the cheek first. This seems to satisfy him. I notice he hid the bite with a turtleneck.

"I really am sorry about...that," I say.

"What? Oh. Don't worry about it, it's nothing."

"You again," a familiar voice sneers behind me.

I turn, and spy a gangly guy with floppy brown hair. "Ben! You're back?"

He narrows his eyes at me, then slowly sticks out his tongue. I roll my eyes, and he cracks into a smile. "Yeah, I'm back."

Benjamin Arrington. Zack's older brother. Only a few years older, but a lot goofier. He's sort of nerdy and quite skinny, like a human Gollum. He's been at a Christian school up in British Columbia for the last three months, training to become a pastor. Zack was sad when Ben first left, and I missed kidding around with him, too.

Ben holds out his hand for me to shake. I do, and he draws me into a one-armed hug.

"They kick you out?" I joke.

Ben withdraws. "Yeah. I wasn't holy enough or something." His dark eyes sparkle.

I laugh. Ben's a good guy. He's very Christian, but not the overzealous kind. I think he'll make a nice pastor one day.

"Actually," Ben says, "they let me loose for some hands-on experience."

Zack claps his brother on the shoulder. "Ben's staying with our parents for awhile. Justin was in Canada on business, so he gave him a ride down."

"Justin?" I say. "Who's he?"

"Oh, our cousin," Zack says. "He'll be here for a few weeks, I think."

"Yeah," Ben says, "it's a veritable family reunion!"

"My parents say you can come over for dinner tonight," Zack tells me. "Seven o'clock?"

I smile. "Sounds good to me."

"Just don't eat all the food this time," Ben teases.

I narrow my eyes at him and pretend to be annoyed.

Zack scans the table of stuff for sale and picks up a medieval-style cross made of silver and amethysts. "Look at this one."

Ben nods. "Beautiful."

A knot tightens in my stomach. "Yeah."

Calm down, Gwen. Just because you're going to a Christian home for dinner doesn't mean you're stepping into enemy territory. The Arringtons are nice. They like you. But would they like me if they knew what I really am?

five

I sit at my desk, my head in my hands, and wait for my computer to load. Now that I've met him, I can't resist inspecting "Takehiko's" blog again. He has a lot of inspired lunacy on there. Last week he posted a comic called "Invasion of the Mutant Tribbles!" An anime-style samurai stands in a bamboo forest as monstrous little furballs jump toward him, fangs gleaming. The samurai says, "WTF? (in Japanese)." Tavian also has a strange fascination with zombies. He likes putting them into sophisticated situations, like zombies golfing, or zombies sipping champagne and saying, "Indeed."

Stuff like that makes me wonder whether Tavian's just a total goofball with a penchant for the bizarre, but he occasionally posts serious fantasy art. At least he calls it fantasy, but the Others he draws look so very realistic.

Today he uploaded a quickly colored sketch of a bay

centaur standing on a grassy hill. The centaur is standing with his back to us, staring at a flaming sunset beyond a grove of olive trees. I can see longing in the tilt of his neck, the tension in his arms. The title: "Home." Oh, the centaur must be in Greece.

Wait. I stare at his dark curly hair. Isn't this the exact same one I saw at the Safeway?

I lean back in my chair and frown. Who is Tavian, anyway? I open up his blog profile. It doesn't say anything about his age or location. Under *Bio*, it says, "I'm a work in progress." But aha, look here. His Instant Messenger username.

"FoxFire88," I murmur.

My fingers hover over the keyboard. I can't resist seeing if he's online. I have a different username for IM, so that my blog can stay anonymous.

> r3dgw3n: Tavian?
> FoxFire88: who is this?
> r3dgw3n: Gwen. We met today at the bookstore.
> FoxFire88: are you e-stalking me?
> r3dgw3n: Maybe. ;-)
> FoxFire88: O_O
> r3dgw3n: lol
> r3dgw3n: I like your new art on your blog. Especially the
>   centaur.
> FoxFire88: thanks
> FoxFire88: brb

After about five minutes of waiting, I wonder if I scared Tavian off. Or if he's just not interested in chatting with me.

FoxFire88: Back. I was typing one-handed while eating.
r3dgw3n: Eating what?
FoxFire88: Tofu. Mmm.
r3dgw3n: Seriously? :-P
FoxFire88: I <3 tofu.
r3dgw3n: Okaaay.
r3dgw3n: So did you draw that centaur sketch from life? It's really realistic.
FoxFire88: Yeah. Saw a centaur at Safeway.
r3dgw3n: Me too!
FoxFire88: Sweet.

A new IM window pops up with a chime. It's Zack.

ThirteenthPaladin: Hi, Gwen. How are you?
r3dgw3n: Fine. You?
ThirteenthPaladin: I'm looking forward to dinner tonight.
r3dgw3n: Me too. :-)
ThirteenthPaladin: Though to be honest, I signed on because something has been bothering me, and I wanted to talk about it with you.
r3dgw3n: Oh, okay.

There's a pause of nearly an entire minute, during which time I chew on my lip. Why must Zack type complete paragraphs with proper grammar?

ThirteenthPaladin: I keep thinking about the drowned couple we found in the pond. They weren't the first dead people I have seen. When I was ten, my Great Aunt Zora passed away. I saw her lying in bed. I can remember being scared and sad, but now I know it was her time to go. The drowned couple just feels wrong. They were going to have a baby. How could God let them die?

My stomach twists. I'm not sure whether I believe in God or not. My other IM window flashes as Tavian sends a message.

> FoxFire88: Still there?
> r3dgw3n: Sorry. IMing somebody else.
> FoxFire88: No prob.
> FoxFire88: I've got to go, anyway.
> r3dgw3n: Why?
> FoxFire88: Dinner.
> r3dgw3n: Tofu wasn't enough?
> FoxFire88: Don't insult tofu or I'll spork you. ^_^
> r3dgw3n: lol
> FoxFire88: We should get together sometime, since we live in the same town. We would piss off coincidence if we didn't.
> r3dgw3n: Yeah.
> FoxFire88: See you later!
> FoxFire88 went away.

I close the window and turn my attention to Zack. I'm not sure how to respond.

> r3dgw3n: Sorry, distracted.
> ThirteenthPaladin: It's okay. Take your time, I'm reading a book.
> r3dgw3n: I wish we could have done something to help those poor people, but I guess it's best not to think about it too much.
> ThirteenthPaladin: Yes. We just have to trust God. He knows what He is doing.

I type nothing. What can I say? I don't trust God because I'm not sure he exists?

ThirteenthPaladin: I have to go now.
r3dgw3n: Okay.
ThirteenthPaladin: I'll see you at seven. My mom is
    making chicken casserole right now, and it smells
    good.
r3dgw3n: Mmm.
ThirteenthPaladin: Until then … Love, Zack.
r3dgw3n: Me too. <3
ThirteenthPaladin went away.

Violet evening softens the sky as I ring Zack's doorbell and hear "When the Saints Go Marching In." The tune makes me wince a little today. Then the door sweeps open to reveal Mrs. Arrington, she of the artfully applied makeup and only fancy clothes. Today she's wearing a beaded tunic and a silk scarf. Her long nails click against the door frame. I feel somewhat shabby in my thrifted peasant blouse and green tie-dye skirt.

"Gwen!" Mrs. Arrington arches her penciled eyebrows. "How lovely to see you."

"You too," I say, mustering a smile.

Mrs. Arrington looks over her shoulder. "Zachary! She's here!" She glances back at me, smiles, and walks into the kitchen.

"Hey, Gwen." Zack pecks me on the cheek. "Survived my mom?" he whispers.

I roll my eyes and mutter, "There's nothing wrong with her."

"Then you don't know her well enough." Grinning, he clasps my hand. "Onward. Time to brave the gauntlet."

"None of that medieval junk!" I whisper.

"Yes, milady."

I dig my nails into his hand, just hard enough to make him stop smirking.

"Zachary, where are your manners?" Mrs. Arrington says. "Escort Gwen inside."

He leads me into their "parlor," a dressed-up extra living room straight out of a JC Penney showroom. The furniture looks unused. Zack says that when he and Ben were kids, they were never allowed to play in there. Like their marble chess set, really fancy, that no one touches. I'm surprised they haven't roped the place off yet. Their house is always cool, even if it's summery outside, and quiet, except for the ticking of clocks. Kind of spooky when nobody's talking. And I don't think I've ever seen them open a window.

My house isn't anything like Zack's. Mine has that stagnant old house feel where there's too much stuff, not enough storage, and familiar clutter strewn about. Old and comfortable, if a bit claustrophobic.

I perch on the edge of a stiff loveseat. Zack flops down beside me. The smell of cooking meat wafts through the house.

"I do hope you like chicken casserole," Mrs. Arrington says. "Zachary's last girlfriend was a vegetarian. Poor girl couldn't eat a thing."

I glance at Zack, who pantomimes zipping his lips shut.

"Where's Ben?" I mutter. "And Justin?"

"They'll be here in a bit. They're buying some ice cream for dessert."

"Can you help set the table, dear?" Mrs. Arrington says.

Zack sighs dramatically and heads into the dining room. I sit alone for a minute, then follow him to help. As we lay silverware—probably real silver—on the damask tablecloth, he keeps pretending to accidentally grab the same ones as me. The touch of our fingers feels like a little electric shock. I stifle a slightly girly giggle.

Somebody rings the doorbell.

"I'll get it," Zack says.

I peer into the foyer. Zack opens the door. A tall man, well over six feet, slouches there in grungy overalls. His bleached hair stands in sweaty spikes. He has a lean, wind-swept look. If he weren't so dirty, he might be handsome.

"Hey Justin," says Zack. "How's it going?"

"Fine, just fine," the man says in a soft, somewhat high-pitched drawl. He looks past Zack with the same pale blue eyes. "Now, who's this young lady?"

"Hi," I say, walking to them. "I'm Gwen."

"I'm Justin Arrington." He holds out his grimy hand, then pulls it back. "Forgive me. I'm a bit dirty." He smiles, revealing dazzling teeth. At least they're clean.

I laugh politely. "Oh, don't worry about it."

Ben elbows past the considerably taller Justin, holding a plastic grocery bag high. "Ice cream!" he shouts, panto-miming a battle cry.

"Benjamin!" Mrs. Arrington calls from the kitchen. "Don't deafen our guests, please."

"Yes, ma'am," Ben says.

Justin sniffs the air. "Aunt Penny, you must be cooking something special."

Mrs. Arrington's voice warms. "Why, thank you, Justin."

Ben rolls his eyes and whispers, "Kiss-ass."

I bite back a smile.

Mrs. Arrington peeks round the corner. "Justin! How did you get so ... filthy?"

"Had to help a friend out with some home improvement."

Mrs. Arrington clicks her tongue, though she can't help smiling. "Go make yourself look presentable." She bounces her hand under her hair-sprayed curls.

"Yes ma'am." Justin touches his brow as if tipping a hat. "I'll see you soon." He bounds upstairs, taking the steps two at a time.

"Where's he from, anyway?" I say.

"Down south," Ben says, mimicking Justin's accent.

"Texas," Zack says.

"Which explains everything," Ben says dryly.

"How old is he, anyway?" I ask Zack. "You never mentioned a cousin."

"I have zillions of them. Justin's twenty-three."

I head toward the dining room. A framed print catches my eye. Some prayer written in flowery calligraphy over a photo of footprints in sand. I don't stop to read it, just like

I ignore the collection of Precious Moments figurines in a curio cabinet.

"Their teardrop eyes always creep me out," Ben says. "Probably creep out God, too."

"Wow," I say. "I can't believe you just said that."

"What?" Ben looks comically innocent.

"Boys," Mrs. Arrington says, "didn't I ask you to set the table?"

"Right," Zack says.

"Didn't ask me," Ben whispers, but he helps anyway.

I focus on setting the table with Zack and Ben. We're done all too soon. With nothing to do, I sit and fiddle with my fingernails.

A key grinds and clicks in a lock. The front door swings open. "Honey, I'm home!"

I try not to smile. I didn't think anybody actually said that in real life.

Mr. Arrington strides inside, toting a briefcase. He's a short man with a pot belly and a shiny bald spot ringed with white hair.

Mr. Arrington spots me and holds out his hand. "Good to see you, Gwen."

"Hi," I say.

He shakes my hand rather vigorously, then heads into the kitchen. I hear a loud smack of a kiss. Zack and Ben grimace, and I smile.

"Dinner's nearly ready." Mrs. Arrington peeks out of the kitchen. "Please, sit."

Zack pulls out a chair for me, then sits beside me. Ben sits across from us.

Mr. Arrington settles at the head of the table and smiles. "How are you, Gwen?"

"Fine," I say.

"So," Mr. Arrington says, "have you decided on a college yet?"

I try to keep my voice light. "Nope! Still looking."

Mrs. Arrington comes into the kitchen with a casserole between her oven mitts. She looks like a housewife straight out of the '50s. She sets the casserole in the center of the table, then heads back into the kitchen.

"It looks just as fine as it smells," Justin says, right behind me.

I glance over my shoulder. My eyes widen. Justin looks ten times better. He showered, slicked his wet hair, and abandoned his overalls in favor of black jeans and a sky blue shirt that flatters his eyes.

"You make me look like a slob," Ben says, tugging at his T-shirt.

I take a closer look and see it's got a nerdy web comic on it. "Wow, real formal, Ben."

He grins. "I'm glad you think so."

Justin sits beside me and rests his elbows on the table. Mrs. Arrington gives him a sharp look, and he straightens, instantly proper. When Mrs. Arrington isn't looking, Ben stares at the casserole with buggy eyes and sneaks a claw-like hand toward it.

I swallow a laugh. "So, Justin," I say, "what brings you here?"

"Doing some traveling for work," he says. "I just wrapped up in Canada, so I thought I'd give Ben a lift and visit you all again."

"So what is your work?" I ask.

"Justin's an *exterminator*," Ben says, like the voiceover in a scary movie trailer.

"I prefer the term 'pest control officer,'" Justin says.

I nod, not sure what to say. I've always thought of exterminators as having a particularly creepy job. I wonder if he came in all dirty because that "home improvement" involved helping a friend exterminate something. Ugh.

"How is it down in Texas?" Zack asks.

"Hot," Justin says, with a lazy smile. "Not much else to say."

Everyone laughs, even me.

Mrs. Arrington sets down wild rice, a pitcher of apple cider, and mesclun salad with arugula, chard, and lettuce. It all looks very nice. "Well!" she chirps. "That's all the food. John, do you want to say grace?"

Mr. Arrington starts to nod, then glances at Ben. "Let's give that honor to Benjamin."

Ben smiles quickly. His face sobers as he begins to say grace. Everybody but me bows their heads and shuts their eyes. I stare at my plate until "Amen." I'm sure Ben said a nice grace, but I'm glad when it's time to eat.

Mr. Arrington saws a piece of chicken with his knife. "How's the game in Texas?"

"Quite lively," Justin says.

"What game?" I ask, thinking football or basketball.

"There's plenty of it where I live." Justin smiles at me. "I prefer deer."

"Oh." My stomach sinks.

I hate hunting. After all, I transform into animals. Their minds don't think so differently than my human one.

"You should come back when it's deer season here," Mr. Arrington says.

"I'd like that," Justin says. "Anybody else interested?"

Ben toys with his fork. "Oh, you know I haven't gone hunting in years. I probably won't be picking up a gun any time soon."

"Fair enough," Justin says. "How about you, Zack?"

Zack glances at me and swallows. He knows I hate hunting. "Maybe."

I poke at my chicken, suddenly aware of it being dead flesh.

"Speaking of hunting," Justin says, "is it true that you folks have a werewolf problem?"

I flinch under his gaze, and my fork scrapes my plate. I talk fast to cover it up. "Yeah. A whole pack of them, apparently."

Ben tilts his head to one side. "Oh? A pack moved down here?"

"I haven't seen any," Zack says with a shrug.

"I live right by the national forest," I say, "and I heard them howling a few times."

Zack shoots me a look. "Really? Why didn't you tell me?"

I stare at my plate. "I didn't want to make you worry."

"We don't have a real werewolf population in Texas," Justin says. "Werecoyotes, though, keep crossing over the border from Mexico."

I nod. "This pack is supposed to be from Canada. Probably came here illegally."

"Probably criminals," Mr. Arrington adds.

"What's sad," Ben says, "is when innocent people are bitten and forced to live as beasts."

I glance at him, wondering if he's joking. If he is, he's deadpanning it.

"I suppose," Mr. Arrington says, his forehead furrowed a little.

"But you hear all these rumors about what they've done," I say. "Theft, rape, murder."

Chloe's voice echoes in my head. *Do you mean that?* But I don't have to defend them just because they're Others. Bloodborn Others, to boot.

Mrs. Arrington shudders, the water in her glass sloshing. "Nasty creatures."

"Definitely," I say.

"Though I do admire them as hunters," Justin says pensively. "Their skill."

"Skill?" I arch my eyebrows. "Brute force is more like it."

Justin fixes me with his pale gaze. "Have you seen them on the hunt?"

"No." My face flames, no doubt as red as my hair. "Have you?"

Justin shrugs and sips his cider, his eyes still on me. I clench my jaw, the beginnings of a headache throbbing in my temples.

"Let's pray we never do," Ben says, his face especially serious.

There's an awkward silence, punctuated by clinking silverware and a cough or two.

"Oh!" Mr. Arrington claps his son on the shoulder. "Zack, tell us about what you and Gwen discovered the other day."

What's he talking about? Wait…oh, not this.

"You probably heard it on the news." Mr. Arrington plows on as if pursuing a juicy bit of gossip. "A couple drowned in Wilding Park."

six

Zack swallows hard and glances at me. I press my lips together.

Ben knits his brow. "In the river?"

"In a pond," Zack says flatly.

Mrs. Arrington lowers her gaze. "Poor things."

"Yes," Ben murmurs. "May God have mercy on them."

I expected him to say "on their souls," but I suppose I've seen one too many melodramatic movies. I stare at his glimmering eyes and wonder if the death of strangers actually saddens him, or if he's just a good actor.

"I heard rumors," Justin says, "that the couple wasn't quite human."

I'm drinking cider when he says this, and it goes down the wrong tube. I sputter, cough, and grope for a napkin. My face burns.

"We can discuss this later," Mrs. Arrington says primly. "I hardly think it an appropriate subject for dinner."

"Mmm-hmm," I agree, rather hoarsely.

The conversation moves to the subject of college. Zack's already been accepted to the University of Washington. I haven't applied yet.

"I'm sure you could get into UW," Mr. Arrington assures me, blatantly winking in Zack's direction.

His parents then grill me about homeschoolers as if I'm a walking library. I force myself to answer their questions pleasantly, despite my worsening headache. At least I've dispelled the myth (much to their disappointment) that I'm one of those super-religious Christian homeschoolers.

"Honestly," I say, "I'm not sure when or where I want to go. My parents say I should save the time and money until I know."

And it has to be a college that is accepting of Others, but of course I don't say that.

"Very true," Mrs. Arrington says.

Justin listens in silence, then shrugs languidly. "I never did go to college. You can get by just fine without it, if it suits you."

Ben nods. "Myself, I found a calling higher than higher education."

Zack cuffs his brother on the head. "Of course, Mr. Holier-Than-Thou."

"Boys!" Mrs. Arrington says, but she bites back a smile.

For dessert, Mrs. Arrington serves something like ice cream lasagna with chocolate between the layers. It hurts my teeth. Soon I have a full-fledged headache, but I hide it behind a polite smile while they talk about the summer.

A grandfather clock chimes nine, and I put down my glass. "I have to catch the bus."

"So soon?" Mr. Arrington says.

I nod. "Before it gets too dark."

"Be safe!" Mrs. Arrington says, with genuine concern.

"Goodbye," I say. "Thanks for the dinner."

Zack follows me to the door. He kisses me, and I feign interest. When we withdraw, I rub my forehead.

"Hey," he says softly. "What's wrong?"

"Headache," I sigh.

He frowns sympathetically. "Do you want me to walk you to the bus stop?"

I shrug.

"I'm going with Gwen," Zack calls over his shoulder.

"Come back soon!" Mr. Arrington chuckles. "No hanky-panky now."

Ben wolf-whistles at that, and Zack rolls his eyes.

Outside, I see a white windowless van parked in front of the garage. Justin's, I assume. On its side it has a cartoon rat with crosses for eyes. In the glow of houselights, I read the motto. *We Get What the Others Leave Behind.*

"Creepy," I mutter.

"Justin can't afford a car," Zack says. "He's been driving in this all over the U.S."

"Oh."

Zack pauses. "He's a good guy. He's been through a lot."

"Like what?"

"Well, he loved this woman a year or so ago, even brought her to meet his family, but it turned out she was a vampire."

My stomach does a somersault. "Really?"

"Yeah. Apparently she just went around screwing with guys. She planned to bite him soon. Needless to say, he broke up with her."

"Yeah," I say weakly.

"I'm still not sure he's over her," Zack says.

We walk in silence toward the bus stop. Amber light pools beneath the streetlamps. In the darkness between them, Zack disappears from my sight. I clasp his hand tighter, glad he's solid and real beside me. He squeezes back.

I don't want to lose him. But I have to tell him.

Next morning at breakfast, Dad drafts me to help out at the hardware store. I grumble and poke at my oatmeal, but can't really think of a good excuse not to. So when Dad fires up his old pickup truck, I'm sitting shotgun.

Mum and Megan wave goodbye from the kitchen. I wonder why my sister never has to help out at the hardware store. Probably all that precalculus and cello practice or something. I, however, play nothing except the harmonica. While math doesn't bore me to death, I'm not titillated by quadratic equations.

The truck rattles and clanks down the driveway. Dad hums to himself. The sun wavers in and out of clouds as if it doesn't want to get out of bed—I sympathize. When I yawn, Dad glances at me. "Tired, Gwenny?"

I sigh at the babyish nickname. "Yeah."

"How was dinner over at the Arringtons'?"

"Meh."

"Meh?"

"So-so." I roll down my window and listen to the hissing wind. "But Ben was amusing."

Dad smiles. "Ben's back?"

"Yeah. Oh, and Zack's cousin, Justin, from Texas."

"All the way from Texas?"

"Yeah. He's an exterminator," I snort. "Pest control officer."

"Hmm." Dad pays more attention to making a left turn than to me. "I guess somebody has to do it."

I grunt neutrally.

The air feels cool, despite it being summer (try telling that to Washington). Goose bumps rise on my arms, so I roll up the window. Dad turns the radio to some folksy music, and it replaces our conversation until we park outside the hardware store. Ever since I was a kid, I've loved the hardware-store smell of fresh-cut wood, rubber boots, alfalfa, fertilizer, and well-oiled metal. I can remember playing in the big bins of nuts and bolts when I was six or so. The saw blades hanging on the back of the wall scared me then.

"Gwen." Dad tosses me a red apron. Time to work.

I start tidying tools. Whenever a customer comes in, I ask if I can help. These two old guys with hearing aids make me yell where to find the paint thinner. I have a nice conversation about petunias with a kooky lady wearing fake flowers in her hair. A couple with three kids comes in, and while the parents argue over greenhouses, I have to keep the little brats from playing lightsabers with PVC pipes.

After they leave, there's not much business for an hour or so, and I sweep the floors. I see Tavian walk past the windows. I wave, but he doesn't see me. My stomach drops. Stop it, I tell myself. You don't want to get his hopes up.

Around noon, Dad says, "Okay, Gwen, you have half an hour off for lunch."

I throw my arms into the air and mime a triumphant cheer. Dad laughs.

When I set foot in the Olivescent, I spot Tavian bending over a book, a slice of pizza drooping in his hand. My heartbeat stumbles, then comes back pounding harder then ever. Maybe it's because I find black eyes sexy. That makes me remember the whole eye candy fiasco, and I blush.

Chloe's voice echoes in my ears. *One word: boyfriend.*

What the heck. He's cute, and probably just friend material.

I stand in line, stealing glances at Tavian as he reads. He has dark shadows under his eyes, and his spiky hair stands up in all directions. Wonder why.

After buying some food, I make my move. "Hey, Tavian."

"Hah? Oh. Hey, Gwen." When he says my name, I smile, and he smiles too, the tired look vanishing from his face.

Damn, he's cute.

He raises his pizza in salute. "Have a seat."

I perch in the chair opposite him, my heart rate still fast, and set down my plate of calzones. "Tavian's an unusual name. Japanese?"

He laughs. "No."

"One of those New Age things?"

He laughs again. "It's short for Octavian. My parents are opera buffs."

I squint. "Which opera?" I've only seen a few on PBS.

"*Der Rosenkavalier*. Octavian is the count."

"What kind of count? Good? Bad?"

"Ugly?" Tavian adds, his eyes sparkling.

I give him a blank look.

"It's an old spaghetti Western," he says. "*The Good, the Bad, and the Ugly*."

"Oh," I say.

"Anyway, Octavian's a good guy. He's the Rosenkavalier, the Knight of the Rose."

Knights again. I wonder if Zack knows about this.

"What's that mean?" I ask.

"He has to deliver a silver rose to Sophie for her wedding with the pompous Baron Ochs. But Sophie and Octavian fall in love." Tavian frowns. "It's kind of weird, because Octavian is played by a soprano."

"What?" I laugh. "Why?"

"Young men in opera are usually played by women."

"That's weird."

"I know. I don't even like opera," Tavian says. "My parents just drag me along." He slaps his knees. "Well. That was an odd tangent."

"It certainly was." I smile. "Octavian."

He groans and shakes his head. "Nobody calls me that. I mean, I only ever hear it when my mom's pissed. Octavian Kimura!"

"Octavian Kimura," I echo. "Cool."

Tavian keeps shaking his head. "Not cool. Weird. I'm forever branded with weirdness."

I laugh. "I like weird."

"Do you?"

We smile at each other, and then I look away. Oops. Didn't mean to start flirting. What would happen if Zack saw us?

Tavian's smile slides away, his face weary again. He looks back at his book.

"Are you actually from Japan?" I say. "Born there?"

He glances up. "How did you know?"

"You have just a teeny-tiny bit of an accent." I pinch about half an inch of air.

"Most people don't notice." He rubs his eyes and yawns. "I'm tired."

"And you said 'hah?' instead of 'huh?' when you saw me."

A smile shadows his lips. "Did I?"

"Mmm-hmm."

My stare zeros in on the title on the spine of his book. *Unlike Us: A History of Paranormal Activity in America.* A tingle dances down my spine. Please let him be Other. Or at least on our side.

"What're you reading?" I say.

"Just some nonfiction." Tavian shuts the book and slips it into his backpack.

"Research?"

Tavian shrugs. His eyes say something I don't understand. A blush rises in my cheeks.

"I've got to go, actually," he says. "But we should hang out some time."

"Sorry." My blush intensifies. "I already have a boyfriend."

"Oh." He doesn't look crestfallen. In fact, he looks surprised. "Not like that. I mean, we're already kind of online friends."

"Oh. Yeah."

"IM me if you're interested."

"Okay."

He gives me a half-hearted wave as he walks away. "Catch you later."

"Yeah," I say, brilliantly.

I watch him leave the Olivescent. Why on earth would he be reading that book if he's not Other? Or interested in Others?

Sunday evening, I think of Chloe, and I can't believe I forgot her all morning and afternoon, moron that I am. She always makes a pilgrimage every Sunday—not to church, but to the forest at Boulder River. Dryads have to sleep in a tree at least once a week or they sicken and eventually die. Of course, this Sunday there are werewolves lurking about. I really hope she had the sense to change her plans.

I grab my cell phone and dial her number. Voicemail. Bollocks. My stomach flip-flops at the thought of shapeshifting to follow her.

I tramp downstairs, calling, "Mum?"

She's scrubbing dishes and setting them in the dishwasher. "What, Gwen?"

"Can I go over to Chloe's? I left something there."

Mum glances over her shoulder. "Now?"

"Yeah. It's important."

She sighs. "Only if you take the bus and come back here by ten o'clock."

"Yes, Mum!"

I grab my coat and hurry into the cool evening air. The last rays of sunlight slide from the cobalt sky, and a breeze steals my warmth. The bus, with its lumbering halts, takes forever to get to Bramble Cottage. A yellow glow spills from the B&B's windows. My heart rises. Could just be guests, though. I round the corner and see Alison at the desk, a prim girl not much older than me. Gah. Alison equals no Chloe.

Without waiting for Alison to see me, I wheel around and leave. I stride through downtown. Cars swoosh past, tires hissing on the rain-wet street. The glistening pavement reflects the topaz streetlights. I give the Half Moon Saloon a wide berth. A man staggers out to his motorcycle beneath the flickering neon sign. He shouts something incoherent yet clearly filthy at me, then grins, baring sharp canines.

Oh crap. Werewolf? I can't see the moon behind the blanket of clouds.

I walk as fast as I can without breaking into a run— that only excites predatory instincts. The man's motorcycle grumbles into life. My back stiffens. I wait for it to advance on me, but it growls in the opposite direction.

Maybe he's just a human with particularly long teeth. His dentist would be proud.

I stifle a nervous laugh and walk faster. Scattered trash skitters in the wind like ugly tumbleweeds. I pass mani-cured shrubbery in a parking lot. The pavement crumbles, yielding to wilderness. Streetlights vanish and stars glit-ter above. It's hard to tell where private property ends and national forest begins.

I follow the deer trails that lead to Chloe's favorite tree, a walk of about twenty minutes. There. An ancient queen of a bigleaf maple towers head-and-shoulders above all the other trees, shawls of moss cloaking its limbs.

I glance around. "Chloe?"

There's no answer. Then, through bristling black foli-age, I see an orange glow flickering ahead. I'm not anywhere near the Kliminawhit Campground … and isn't it awfully wet for wildfire?

Howls pierce the night. I jump, then grit my teeth. Not *again.* This is getting really annoying.

Silently, I creep nearer. There are people standing, silhouetted, around the flames. Sparks fountain skyward. What idiots, I think. Do they plan on burning down the entire national forest? I hear rowdy voices, a belch, then laughter. They sound drunk.

"Quit being so fucking loud, man," says a guy, just as loudly as the rest.

"Shut your fucking mouth, then," says another guy. "You tell him, Blackjack."

A low growl replies. A brindled pit bull lies at their feet, gnawing and slobbering on a rock. What kind of dog chews on a rock? What kind of werewolves own a dog? Frowning, I tiptoe even closer.

Four guys are standing by the flames, each holding a beer bottle. I recognize the Koeman brothers from the Buttercup Dairy: Chris, a bald guy with pale blond eyebrows, and his younger brother Brock, a standard issue hulking jock. I can't remember the name of the fat pimply guy, and I don't think I've ever seen the little skinny guy before.

"Mikey, aren't we supposed to be loud?" Brock cups his hand to his mouth. "Awooo!"

The fat pimply guy—Mikey, apparently—giggles rather girlishly. "Awooo!"

Chris laughs. "Man, you guys sound just like werewolves." He swigs his beer. "Let's hope those curs think so."

The littlest guy glances around. "I got to pee. You guys watch my back, okay?"

"Can't you piss here, Josh?" says Brock.

Josh shrugs, his cheeks pink. He edges toward the bushes and unzips his fly.

"You know," Mikey says, with a philosophical expression, "I've heard werewolves don't like people pissing on their territory. It pisses them off."

Josh stops peeing abruptly.

"Jesus Christ," says Chris, his face twisted with disgust. "This isn't their territory." He lifts a rifle from the ground. Its barrel gleams in the firelight. "That's why we brought this, remember?"

Mikey holds up his pudgy hands. "Yeah, Chris, I remember! Put that down, okay?"

Chris strokes the rifle, then props it against a tree.

Icy fear trickles down my spine. They think they can provoke the werewolves and fight them off with a rifle and a dog?

The pit bull lumbers to his feet, snuffles around, and cocks his leg. A stream of urine patters on leaves. The guys burst out laughing.

"That dog's so fucking smart!" Brock cackles. "Good boy, Blackjack!"

Idiots! Stupid, stupid idiots. I need to stop this. A burning log cracks and spits sparks high. I stride toward the orange glare.

Chris sees me first. "Who's this?" He narrows his glittering eyes.

seven

Blackjack lunges toward me, bellowing. I leap back, my heart hammering. My muscles tighten on the brink of transformation. Brock yanks Blackjack's choke-chain and drags the pit bull down.

"Who the hell is this?" Chris says.

Brock squints at me. "Uh … I've seen her around. Like, at the hardware store."

Damn. Klikamuks is too small of a town.

"Yeah," Chris says slowly, all twelve of his brain cells working hard. "She's that homeschool girl. What's her name?"

How irritating. Talking about me like I'm not here. "Gwen," I say.

"You sure she's not trouble?" Josh whispers, his eyes round and guilty.

Brock shrugs. "We can handle her."

Chris's face relaxes into a smirk. His gaze lingers on my body. I fold my arms tight, trying not to look uncomfortable, or, worse, afraid.

"Care to join us?" he says. "Gwen?"

I look coolly at him. "I barely know you, and I'm not interested in getting drunk."

"How about getting drunk and getting laid?" Chris snickers at his own cleverness.

"Oh, how appealing," I sneer. "Does that line usually work with girls?"

Mikey laughs, and Chris whacks the back of Mikey's head, none too lightly.

"What do you think you're doing out here?" I say. "Howling at werewolves?"

Josh licks his thin lips. "Uh…"

"Just having some fun," Brock says.

I point at the rifle. "And that?"

"Protection." Brock arches an eyebrow. "You need to loosen up, baby."

"You shouldn't provoke werewolves," I say.

"What," Brock says. "You on the side of those gicks?"

Gicks. Magicks. I haven't heard that slur in years.

My face heats. "I'm not on anybody's side. Just saying that they could kill you."

Chris sidles closer, close enough to breathe beer fumes on me. "You worried about us?" He drapes an arm over my shoulders.

I shrug him off. "No."

He grabs my arm. "Why'd you come all the way out here? Huh?"

I yank away.

Chris grabs me again. "Huh?" He says it louder.

My heart pounds against my ribs. I clench my hands to stop their shaking.

"Chris." Brock tugs his brother back. "Quit."

Somebody grabs my butt. I whirl.

Mikey giggles. "Nice ass."

I want to punch him. I want to turn into a cougar. But I can't. Not in front of them. They know me. They know me, and they are still treating me like this. Tears prick my eyes, and that only makes me angrier.

Arms encircle me from behind. "Cool down, fire-crotch." Chris presses against my back.

Oh, isn't that clever. "Let go of me," I say.

Chris squeezes my hips, bruising me. "Shhh." His breath warms my ear.

"Let go of me, or you'll regret it." My voice sounds surprisingly level, considering how much I'm shaking.

"I don't think I'm going to regret anything," Chris murmurs.

"Oooh." Mikey swigs his beer like a spectator at a game. "Hey, aren't redheads supposed to be horny?"

Josh backs away, his face pale. Brock glances at him, looking equally uneasy.

I shut my eyes to hide their glow. Magic is burning inside me. My skin feels feverish. I concentrate on my hands.

I dig my nails into Chris's arms, and he doesn't flinch. But he does more than that when my nails become cougar claws.

"What the fu—" Chris screams as I dig deeper.

Blood wells beneath my fingers. I keep my eyes shut tight and hope the glow doesn't leak out. I quiver on the brink of cougar. A growl rumbles up in my throat, but I force it down. They can't know.

Chris yanks back, and I throw myself into girl form with a gasp. My eyes snap open. I raise my blood-slicked hands before my face. No golden glow shines on them. Shaking and giddy, I face the guys.

Chris clutches the gashes on his arm and stares at me. "Bitch!"

"What'd she do?" Josh asks, looking paler.

"Dug her nails into me!" Chris says.

Brock whistles under his breath. "She's got some fucking long nails."

Chris grabs my wrist. He stares at my short little bloodstained nails.

I twist out of his grasp. "I'm leaving. And you'd better get out of here before the werewolves kick your butts."

The guys are so shocked they let me walk away.

"Wait a second," Brock says. "Her nails. Claws! Is she…?"

"Get her, Blackjack!"

Not the rifle, I mentally urge them. Don't remember the rifle. I break into a run, pursued by Blackjack's panting.

Crap. This time I'm really in for it. Can I possibly shapeshift fast enough?

I hear a *whoosh—thwack—yelp*. I wheel around to see a low branch flinging Blackjack aside. The pit bull hits a trunk, slides, and scrambles to his feet. Whimpering, he flees with his stumpy tail between his legs.

Yes! Here comes the cavalry. Chloe, at least.

The boys shout and curse. Chris raises his rifle, but another branch smacks it from his hand. Josh shrieks. Mikey runs away, surprisingly fast for a fat guy. Chris grabs his brother's arm before he can follow.

"Get the gun!" Chris bellows.

Brock dives for it, but a root rises from the dead leaves like the Loch Ness monster and twists around his ankles. He cries out, groping for the rifle as another root drops it neatly into the bonfire. Chris starts yelling and waves at them to flee. They scramble away, tripping over serpentine roots. Cowards!

A branch coils around my waist and hoists me high into the air. I shout, my stomach lurching, as it lifts me even higher. My feet are dangling twenty feet above the ground. Then a sound like firecrackers makes me clap my hands over my ears. Ammo explodes from the rifle and peppers the trees. The tree holding me—a towering Douglas fir—shivers as if in pain. Chloe's face surfaces from the bark and glares at me.

"What took you so long?" I say.

"What are you doing here?"

"Looking for you." I fidget within the branch's grip. "Can you put me down?"

She sets me down, well away from the bonfire. Her

face sinks into the tree, and she steps from the trunk and strides toward me.

"Gwen! Are you insane?"

"Are *you*? Don't tell me you were actually sleeping out here with werewolves around."

"I can take care of myself," she says coldly.

I feel an awful twisting in my stomach, like I always do when Chloe's mad at me.

"Great," I say, "just great. I blundered into moronic guys for nothing. And why did you wait so long to help?"

"I decided to sleep as far away from those young men as possible. They didn't wake me until I heard them shouting at you." Her steely expression wavers. "Thank you for worrying about me, but you shouldn't."

"Humph," I say, but I'm not pissed off anymore.

Chloe grabs my shoulders and spins me around. "Not hurt, are you?"

"No."

She purses her lips. "Gwen, you shouldn't be so reckless."

I stare steadily into her eyes. "You shouldn't, either."

"True." Chloe's gaze flickers away from mine. "I…"

"What?"

"Nothing."

"It's not nothing, I can tell."

"Have you ever had the feeling that you're being watched?" she asks.

The hairs on my arms bristle. "Of course."

"I've felt that way for the past week or so. This morning,

someone left a bouquet of roses on my doorstep. With no note."

I laugh. I can't help myself. "Randall."

Chloe frowns. "It doesn't seem like something he'd do."

"He's staying at the B&B, right? Maybe he picked some roses from the garden." I'm still smiling. "See? I said he liked you."

She shakes her head. "What about a stalker?"

"Nah. Probably just some secret admirer." I make a face between a grin and a grimace. "Hopefully not Chris or Brock."

"It was rather amusing when their dog ran off," Chloe says in a conversational tone.

I laugh. "It was funnier when they did." I scratch at the blood under my nails. "Yuck. I'd better wash this off."

Chloe nods. "You should head home."

"Yeah. By the way, thanks for saving my butt."

"Any time." Her smile doesn't touch her eyes. She looks away, then back at me. I'm not sure what I see in her face. "Randall is…"

"What?" I raise my eyebrows. "Are you guys officially together?"

She squints, then sighs. "Yes."

"Ah, I knew—"

"And he's a werewolf."

"*What?*"

"I've known it for a while now," she says. "And before you ask, it doesn't bother me. In fact, I don't think it should affect how I feel."

"You're crazy," I say, shaking my head. "A werewolf? Seriously?"

Chloe leans against a mossy tree, her gaze distant. "He told me soon after I told him, but I already knew."

"Told him what? Wait, you didn't—"

"Gwen." She meets my gaze. "Don't worry. Randall's a good person."

"He's a *werewolf.* He's *dangerous.*"

Her eyes sharpen. "How do you know?"

"Haven't you heard? Werewolves and vampires just love to seduce women right before they bite them. And did you really—"

"That's not true, and you know it."

I fling out my arms. "It's in their nature to do that. Why do you think there are so freaking many of them?"

"Them? They're Others, like us. Randall understands me."

"Chloe! This isn't Beauty and the Beast. You're not going to somehow tame him. And wait, is he with that new pack?"

"No."

"Did he tell you that?"

"Yes." Her voice chills. "We obviously disagree on this topic. Can we let it go?"

"I . . . I guess." I exhale noisily. "Just be careful, okay?"

"I will if you will," she says, and she smooths her hair back and walks away.

You know, I thought getting my driver's license would be one of those empowering, rite-of-passage kind of things. But instead it just sucked. No, "sucked" is too kind of a way to say it. More like sucked monkey balls.

Outside the Department of Licensing, Dad tries to smile. "Want to drive home?"

I shake my head and yank open the passenger-side door. How can he honestly think I still want to drive after what just happened? While Dad backs out of the parking lot, I stare at my temporary black-and-white paper license. My photo beams at me, foolishly happy. Next to the line "HT: 5-07" and "EYES: HAZ," it says "50% POOKA."

"For identification purposes," the guy at the DOL said, which of course is total bull.

How can I ever show this to Zack? To anyone?

A lump smolders in my throat all the way home. Mum frowns when she sees me and assumes I failed my driving test, but Dad explains. I run to my bedroom, grab a pen, and bury "50% POOKA" under black scribbles. Then it looks nearly normal.

Nearly normal. As if I am.

That afternoon, I work at the hardware store, the monotony a comfort. Dad lets me sort merchandise while he handles the customers. When I return from lunch, I see Justin's white van parked outside. What's he doing here?

I freeze at the edge of the parking lot, my fists clenched.

Bollocks. Chris and his stupid friends are loitering by the doors.

I breathe deeply and stride toward them, my face blank.

"Red," Chris calls. "Hey! You listening to me, Big Red?"

I ignore him and keep walking. Brock steps in front of the door.

"Excuse me," I say, in a mild voice.

"Aren't you happy to see us?" Brock asks.

Mikey giggles. I hate that giggle. Josh fidgets and twitches like a little ferret.

"Redheads are my favorite flavor of lady." Brock leans closer, smacking a wad of mint gum, and pretends to lick me. "Spicy."

There's a snowball's chance in hell I'd find these assholes sexy.

They're blocking my way, but I try to keep moving. "I have to get back to work."

I notice that Chris didn't bandage the ugly red wounds I gave him. Apparently he wants to look macho or something.

Chris leans close. "I know what you are," he hisses, beer-and-cigarette breath in my face.

I rummage in my purse. "Breath mint?"

"Bitch," he spits.

I pretend not to have heard, but I'm sure my face is stoplight red.

"What breed of gick are you?" Chris lowers his voice to a whisper. "Cur or leech?"

Oh, I just love it when people assume all Others are

werewolves or vampires. I've had enough of these Nean-
derthals. My heart hammering, I advance on Brock. At the
last minute, he steps away with an insolent sneer. Magic
simmers inside me.

Inside, I see no sign of Dad. Justin, in overalls and a
cowboy hat, is browsing axes.

I tie on my red apron. "Can I help you?" I ask, in my
fake-chirpy work voice.

Justin turns and gives me a lazy smile that feels like
warm sunshine. "Fancy seeing you here, Gwen."

"I work here," I say, now blushing for a different reason.

He nods. "I'm looking for some chain."

The spools of chain lie at the back of the store. I'm
glad to get away from the door.

Justin ambles behind me. "I want extra strong."

"Right here," I say, pointing at the thickest we carry.

I glance out the windows and see the four guys loitering across the street. I exhale. Justin takes about five yards
of chain to the checkout, along with a camouflage poncho,
three pairs of thick gloves, a shovel, and an ax.

As I scan the items, I say, "What's all this for, anyway?"

He shrugs languidly. "Hiking, geoducking, that sort of
thing."

I raise my eyebrows. "Geoducking?"

"Digging for clams," he says.

"You need an ax for geoducking?"

Justin's laugh surprises me. "I doubt that would be a
clever way to get geoducks. The ax does a much better job
cutting firewood."

"Oh." I'm blushing, but smiling. "Yeah."

"Actually," he says, "Ben would be the one—"

"Zack!" Dad strolls up to us. "My, you've grown. And you cut your hair."

"Dad," I groan, "it's Zack's cousin, Justin."

When Dad grins, I know he's teasing. "From Texas, right?"

"Born and bred," Justin says.

"I've got to use the restroom," Dad says. "Woman the store, Gwen."

I roll my eyes. "Okay."

Justin tips his hat to me. On his way out, he holds the door for an elderly man who's shuffling in.

I recognize the man: Mr. Quigley. He lives in an ugly little pistachio-colored cottage with plastic windmills stuck in the flowerbeds, and he doesn't get out much. When he does, it's mostly for numismatist meetings. He keeps asking people for coins to add to his collection. I gave him an old penny once.

"Hi, Mr. Quigley," I say. "Can I help you?"

With his five-foot-one height, wire-rimmed glasses, and curly white beard, he looks like he should be a jolly old man, but he scowls at me. "Eh?"

I raise my voice. He's probably hard of hearing. "Are you looking for something?"

He nods sharply. "Some hooligans smashed my mailbox." His strong Boston accent gets on my nerves sometimes.

"I'm sorry to hear that," I say. "Do you need a new one?"

"Of course I need a new one," Mr. Quigley grumbles. "They're in this aisle."

He follows me, muttering under his breath. After one glance at the mailboxes, he jabs his finger at the cheapest one. I carry it to the checkout for him and ring it up, then hand him a dollar bill and two quarters in change.

Mr. Quigley perks up. "What's this?" He squints at one of the quarters. "Wisconsin...2004-D...extra leaf!"

"Extra leaf?"

He holds it up to me. "The corn has an extra leaf. This could be worth five hundred dollars, easy!"

"Wow," I say, mentally kicking myself.

Mr. Quigley beams, his cheeks rosy. He carefully folds the five-hundred-dollar quarter in a handkerchief and tucks it into the pocket of his shirt. "Thank you very much, young lady! Keep the rest of the change."

"Uh, have a nice day," I manage. "Don't forget your mailbox."

Mr. Quigley carries it under his arm. Whistling, he leaves the store. I see Chris, Brock, and company crossing the street again, advancing on Mr. Quigley. The fine hairs on my arms bristle. I think I know who bashed his mailbox.

Damn. Dad's still in the restroom. I start spray-cleaning the windows in order to watch.

Mr. Quigley tries in vain to step around the guys. They jeer and dance around him, blocking him. Justin peers around his white van and frowns. I brace myself for trouble.

Then Justin says something to the guys I can't hear. They hesitate, then slouch back toward the store. Mr. Quigley climbs into his rickety car and leaves.

The door opens, and a prickle crawls down my spine. Apparently they've found enough balls among the four of them to actually come inside. Footsteps approach behind me. I scrub the windows harder.

"Hey, firecrotch," Chris says.

Play innocent, I tell myself. Wait until they screw up, then nail them.

I feel stinky breath on my neck. That has to be Chris.

I make my face blank and turn around. "Can I help you?"

Chris is standing only a few inches from me, his hands at his sides, his fingers twitching.

"Uh, yeah," Josh says. "We're looking—"

Brock elbows him, and he shuts up with a squeak of protest.

Chris bends closer. "Quit playing dumb," he whispers.

Oh, I think I'm going to keep playing dumb. "I'm sorry I snapped at you guys in the woods." I smile through clenched teeth. "I was just worried about you. But I'm sure you can take care of yourselves, being as tough as you are."

The guys inflate like proud roosters—except for Chris.

"You're a filthy liar," he hisses.

I wrinkle my brow. "What are you talking about?"

"Your eyes are this fucked-up color," Chris says.

"Hazel," I say.

"What?"

"They're called hazel."

Chris's face twists. He shoves me in the chest, his fingernails digging into my breast.

"Okay," I say. "That's sexual harassment. Get out of the store before I call the cops."

Mikey bites back a nervous giggle. Josh edges toward the doors.

"Oh really?" Chris says. "Think they'll believe a gick like you?"

I laugh. "Think they'll believe an asshole like you?"

"Is something going on?" Never have I been so glad to hear Dad's voice. "Gwen?"

Chris backs away from me. "We're just browsing," he says. "Come on, guys."

They slouch off in the direction of the machetes.

Dad pulls me aside. "Gwen," he whispers. "Were they bothering you?"

I shrug. "They were just being dickheads, as usual."

"Hey. Watch the language."

I narrow my eyes, two seconds away from telling Dad that Chris shoved me, but that would lead to me explaining why he did it in the first place. So I inhale slowly, then sigh. "Okay. Sorry. Wouldn't want to scare off customers."

Dad claps me on the shoulder. "Next time, let me know, okay? I'll deal with them."

I stay close to Dad until the guys buy a machete and leave the store. I shudder.

eight

The night breathes rain-cooled air into my bedroom, rippling the curtains by my window. I inhale, savoring the tang of woodsmoke. It helps me sleep if I can see the sky. Tonight it's cobalt blue, etched with the silhouettes of trees.

An owl starts hooting outside my window. After about five minutes, it starts getting annoying. Stupid bird. I jump out of bed and slide open the window. Surprised, I laugh. Zack is perching in the vine maple, his hands cupped to his mouth. I roll my eyes at his hoodie and pajama pants.

"Gwen!" He grins at me. "You heard."

"What are you doing here?"

He hops onto the roof. "Your virtue is in no danger from me, milady," he says, his hand over his heart. "May I come inside?"

I laugh—it sounds a bit rusty—and shove the window

open wider. Zack climbs into my bedroom, kicks off his shoes, and smooths his hair. I hurry to lock the door, then face him. My heartbeat thumps against my ribs. Just the sight of him in my bedroom excites me, but I don't want to wake my pooka half.

Zack sits on the edge of my bed. "You've seemed kind of down lately."

My smile fades. "Yeah." I sit next to him, my hands clasped in my lap.

"Especially this past week."

I laugh curtly. "I've had a lot going on."

"I know, but it's more than that." He hesitates. "You seem uncomfortable around me."

"Zack!" I sigh and lay my hand on his shoulder. "It's not your fault."

He frowns, as if my casual gesture belittles the moment.

"I've just been … dealing with some personal issues," I add.

"Why won't you tell me about them?"

Something inside me hardens, goes cold. I stare at the carpet.

"See?" He slides off the bed. "You're uncomfortable around me."

"It's not that! Zack, you have to believe me. My feelings for you haven't changed."

He says nothing, just stares at me, his eyes glimmering.

I stand and kiss him, trying to tell him everything without words. He doesn't move. Then he embraces me, and the kiss deepens. His hands slide from my neck to my hips. Blood whooshes in my ears. He drives me backward, up against my bedroom wall. I arch against him, my body as taut as a bowstring about to be loosed. We break apart, breathing raggedly, our faces close enough to kiss again.

"Gwen," Zack whispers, his eyes closed. "I believe you."

I press my lips against his and run my hands over his strong shoulders. Heat rushes through me, melting the numbness inside. Nothing else matters but us, together, so close, yet not close enough.

My heartbeat's pounding so hard I wonder if Zack can hear it, but still, I feel nothing alarming from my pooka half. So long as I don't think about biting or other wild things, I'll probably be okay—I hope.

"I know just the thing," Zack says, "to make you feel better. Lie down."

"What?" My heartbeat stumbles. "Why?"

Zack smiles. "Trust me. It's not what you think." He glances pointedly at my bed.

"Wait," I say. "Let me tidy up a bit."

I clear my stuffed toys off the quilt. I don't want them staring at me with their big innocent eyes, reminding me of the people who gave them to me. Last into the closet: the fishbowl of toys from my nightstand. Zack watches me, his face shadowed—I wonder if he thinks I'm childish. Not looking at him, I lie down.

"On your stomach," he says.

I roll over. He tugs my hair aside and starts massaging

my shoulders. When my tension melts away, I realize just how uptight I was.

"Mmm," I say, muffled by my pillow.

Zack kneads my back in deep, satisfying circles. I love his touch around the lower curve of my spine. I drift into a half-sleeping daze. His fingers slow, then slide along my waist. He kisses the clover tattoo on my neck.

"Gwen?" he murmurs. "Are you asleep?"

"Almost."

I'm so sleepy my pooka side seems to be snoozing, blissfully unaware. Maybe it won't wake up. Maybe I'm safe. I roll over and stare at Zack. The soft look in his eyes makes me melt. I'm so lucky to have him as a boyfriend.

I draw him into a kiss. When he pulls away, I catch his arm. "Stay."

Zack raises his eyebrows. "Stay?"

"You can sleep here." My face burns, but I stare steadily at him. "I mean, in the most innocent sense of the word."

"Sure."

He tugs the hoodie over his head, giving me something to stare at, and climbs into bed next to me. The bed jiggles and creaks as we get comfortable. He lies beside me, not touching. I'm acutely aware of the space between us. Frogs chirp in the silence.

Okay. Try to fall asleep.

Zack laughs.

"What?"

"I have to pee," he whispers.

I sigh. "Really?"

"Yes. I drank too much water before I got here."

"The bathroom's across the hall. But if you wake anybody up…!"

"I won't." He slips out of bed. My gaze meanders over the moonlight on his bare chest.

"Watch out for my sister. She sometimes goes late at night."

"Okay." Zack unlocks the door and tiptoes out.

I brace myself for Megan shrieking or Dad bellowing. How could I explain? I hear the toilet flush, the sink run, and soft footsteps approach. Zack slips back into my bedroom, locks the door, and climbs into bed.

I smile. "I hope you washed your hands well enough."

"Yes ma'am. But they're cold." He grabs my arms with a hissing noise.

"They're icy!" I wriggle away, laughing.

Zack rubs his hands together. "How's this?" He wraps his arm around my waist.

"Better." I snuggle into the curve of his body. "Much better."

I watch digital minutes pass on my clock. An ache gnaws inside me. I can't stop thinking about his hot breath on my neck.

I whisper, "Zack?"

"What?" he murmurs.

"Are you awake?"

"Obviously."

Long pause.

"I can't sleep," I say.

"Me neither."

I rest my head on Zack's chest. His heartbeat thumps in my ear, slower than mine. I stroke his long hair, and he buries his nose in my curls. Our ankles cross beneath the sheets. It feels so sweet just to lie so close.

Zack sighs, and he doesn't sound content.

"What?" I say.

"I don't want to pressure you, Gwen, I really don't, but we've been together long enough that it seems like we should be ready."

I stare at his silhouette. "For sex?"

"Yes."

I flick on my bedside lamp so I can see his face, but I still can't read his expression. "It has to be the right moment."

"There have already been many right moments for me."

His words sting. "But it has to be for both of us."

"Of course," he murmurs. "I didn't mean it that way."

It's my turn to sigh. "Maybe I'm just scared. I mean, once we do, there's no turning back. How will it change things?"

"Gwen," he says, "don't worry about it. It'll be okay."

I exhale slowly. "Well, this is certainly not the time or the place."

He nuzzles the hollow of my neck. "I can wait."

I manage to smile and kiss him, then flick off the light.

Around dawn, Zack wakes me by getting out of bed.

Half-asleep, I catch his arm and make a soft moan of protest.

"I have to go," he whispers.

"Why?"

He smiles. "This is your bedroom."

"Oh." I shut my eyes again. "Goodbye."

He kisses me, then leaves me with the memory of his lips.

I drift off again, then wake at my normal time. Nothing remains to say Zack spent the night. I grin to myself. Something does look different though ... oh, I put away all my stuffed animals. I take them back out of the closet. There. All my toys look at me with little black eyes. They seem too innocent to know about sex. I wonder if I will give away my virginity in this room, or somewhere else.

Should I tell Zack the truth about me being Other before? Or after? I bite the inside of my cheek. What will happen? A thorn of fear pokes my heart. I don't know what he'll say. Not exactly. Not at all.

Much to my chagrin, Dad says I've got to help out at the hardware store again, since he's so busy with a wayward shipment of lawn mowers. Sure, I'm getting paid, but I'm skittish all morning, keeping an eye out for Chris, Brock, and Co. Dad doesn't seem to notice, his ear glued to the phone. When lunchtime comes, I'm glad to escape the store.

Just when I'm turning the corner, somebody calls, "Gwen!"

I hesitate between steps, not sure whether to stop or walk faster.

"Gwen, wait up."

I recognize the voice. "Tavian?" I face him. "What are you doing here?"

He looks even more tired and pale than he did last time I saw him. "Looking for you."

"Since when do you know where I work?"

"I asked a waitress at the Olivescent." Tavian ruffles his hair to a new level of spikiness. "Which reminds me. Do you want to get something to eat?"

"Tavian ... I'm really not planning on dating behind my boyfriend's back."

He sighs. "It's not that. I want to talk somewhere not so public."

"About?"

Tavian presses his lips together and jams his hands deep into his pockets. "Bad news."

"What happened?"

He starts to wave me closer, then just grabs my hand. "Come on."

All right. Let's see where this leads. Actually, Tavian doesn't lead me very far at all. Just to a little garden outside a café.

He sits on a bench. "I didn't want to tell you in the street, but ..."

I don't sit, and cross my arms. "Tell me what?"

"You know Mr. Quigley, right?"

"Yeah. A lot of people do. Kooky old man."

"He's dead."

We stare at each other.

I don't know what to say, except, "Really?"

"I saw him." Tavian rubs his hands over his face. "He's— he was—my neighbor. I saw him … lying in his yard."

"Was it an accident?" I say in a small voice.

"Not unless he accidentally strangled himself." Bitterness saturates Tavian's voice. "And the weird thing is …"

My heart's thumping with dread. "What?"

"He was dressed all in green, with a whiskey bottle in his hand and a couple dozen coins scattered around him."

"What! Why?"

Tavian stares at me. "His coin collection, I suppose. I don't know why."

"All in green?" I say. "Was he trying to make some kind of a statement?"

"I don't think *he* was."

I try my best to ignore the sick feeling in my stomach. "You're saying … ?"

"Gwen," Tavian says in a low voice, his head tilted in my direction. "There was no noose. Nothing around his neck. If he killed himself, how did he get himself out in his backyard, so neatly arranged like that?"

I sink onto the bench, my knees suddenly shaky. "Unless it was a murder."

"Yes. And I think," Tavian adds, in an even lower voice,

"that the murderer wanted to tell us something about Mr. Quigley."

"What do you mean?"

His voice is barely above a whisper, his black eyes intense. "Mr. Quigley was Other."

I jerk away as if his words burned me.

"You knew, didn't you?" he says.

I shake my head. "Tavian, I don't know what you're talking about."

"Gwen," he says, his eyes saying he doesn't believe me.

"And why *would* Mr. Quigley be Other?"

"Think about it. Green clothes, coins, short old man."

I laugh hollowly. "Being a short old man makes you an Other? That's news to me."

"He was a leprechaun," Tavian hisses. "I'm sure of it. And I think the murderer killed him because of that."

"That's speculation," I say, not wanting to believe it.

"What about the vampire they found dead outside the 7-Eleven? What about that couple who drowned in Wilding Park?"

The water sprites. He must have heard rumors about me finding them.

I turn away and press my knuckles to my mouth. "Why are you telling this to me?"

"Gwen." Tavian softens his tone. "I think you know."

With that, he stands and walks away. I don't have the guts to follow. He has to be Other. Does he know I am?

That night, I huddle on the couch with my family, watching the news. It isn't good. A streak of apparently random killings in Seattle. A homeless teenage boy, a solitary middle-aged woman, two brothers on vacation. They don't have a photo of the homeless boy, but they do have one of the woman: pale-faced, without makeup, her seal-brown hair parted down the middle. She looks ordinary, not Other. But with the two brothers, even the police can't deny their quicksilver eyes, ivory hair, and ice-water blood—sightseeing frost spirits from somewhere in Norway. Flamboyant, obvious targets.

It would be so easy to kill Others in a big city like Seattle. Pick them off, one by one.

I leave the living room in a cold, numb daze and trudge upstairs to my bedroom. The water sprites. The vampire. Mr. Quigley. How easy was it to kill them? I lie limp on my bed, blood whooshing through my ears. I drag the covers over my head and curl into a ball. Hot tears leak past my eyelids.

The hatred finally boiled over. Someone's killing Others.

I toss aside my covers, grab my cell phone, and call Chloe. I gouge a hangnail as it dials.

"Hello?" she says.

Words tumble out of my mouth. I want to tell her everything: Mr. Quigley, the boys harassing me again, Tavian, the murders in Seattle.

"Slow down," she says, in a voice of forced calm.

I draw a shaky breath and start over, digging at my hangnail until it starts bleeding.

She listens, then at last says, "You think there's a serial killer out there?"

"I don't want to." By now I'm gulping air and trying not to cry. "Do you?"

She's silent for a moment, and that tells me everything.

"Do you think Tavian's right?" I say. "Do you think they're Others?"

"Can we trust him?"

I heave a shuddering sigh. "I don't know. Do you think *he's* Other?"

"There's a possibility. I haven't a clue what kind, though." Chloe pauses. "You know, these killings make me think of the White Knights."

"The White Knights?"

"An ultraconservative organization that's built around a hatred of Others. They're famous for burning crosses and lynching Others. Around the turn of the century, the White Knights had over four million members in America alone."

"Oh! I remember reading about them. But I thought they disappeared in the 1930s."

"That's merely what the history books say. So long as people hate Others, the White Knights will never truly die out."

I shudder. "You think it's them?"

"Or perhaps someone who aspires to the ideals of the White Knights. Gwen, if a killer is targeting Others, we'll simply have to lie low."

"What, you trust the police to do their job?"

She speaks in a cool tone. "Don't try to do their job for

them. Now would be an exceedingly poor time to make ourselves known."

"Yeah." I grab a tissue and blow my nose. "Sorry. I didn't mean to get all emotional."

"That's all right. It frightens me too. Promise you'll be careful?"

"Of course. You too."

I stare at my reflection, red-eyed and blotchy, in the mirror above my bookcase.

Chloe pauses. "How are things between you and Zack?"

"Not bad, actually. I think I'm going to tell him soon."

"Good." Her voice sounds warm with relief. "I'm proud of you, Gwen. It takes guts."

I'm quiet for a moment, a little embarrassed, and then a thought crosses my mind. "How about you and that— you know, Randall?"

Chloe coughs. "We're both fine."

"I still can't believe you're dating him," I mutter.

"I trust him."

"I can't believe you do."

"Are you implying I have poor judgment?" Chloe says frostily.

My face reddens, and I'm glad she can't see it. Part of me wants to ask what he's like. I've never knowingly had a conversation with a werewolf.

She sighs. "Well, I should go. We can talk more later, okay?"

"Yeah. Thanks for listening to me. I feel better now."

"You're welcome." Chloe's voice thaws a bit. "Good night."

I set down my phone and bite a hangnail. Really, of all the crazy things … dating a werewolf has to be near the top of the list.

I sign on to the Internet and scour Tavian's blog for any signs of Otherness, but it's so full of the bizarre and fantastic it's almost impossible to tell. He's uploaded a new piece of artwork, in the style of a Japanese woodblock print—a little black-haired boy standing among foxes in kimonos. The boy looks lost.

I frown hard. What does it mean? Who *is* Tavian?

nine

When I open my bedroom curtains the next morning, I think it's snowed in the middle of summer—but only for a few groggy seconds. The white is toilet paper. It loops and tangles through the trees in our backyard.

I stare numbly at the TP. Who did this?

Chris. Brock. And the rest of those stupid boys.

I glance at my alarm clock. Still 6:40. I'm the early bird of the family. Maybe I can clean it before the others wake up.

I don't bother changing out of my pajamas, just slide open my window and crawl onto the roof. Gritting my teeth, I grab a piece of TP fluttering in the wind. The moist air makes it somewhat soggy. It tears into little pieces. I curse and pull myself into the nearest vine maple. I grab fistfuls of TP and toss it down.

This is going to take forever. My stomach sinks to somewhere in the region of my toes.

Damn it! Why did I ever try to talk to those guys in the woods? Why did I talk to them again at the hardware store? I should've just ignored them and told my parents. But then they'd be pissed at me, too.

I work faster. I can't reach the highest branches. Should I transform into some sort of nimble animal? Would anybody see? A dog barks, and traffic whooshes on the nearby highway. A car door slams, an engine starts.

Maybe if I go down and get a stick. A rake. Or something.

I descend from the vine maple, scraping my knees and bloodying some knuckles. I drop to the ground. A sharp rock jabs my foot. I yelp and hop on one leg, cursing through clenched teeth. Crappity-crap.

The front door scrapes open. I freeze like a deer in the headlights.

"Gwen?" Dad blinks owlishly at me. "What's going on?" His eyes widen as he glances around the yard. "Who did this?"

"Not me." I laugh, on the verge of hysteria. "Not my fault."

But it is, to some degree. My throat tightens until it hurts.

Dad tramps outside in his slippers. He stalks around the yard, glowering at every tree, and rakes his fingers through his tousled hair.

"I'm sorry." My voice quavers, and I have to look away

for a whole second before I can get a grip on myself. "I didn't mean to piss them off."

Dad stares at me. "Who?"

"Chris and Brock, those brothers. Mikey. This guy named Josh."

Dad looks dumbfounded. "But *why*?"

"I need to talk with you and Mum."

Mum isn't very happy to be woken up for this. As soon as she sees the mess in the yard, the Welsh swearwords fly. I make a mental note to look them up later, if I can manage to spell them.

My parents sit at one end of the kitchen table. I sit at the other. Why does this feel like the interrogation room in a police station?

"All right, Gwen. Tell us," Mum says, her accent suddenly strong. Uh-oh.

I draw a shaky breath. The story spills out of my mouth. Everything, including me digging claws into Chris's arm and drawing blood. When I repeat the word "gick," tears sting my eyes, but I set my jaw. I end with a pathetic, "I'm sorry."

"Gwenny," Dad says, "it's not your fault."

"Isn't it, Nicholas?" Mum's voice lilts like a furious songbird. "She knew very well what sort of trouble she was getting herself into."

I let my head drop to the table and fold my arms in front. "I know," I moan.

"Those boys were being assholes!" Dad says.

"Of course they were," Mum says. "But Gwen has to

learn that just because she's half pooka, she's not bloody invincible."

I hate it when they start talking about me like I'm not in the room.

Dad sighs. "You're right." Anger returns to his voice. "Gwen, what happened in the store? Were they harassing you?"

I nod. Hot tears roll down my face. I keep my head down.

"Those little pieces of—"

"Nicholas," Mum says.

Dad glares at the floor, his jaw taut, and I know he's trying not to rant around Mum.

"Gwen," Mum says, softer. She can always tell when I'm crying. "Those boys had no right to treat you that way, but what you did was dangerous. There's a better way to handle things. You have to be nonconfrontational."

"What?" I lift my head, frowning. Is she going to go all Gandhi on me?

"Talking to those boys only provoked them," Mum says.

"Obviously," I mutter under my breath.

Mum narrows her eyes, and I flush.

"Nonconfrontational," Dad repeats. "It's best to ignore them and report them to someone who can handle them."

"What, the police?" I say with a bitter laugh. "They don't care about Others."

"They'll care about this," Mum says, waving at the TP on the trees. "Believe me!"

She has this tone that makes me believe she'll march down to the police station and kick butt if they don't cooperate. I feel a little bit better.

"I don't think TPing is actually illegal in this county," Dad says, somewhat mournfully.

"Well then." Mum sighs. "I suppose I'd better call their parents before the police."

"I hope they get grounded for life," I mutter.

Mum goes over to the telephone. As she flips through a phone book, she glances at me. "As for you, Gwen ... I don't want you out of this house after dark. As soon as the sun goes down, you're staying in."

"Okay," I say.

"That includes nighttime flying," Mum says.

"What?" How did she know about that? Bollocks. I underestimated her motherly radar.

Mum gives me a scorching look.

"Yes, Mum," I sigh.

I still don't feel right. Shaky, sick with fear. Chris, Brock, and the other guys seem to think I'm Other. But if they'd do something as silly as TPing my yard, they don't seem like the kind of people to actually kill anyone.

Then who did?

Of course, the werewolves are the most likely suspects. They're not very friendly. I mean, heck, they're fugitives from Canada. Frowning, I lean my elbows on the table and knead my forehead. Why do I have to have problems in the boyfriend, family, and possible-serial-killer departments all at once?

My life officially sucks.

My cell phone rings, and everybody jumps. It's Zack. I unplug it from the charger on the kitchen counter and hurry upstairs.

"Hey, Zack," I say, trying to sound like I'm glad to hear from him.

"How's it going?"

"Good," I lie.

"I just remembered something I wanted to tell you the other night."

My stomach sinks. "Oh?"

"My parents and Ben are going to an art fair this Sunday. They'll be gone until the afternoon. We can have the whole house to ourselves."

I perk up. "Really?"

"Yes. What do you think?"

"Yeah!" Suddenly I feel alive again, my skin tingly. Now's my chance to tell him.

"I want to make things perfect," Zack says, his voice suddenly velvety.

"Oh!" Of course that's what he means. "I…"

"I'll let you think about it. Call me if you're interested, okay?"

"Okay. Thanks for letting me know."

Zack hangs up, and I set down my cell phone with wobbly hands. I clench them into fists. Why do I have to be so naïve and scared? I chew on my lower lip. After a minute or so, I tell myself that I'm making my decision and there's no turning back. No chickening out now, it's too late for that. I'm going to go.

Sunday morning, I keep glancing at my cell phone. It rings, and I lunge. Gah. Just one of those random telemarketer numbers.

Deep breaths, Gwen. I pretend to swoon onto the bed. Giggling, I hug myself. Okay. I know I want to do this. I've been thinking about it practically forever. Now we'll finally be as close as we can be.

And somehow or another, I'll tell him the truth about me being Other.

With sweaty hands, I call Zack.

"Gwen?"

"Yeah, it's me." I draw a deep breath. "How's it going?"

"Great. My parents just left. You want to come over?"

The way he says it, I can imagine his eyes smoldering. "Sure."

I shut my cell phone and rub off the fingerprints. After half an hour of trying on clothes, I settle on my favorite jeans and a moss green blouse. I brush my hair, watching myself in the mirror, then run downstairs, taking the steps two at a time.

"What's the hurry?" Mum calls, peering from her office.

"I'm going to Zack's," I say.

"For how long?"

I flush. "Oh, I don't know. An hour or two."

She eyes me, then looks back at her computer. "Okay. Be safe."

What's that supposed to mean? Be safe on the way there, or be safe with Zack?

"I will," I say, since I plan on both.

The bus ride to Zack's neighborhood lasts several eternities. I cross and uncross my legs, my skin hypersensitive, and keep reapplying my lip gloss. Finally I hop off the bus and walk to his house. When I knock, he sweeps open the door.

"Hey," he says. "You look nice."

"Thanks." I flash a nervous smile.

He ushers me inside with a wave of his arm. I cross the threshold, my heart racing. I stride to the living room and perch on the couch.

"Zack?"

He's standing in the doorway of the living room. "What?"

"Uh…" I break into a grin. "This is kind of awkward, isn't it?"

"Not really."

I can't stop staring at his eyes, so blue, and his long loose hair. I realize I'm pressing my knees together. I force myself to relax.

"Do you think we should talk more?" I say.

"We already talked," he says. "Isn't that why you're here?"

I blush. "Well, yes."

He flicks his eyebrows upward. "Come upstairs. You're going to love what I found."

The moment of no return. I can back out later, but it will be harder emotionally. A grandfather clock fills the silence with ticks.

Excitement bubbles inside me, boiling over as one word. "Okay."

Zack heads upstairs. I follow, clutching the banister. My heart hammers at my own daring. He peeks inside his bedroom.

"Uh, wait here," he says.

He darts inside and shuts the door behind him. I see his shadow through the crack under the door. What's he doing?

"Okay," he calls. "Come in!"

I push open the door. The window curtains are closed. Silver candlesticks stand on his dresser and cast a warm, flickering glow.

"Oh!" I say, sounding unusually coy. "How lovely."

"Yeah." He smiles, a smoking match in his hand. "I found them in the attic. I almost did roses too, but that would be overboard."

I try to smile in return. I can tell him now. But I really don't want to ruin the moment.

"You look nervous," he says. "Relax."

That was blunt. I press my lips together.

Zack stands so close behind me I can feel the heat of his body. His breath stirs the hairs on the nape of my neck. I tense.

"Zack…" I face him. "I…"

He kisses me on the mouth, and words melt from my mind. I pull back, my pulse racing. His eyes are flame-blue.

"I have to tell you something," I say quickly. "You don't know everything about me."

He frowns, then makes an effort to look understanding. "Okay."

"I…I'm not sure how to say this, but I'm…"

He exhales, relief dawning on his face. "It's okay."

"Really?"

He nods and steps very close. Before I can speak, he scoops me into his arms.

"Zack!" I make a noise between a laugh and a shriek. "Don't drop me!"

He smiles down at me. "Don't worry. I've got you."

I cling to his neck, feeling like one of those women on a romance novel cover. Heat radiates off his body, and desire clouds my mind. I want him, all of him. He lays me on his bed and kisses me so fiercely I wilt.

"Zack," I whisper.

His golden hair curtains my face. He kisses the hollow of my neck. I swallow, feeling his lips against my throat.

"Zack, wait."

He pulls back. "Too fast?"

I struggle to catch my breath, my hand above my heart. He stares at the rise and fall of my chest. My blouse rides up past my bellybutton, and his fingers skim the bare skin at my waist. I catch his hand.

"Stop," I say, trying to be gentle but firm.

He frowns, looking more and more confused. "What's the matter?"

"It's not you … it's just … I …"

Tenderness fills his eyes. "Gwen. I totally understand."

"Do you?"

"Yes," he says, and he kisses me as if to prove it.

When he pulls back, I know he can see the hesitation on my face.

"Do you want to or not?" he asks.

"It's more complicated than that."

"It's kind of a yes-or-no question."

I sigh. I'm such a coward. How can I break it to him?

"Don't worry," he says. "I have protection."

He opens his nightstand drawer and gets a condom. He seems embarrassed to hold it, so he sets it on the nightstand and kneels on the floor beside me. He tilts my face toward his and kisses me. I moan softly with protest and pleasure. His touch drives me wild. Thoughts fight to surface in my mind.

When I can speak again, I say, "You really know what I mean?"

"Yes. Of course. I guessed you were quite some time ago."

I want to smile, but I'm too scared. Is it that obvious that I'm Other?

"Really?" I repeat. "It's okay that I'm not like you? That I'm …" My lips move for the word "Other," but no sound comes out.

He draws back to meet my gaze. "Yes."

Relief thaws the cold fear inside me. I exhale, then hook my hands behind his neck and kiss him. His chest presses against the side of the mattress. His hands slide down my body and find the zipper on my jeans.

I shiver, thrilled and scared by the reality of the situation. "I … you … could you …"

"I'll go slow. You can just say stop."

"Okay," I breathe.

He climbs onto the bed, and I start unbuttoning his shirt. A button gets stuck. He fiddles with it, then yanks off the shirt at the expense of the remaining buttons. I laugh, a short, breathless laugh. He tugs my blouse over my head, then unhooks my bra and tosses it away. I fold my arms over my chest, shy in the candlelight.

"You're beautiful," he says, and he gently pulls my arms away.

He kisses between my breasts. Tingles dance over my skin. The rest of our clothes soon follow, and at last he climbs into bed with me. Just being naked together seems so deliciously intimate. I want to savor everything.

"I can't believe we're finally doing this," I whisper.

"Yeah," he says hoarsely.

He keeps kissing and touching me until I can't bear it any longer. I stare at the ceiling, breathing in quick gasps. He asks if I'm ready, and I nod, too excited to speak. He snatches the condom from his nightstand.

I shut my eyes, then suck in my breath at the sharp twinge.

"Okay?" he says.

I nod. "It didn't really hurt like I thought it would."

Then, without fanfare or a choir of angels, we're having sex. It's still somewhat painful, but pleasurable as well. A flock of thoughts flits through my mind. So simple? Yet more than I ever imagined. I stare over his shoulder, my eyes unfocused, and curl my fingers around his neck. He sees my face and freezes.

"What?" I say.

"Wait," he says. "Wait... God, I don't think I can..."

I feel him stiffen, then shudder. He blows out his breath and lowers himself onto me.

The weight of him makes breathing uncomfortable. "Zack," I wheeze.

"Sorry." He rolls off me.

Was that it? The whole deflowering thing?

I frown at the ceiling and ache with unspent energy. "I didn't—"

"I know." Zack gives me a half-smile. "We're not done yet."

In a few minutes, I groan and clutch the sheets.

Afterward, I lie beside him in a dreamy daze. "I love you, Zack." I can say it so easily, now that it isn't caged up inside me.

"Me too," he murmurs, his eyes closed.

"I can't believe I waited so long."

"Well, it's good to wait until you're sure."

I smile. "I'm so glad you're okay with who I am."

He opens his eyes a crack. "Hmm?"

"With me being Other," I say.

"Other than what?"

"Very funny," I say dryly.

He rolls onto one elbow. "What's funny?"

I poke his arm. "Don't act so innocent."

Zack's face clouds. "Gwen..."

"If you're wondering," I say, "I'm half pooka."

I wait for Zack's face to clear, but it remains shadowed. "You're...what?" He laughs hollowly. "Half pooka?"

What does he mean? Why did he laugh like that?

"Pooka," I repeat. "My real dad's a shapeshifting spirit from Wales."

Zack slides to the edge of the mattress. "You're Other," he says slowly.

I try to smile. "Of course."

"You're kidding me." Now he's on his feet.

My stomach plummets. Something isn't right. "What are you talking about?"

"What are *you* talking about?"

We stare at each other.

"You said you understood!" I cry. "I thought you knew!"

"I was talking about your virginity," he says, and he sounds so cold.

Tears sting my eyes. "Zack." My voice quavers, and I hate it. I realize I'm curling on the bed to hide my nakedness.

"You...all this time..."

"Yes," I whisper, "of course."

He sits down at the foot of the bed, not close enough

to touch me, and kneads his brow. "It's not like werewolves or vampires, is it?"

"What? You can't just lump me with *them*."

"Yes, but is it... contagious?"

"No!" I glower at the back of his head. "I inherited it from my dad. Like I just said."

He exhales shakily and starts pacing around his room.

"You said you wanted this to be perfect." My voice catches. "You're ruining it."

"It's just... Jesus, Gwen! Why didn't you tell me sooner?"

"I tried to! A few dozen times! I know this sounds really bad, but... I... I don't know."

"Gwen." Zack won't look at me. "I think you should go. My parents will be back soon."

"Yes," I say, my throat aching. "I should."

I yank on my clothes. Hot tears roll down my face. I march toward the door, and Zack catches my arm.

"Gwen." His voice softens. "We can talk later."

I nod, not meeting his gaze. He hands me a tissue. I snatch it from him, and it tears in half. He tries to give me the other half, but I shake my head and leave.

It was so wonderful, before he knew.

ten

When I get home, I cry in the shower until the water goes cold. I towel myself roughly, then tug on my dirty clothes. I notice a small bloodstain in my underwear. I feel strange, vulnerable. Like I'll never be myself again.

I leave my hair wet. Usually I hate it dripping down my neck, but today I don't care. I sit on the edge of my bed, shivering, though it isn't that cold. I pick up my cell phone and dial Chloe's number.

It rings endlessly. Then I get her voicemail.

"Hi Chloe," I say. "It's me, Gwen. I really want to talk." I hesitate. "It's about Zack. Call me back soon. Bye."

I shut my cell phone, check the battery, then set it on my bedstand.

I lie back on my bed. My hair wets the pillow. I stare at the milky round light on the ceiling until it blurs and looks like the moon.

My limbs feel leaden. I count my stillborn hopes, then shut my eyes and drift off.

When I wake up, an hour or so has passed. I call Chloe again. She should still be at work, and she always has her cell phone with her.

"Chloe? Are you there? It's me, Gwen." I hesitate. "Maybe I'll stop by later. See you."

I drag a comb through my matted hair. It hurts, but I like the distraction. I grab the Bean and head out.

It starts to rain when I get off the bus. I only have to walk two blocks to get to Bramble Cottage, but I still get soaked. Ironically, the shower passes as soon as I reach the B&B. The story of my life. Clouds always wait for me.

Raindrops glisten on the rosebushes like tears. In the B&B, opera meets my ears, a sad aria I don't recognize. Odd. Chloe doesn't really like any classical music. I think it's because it reminds her of her age.

A grating sound, metal against wood, punctuates the music. It comes from a parlor by the foyer. I slowly push open the door to see Randall on his knees. The carpet has been ripped back. Hammer in hand, he's wrenching staples from the floorboards with a strength and ferocity that makes me stare. I realize my heart's pounding, and that I'm a little afraid to be around him. I've never knowingly been so close to a werewolf.

Just pretend you don't know, Gwen. He won't reveal himself.

"Randall?" I'm not sure he can hear me over the music. "Randall!"

He shuts off the radio and faces me, his expression dark. "What is it?"

"Where's Chloe?"

Randall wipes sweat from his brow. "I don't know. She hasn't been here since this morning." His jaw moves as if he's gnashing his teeth.

"Did she say where she was going?" I ask.

Randall nods. "The forest." He hesitates, but doesn't say more.

My heartbeat quickens. "Why?"

He sighs and sits on the floor. The hammer drops from his hand with a thunk. "We kind of got into an argument."

My eyebrows shoot up. "An argument? About what?"

Randall meets my gaze. I notice, for the first time, that he has striking eyes. Not a remarkable color—dark brown—but intense. "We've gone out a few times. Unofficially." He wiggles his fingers in air quotes. "Then Chloe said we should stop, it would compromise our working relationship. She wouldn't listen to me."

Finally! Chloe wasn't seriously thinking about a relationship with a werewolf. Maybe she just wanted to see what it was like. I'm no expert on her dating history, but she does seem to have a thing for dangerous guys.

I see Randall's staring at me, so I mutter a quick, "I'm sorry."

He shrugs. "Why are you looking for her?"

"I want to talk."

"Find her, then. I would, if I didn't have to work." He

nearly snarls the last word, and it's all I can do to keep myself from recoiling. He drops to his knees and starts yanking staples from the floor again.

I wince at the sound and leave Bramble Cottage. Bollocks. Why didn't I bring the car? I don't feel like walking all the way to Chloe's maple.

I drift through Klikamuks like a ghost among the lively passersby. A knot tightens in my chest, as if something's going to snap if I don't shapeshift. I leave the stores and sidewalks behind for abandoned lots where weeds edge into the forest. As soon as I reach the trees, I peel off my clothes and urge myself into horse form, with a shudder that reminds me of Zack and myself. No. I don't want to remember.

I run, my hooves pounding an angry beat.

What should I say to Chloe? It's funny how we both ran into relationship drama on the same day. Though she did the smart thing, breaking up with a werewolf, and I...I gave my virginity to someone who now looks at me like *that*. Just because I'm not totally human doesn't mean I'm not a person. Zack has to understand. Eventually. What's really stupid is that I knew this would happen, but I let lust take over.

Screw it. Screw the whole thing.

I run faster, at a full gallop. The road flashes past through the trees. I picture drivers glimpsing me, staring at the runaway horse. My muscles burn, but I push myself harder. I plunge into the deep forest. A startled stag bounds from the ferns and zigzags in front of me. I race it to a stand of salmonberries, and win. I skid to stop and the stag vanishes. Sweating, my sides heaving, I halt by the giant maple.

No sign of Chloe. I whinny, then circle the tree, scanning the branches. Still no sign of her. With a sigh, I trot away in search of my friend. The sun slips lower and lower. Puddles of light pool among the shadows, then fade into darkness. When evening falls over the forest, I know I have to quit.

Bleary-eyed, I shapeshift into a girl again, yank on my clothes at the edge of the woods, and plod home.

We keep a spare key in a fake rock, so I let myself inside. My family is sitting in the living room, their eyes reflecting the light of the TV.

"Did you all eat already?" I ask.

"There you are, Gwen!" Mum says. "Did you have dinner over at Chloe's?"

I shake my head. "She isn't there."

"Dinner's in the oven," Mum says absently.

Dad furrows his brow. "Why are there twigs in your hair?"

"I went looking for Chloe in the forest. I can't find her."

"Hmm," Dad says, his gaze gravitating to a commercial on TV.

I sigh and go upstairs. An unnameable emotion gnaws inside me. Nibbling away my sanity, no doubt. I lie on my bed and wonder if things could have gone any differently today. What if I showed Zack my pooka side? Would it help him understand?

The minutes blur together as my eyes blur with tears.

"Dinner's ready!" Mum calls.

I go downstairs, dutiful and robotic. Mum slices a steaming potpie. I usually love potpie, but I can't stomach any tonight.

"What's wrong, Gwen?" Dad asks.

"I'm just not hungry," I mumble. "Can I go to bed?"

Mum lays her hand across my forehead. "You don't have a temperature."

"I'm just tired," I say.

If Mum and I were alone, I would be tempted to blurt out the truth about what happened between Zack and me. But since Dad and Megan are staring at me, I trudge upstairs. My feet feel like bricks. Where could Chloe be?

My clock only says 8:45, but I crawl into bed and fall into mercifully dreamless sleep.

My cell phone wakes me. I crack open my eyes and squint in the morning light. Groggy, I grab the cell phone. Zack's number. I half-open the phone to answer. Then anger clenches my chest and I slap the cell phone down.

I don't think I can talk to him. Not yet.

He tries calling me again, and again. After five calls, I turn my cell phone off, get dressed, and go downstairs.

Halfway through breakfast, someone knocks on the door.

"Who could that be?" Mum says.

I half-stand, ready to dart away, but Mum gets up first. I drop back down and clutch my spoon so hard it digs into my palm.

Mum opens the door. "Hello, Zachary. Why the early visit?"

"Oh, nothing, just wanted to talk to Gwen." Zack tries to sound casual and fails.

Surely Mum knows something's up, but she lets him in anyway.

Zack stands in the doorway of the kitchen. I'm half angry, half glad he's here.

"Gwen." He waves at the door. "Do you…?"

I shake my head, my lips a thin line. Hurt sharpens his eyes. Act normal, I tell myself. Don't burst into tears in front of everybody.

I suck in air through my nose. "Let's go to my bedroom."

"Oho," teases Dad. "Leave the door open, you two."

I feel sick. Without looking at Zack, or at anyone, I go upstairs. He follows.

In my bedroom, I shut the door and lock it, forcing myself to face him. "Okay." I lean against the wall. "It's time to talk."

Zack sits on the edge of my bed. I want to tell him to get off and sit somewhere else.

"Gwen." He stares at his hands. "I'm having a hard time…believing…"

"Believing what?"

He glances at me, then away. "That you're Other. I mean, you seem so normal."

I narrow my eyes. "Others can be normal."

"That sounds oxymoronic." He laughs bleakly. "But I'm serious. You're only half pooka, right? How...how different are you?"

"What do you mean?"

He pinches his neck in little nervous movements. "What kind of magic do you have?"

Hope stirs inside me. Maybe if I show him, he'll understand.

"I can shapeshift," I say.

"Shapeshift," he repeats. "Really?"

"Of course."

He keeps staring at me. I twist my toes and fidget under his eyes.

"Can you...show me?" he says, cheeks red.

"Oh. Okay."

I turn my back on him and undress. Of course he's already seen me naked, but it's different now. I clench my fists and tighten my thighs. My muscles shake, and I keep waiting...waiting for it to happen.

Do it. You have to show him. You have to.

I think I'm going to cry. I clench my jaw and shut my eyes, then finally shapeshift into a horse. My hooves hit the carpet. I step toward Zack, my head held low, and whicker.

He slips off my bed and slides down to the floor. He looks so pale, with a sheen of fear or shock in his eyes.

I change again, shrinking into a cat. Perhaps he'll find a marmalade tabby safer. But he still looks pale, his mouth twisted tight. No, please don't be afraid. I pad silently over to him and rub my head under his hand. He yanks away.

I change back into a girl and kneel, naked, my head bowed. My hair hides my face.

"Oh God," he says, still on the floor. "It's true."

I grit my teeth. "Don't look at me like that."

Now he won't look at me at all.

I tug on my clothes, brusquely. "It's because you're Christian, isn't it?"

He says nothing.

"I'm right, aren't I? Christians hate Others." If he believes the Bible, he must think my very existence is a sin.

He shakes his head. "That's a stereotype."

"But the Bible says we're devils and demons. That's a bunch of bull—"

"Don't say that," he says, glowering at me.

I step back under the force of his glare. "Hey. I'm not talking about the whole Bible. Only the stupid parts."

"Just stop it, Gwen."

"Me?" Anger rises inside me. "Why is this my fault?"

"I didn't say it was anybody's fault."

"Did you wish I was a good little Christian home-schooler, virginal and pure?"

Now I'm crying.

"Don't cry, Gwen." He stands up with a sigh, exasperated.

"Shut up!"

He looks surprised, as if I slapped him.

I look away, tears rolling down my cheeks. "I'm sorry," I say, my words broken. "I wish none of this ever happened."

"It shouldn't have happened," he says in a low voice.

"What's that supposed to mean?" I step toward him.

"This isn't going to work."

"We can work things out!"

He's shaking his head, already halfway to the door. "No. I can't."

I'm not going to let him go. "Why not?"

"My family...my *mom*..." He slides his hands over his hair. "Everything I've ever known, everything I've ever believed."

"Zack," I say, swallowing hard. "I still love you."

"Gwen!" His voice snags on my name. He turns his back on me and leans his head against the door, his hands pressing on the wood.

"If I weren't Other, would you stay with me?"

He won't answer, but I know what he'd say.

"No one else has to know."

He whirls on me. "No more lies!"

We lock gazes, tears in our eyes.

"Fine," I say. "Great. It's over. Get out of here."

Trembling, I reach past him and grab the doorknob. I yank, but it won't move. I remember the lock and wrench it open.

Zack hesitates on the threshold, but won't look back. "Gwen."

"I don't want to hear it, Zack. I don't want to see you again."

His back stiffens as if my words have hit him like bullets. Without a word, he runs down the stairs, nearly colliding with Mum at the bottom.

"Zack?" she says. "Leaving so soon?"

"Goodbye," he says, loud enough for it to be meant for me.

I stand at the top of the stairs and watch him slam the door. Mum stares at me, her mouth and eyes an "O."

I sit on the top step and begin to sob.

"Gwen!" Mum rushes upstairs. "What happened?"

"We broke up."

She sighs and wraps her arm around me. "Oh, Gwen. I know how hard that can be."

I glance downstairs. Though I can't see Megan or Dad, they can probably hear me. Mum guides me into my bedroom, shuts the door, and sits with me on my bed. I rest my head in her lap and keep crying.

"Why did you break up?" Mum says.

"I ... we ..." I lower my voice to barely above a whisper. "We had sex."

Mum doesn't seem as shocked as I expected. "And?"

I draw a shuddering breath. "I tried to tell him before we did it, but he thought I was talking about my virginity."

"Tell him what?"

"That I'm Other." I moan. "Now he knows."

Mum exhales slowly. "It's not your fault. Some people are just like that."

"But why does it have to be him? Why Zack?" My jaw trembles. "I thought I knew him."

Mum just sighs and holds me close until my tears die to sniffles. After about five minutes, she says, "I'd better start lunch."

"Okay." I pull back and rake my fingers through my hair.

"Macaroni and cheese. How does that sound?"

I manage a wobbly smile. "You know it's my favorite."

Mum stands, smooths her clothes, and heads for the door. "You'll feel better later. And remember, Mr. Right is still out there, waiting."

"He'd better be," I say, pretending to shake my fist.

Mum smiles and shuts the door behind her.

I hunch on my bed. The tears washed away some of the ache inside me, but I can't stop thinking of Zack. One minute I wish I'd hit him; the next, my mind races through all the possibilities of us getting together again.

Through my closed bedroom door, I hear muffled voices. I tiptoe over.

"Whoa," Megan says. "What happened?"

"She broke up with Zack," Mum says. "It's best to leave her alone."

There's some quieter comments I can't hear, then silence. I crawl back into bed, intending to stay there forever. Mum brings the macaroni and cheese up to me. When night falls, I keep drifting into sleep, then lurching awake. By morning, I'm emotionally exhausted.

I need to talk to Chloe. When I try calling her, I get

no answer. Maybe her cell phone's broken. Instead, I call the B&B.

Alison answers the phone. "Hello, Bramble Cottage."

"Hey, Alison," I say. "It's Gwen. Is Chloe there?"

"No, actually. She was supposed to be here this morning. I suppose she's just late."

My stomach sinks. Chloe's very rarely late. "Okay, thanks."

When I hang up, I decide to just go over to the B&B and see what's going on myself. On the bus, I lean my forehead against the cool windowpane and try to block out the chatter of excited friends. A couple cuddles on the seat in front of me, and their quick kiss feels like a needle pricking my heart.

I get off at Bramble Cottage and step into the lobby. Alison's distracted by a customer, so I slip upstairs, stepping over a rope with a sign that says *Employees Only*, and head for Chloe's attic bedroom.

Her door's locked. I rap on it. "Chloe?"

Silence.

She's probably still in the forest, enjoying her time with the trees. Or... maybe she made up with Randall, and they're together somewhere. Frowning, I glance out a narrow window. Somebody's standing in the garden.

Randall. I guess that rules out one of my hypotheses.

I peer at his shaggy brown head. He's holding a pair of small gold items. He tilts his hand, and they glint in the overcast light. I squint and lean closer. Are they... Chloe's maple-blossom earrings? Randall lifts them to his face—

kissing them? He drops them into the pocket of his jeans and steps into the B&B.

My heartbeat thumping, I hurry downstairs before he can come up. We jostle shoulders in the doorway to the lobby.

"Hey," I say. "Have you seen Chloe?"

Randall shakes his head, his eyes dark. I shiver and hurry to catch the bus home.

No, Gwen. It can't be what you're thinking, what you have been thinking all this time. Werewolves are bad, in general, but not by default...and would Chloe really be that naïve? A weight sits in the pit of my stomach.

It's almost too obvious. And I don't want it to be true.

I play dead on my bed, curled around a clump of quilts, and stare out the window. Afternoon clouds curdle, souring the sky. The scent of coming rain dampens the air. I shove open the window and get ready to shapeshift. Should I tell Mum? But it's not like I usually tell her. Besides, she only banned nighttime flying.

With clumsy fingers, I tug off my clothes and toss them aside. My skin prickles as glossy black feathers unfurl. Now a crow, I pump my wings, glide through my bedroom window, and ride the wind toward the Boulder River Wilderness. A chilly breeze fingers my feathers. I can feel it in my hollow bones—a storm soon.

Soon I reach the Kliminawhit Campground. It's not

far from my house, as the crow flies. Lame joke, but the truth. Hardly anybody is camping today. I suppose nobody sensible would, given the murders and the werewolves.

I glide low over the trees. I hear the whispery pattering of beginning rain, hopefully not the prelude to a down-pour. Wet feathers don't fly well, so I dive between a gap in the canopy, flare my wings, and land on the ground.

Squeezing my eyes shut, I change into a girl. Naked, I shiver. I feel huge and heavy, and plod through the for-est until I settle back into my bones. Chloe's favorite maple looms ahead. Rainwater rolls from its leaves. Silently, I walk around the maple's trunk.

A scream snags in my throat.

Chloe hangs from a branch by a noose, her eyes closed, her face white. A pine-tree air freshener dangles from her neck, horribly ridiculous. Pale gold liquid oozes from her slashed throat. I never knew her blood was like sap.

My legs crumple, and I crawl forward.

"Chloe?" I whisper, so faint that she wouldn't hear me even if she could.

I touch her hand—her cold hand. I yank back as if she's disgusting, then immediately feel ashamed. The wind blows tears slantwise across my face, and rain washes them away. I shake my head. Chloe can't be dead.

Who killed her?

Fury flames inside me, igniting my magic. I double over, wracked by transformation. Spikes of fur bristle along my spine—talons sweep from my fingers—fangs pierce my lower lip. I taste blood. I stare at my hands. Scales, striped fur, black insect armor. My size shrinks and swells out of control.

What's happening? What am I becoming?

Panic constricts my chest. I have to stop. I dig my claws—hooves—fingers—into the dirt. I shut my shifting eyes. When it stops, I gasp. Human again, I climb to my feet, shaking so violently that I have to lean on the tree.

Chloe dangles beside me. Vomit rises in my throat. I turn away, then turn back.

The pine-tree air freshener twirls in the wind. I yank it off her neck. What kind of sick joke—oh. Whoever killed her knew. That she's a dryad.

I climb partway up the tree and brace myself in a fork of the trunk. I attack the knot in the rope with desperate strength. It scratches my fingers and rips a nail, but at last it gives way. Chloe crumples face-first on the ground, her rain-wet hair shining on the leaves like liquid gold. I jump after her and land on my knees.

I can't do anything but stare. Rainwater trickles down my skin, and I feel so cold.

eleven

I sit on my couch, flanked by Mum and Dad, and stare at Officer Sharpe. Rain trickles from my hair and slides down my face.

The policewoman clears her throat. "So I understand you found the victim hanging?"

I can't stop trembling. I nod.

"But then you took her down? And removed a…" Sharpe glances at a notepad. "An air freshener from her neck?"

I nod. If I answer her questions, maybe she'll go away faster and leave me alone.

Sharpe purses her lips. "You shouldn't have tampered with the evidence."

"I couldn't just leave her hanging there," I rasp. My throat feels raw.

"You should have."

I stare at her with undisguised revulsion. Dad squeezes my arm.

Sharpe flips through her notepad. "This is the third victim you discovered, correct?"

"Yes." What is she getting at?

"And I understand that a certain Mr. Quigley shopped at the hardware store where you worked. Can you verify this?"

"Yes," Dad says, frowning. "Mr. Quigley was a customer at my hardware store."

"Gwen Williams." Sharpe stares at me with her gunmetal gray eyes. "Did you interact with Mr. Quigley prior to his death?"

I start to nod, then cross my arms. "Are you implying—"

"Please answer the question, Ms. Williams."

"Yes, I *interacted* with Mr. Quigley. I interacted with Chloe, too. She was my friend." My voice cracks on the last word.

Sharpe's face looks masklike. "Can you describe how you last saw Mr. Quigley?"

"Ms. Sharpe," Mum says, in a tone I recognize as dangerous.

"Officer Sharpe," she corrects.

Mum plows on. "Gwen's been through a lot. Do you really need to question her now?"

"I'm afraid so," Sharpe says. "We have to act fast."

"Will you?" I say, my eyes still locked on hers.

The officer dips her head. "Of course."

My teeth chatter, though anger burns inside me. "Even though she's Other?"

Sharpe lifts an eyebrow. "Why do you think that?"

"Her blood's not red," I say. "Can't you see she's—was—a dryad?"

"Did she tell you that?" Sharpe says, scribbling on her notepad.

"Why the hell does that matter?" My voice cracks. "Why do you care?"

"Gwen!" Mum says, eyes wide.

Sharpe looks mildly interested by my outburst. "We care because we're the police, and it's our duty to handle these matters."

I get to my feet. "So this is how you handle matters?"

"What do you mean?" Sharpe says, still calm.

"You hush things up when Others are murdered?"

"Gwen!" chorus my parents, both trying to drag me down.

"She's obviously upset," Sharpe says. "It's understand-able."

"I'm still in the room," I say, my teeth bared.

Sharpe ignores me. "Maybe I should come back later."

"Yes, of course," Dad says. "Thank you for trying to help."

"Help?" I laugh harshly, then cough. "If that's help, we're all doomed."

I break free from my parents and storm outside. Officer Sharpe's shiny cruiser sits in the driveway. I kick a tire so hard my toes sting.

"I hate this!" I scream to the sky.

Rain pours onto my face. I feel like somebody picked up a chessboard and tilted it so all the pieces are sliding off the edge. I grab a rock, ready to smash the police cruiser's windshield. I think better of it, and hurl the rock at the ground. Pathetic. Mum and Dad and Officer Sharpe watch from the windows.

My legs numb, I stalk into our backyard and sit behind a rhododendron where they can't see me. I dig my fingers into the lawn and tear out hunks of grass, like I'm yanking hair from a scalp. I throw dirt clods toward the forest.

A car door slams, and I glimpse Officer Sharpe driving away.

"Gwen?" Dad calls.

I don't reply.

"Gwen, we know you're out there. Come inside!"

"I don't want to."

"Don't be ridiculous," Dad says. "You're going to catch pneumonia."

"Maybe I should."

Footsteps swish across the wet grass, and Dad stops in front of me. "Come on."

I shake my head and fold my arms.

"You have to come inside," he says. "We're worried about you."

I stare at his knees.

He hauls me to my feet with a grunt. "You're not so little anymore, Gwenny," he says, a lame attempt at a joke.

I sniff, but let him steer me into the house.

Mum is waiting by the back door. She starts toweling me with excessive force.

"Ouch, Mum!" I say, trying to fend her off.

"Hold still," she says.

I grimace and let her wring out my hair.

"Now go upstairs and change your clothes," Mum says.

Too tired to argue, I trudge upstairs. As I stand naked in my bedroom, I stare at my reflection. My puffy red eyes and pinched face look ugly. I curl my lip, turn the mirror toward the wall, and get dressed.

What now? I stand in the middle of my bedroom, my arms limp by my sides. I can't just go on living my life as if nothing's different. I want to think of something—any-thing—to get rid of the empty gnawing inside. My mind circles back to the thought of Zack, and I flush with anger, then shame.

I sit on the carpet and curl into a ball, feeling small and vulnerable. I imagine Zack seeing me like this, hesitat-ing in the doorway, then kneeling by my side, unable to hide the way he really feels about me.

I laugh harshly, willing myself to cry, but the tears don't come.

My computer catches my eye. I turn it on to delete my desktop wallpaper: a photo of me and Zack, smiling and hugging. As soon as I delete it, I regret it, then tell myself I shouldn't. Might as well delete his number from my cell phone, too. I can't bear to touch Chloe's number, though of course she's never calling again.

I don't eat anything for dinner. Mum doesn't say anything, and lets me go to bed early.

As soon as I turn off the lights, the darkness feels suffocating. I turn on my desk lamp and huddle inside its pool of light. Shadows loom on the walls around me. I'm not afraid of the dark. It's more the … nothingness.

I drag my desk lamp closer to my bed and crawl back under the covers. Rain lashes against my window and drums on the roof. Usually it lulls me, but not now. I don't want to sleep. What if I dream of her?

But I don't sleep that night. I cry so much my pillow grows cold and wet with tears.

When I don't eat breakfast the next day, Mum frowns. "Aren't you hungry, Gwen?"

"No." I slump in my chair and stare at the pancake on my plate.

Megan won't look at me. She seems scared of me. Quietly, she gets up and opens a kitchen cabinet. I stare at my hands, clasp them to stop their shaking, then look up again. Megan drizzles maple syrup on her pancake.

Pale golden blood. I can't look away, though I desperately want to.

"What's wrong, Gwen?" Mum says, her voice tight.

I shake my head.

"Gwen? Are you all right?" Mum grips my arm.

"That." I point at the maple syrup. "It—looks like— her blood."

Megan gapes at the bottle in her hand.

"Put it away," Mum says.

Megan hurries to shove it in the cabinet. Mum whisks away the pancake.

"No," I whisper, "It's okay. I'll just go upstairs." I shove my chair from the table and leave. Try to, anyway.

Mum catches my wrist. "Gwen, do you want to talk?"

"Not really," I say, which is halfway a lie. "Maybe later."

Time flows past me. I scarcely eat. I often feel faint enough that I have to lie down. At night, I become good friends with my clock, watching the red digits blink past. My sleep cracks into shards of dreams.

The police, as usual, prove to be useless. Fifteen seconds on the news. No mention of Chloe being Other. I hide in my house like a rabbit in its burrow, waiting for the killer to strike again, amazed that we remain safe.

I don't talk to anyone about her. How can they understand something even I don't? Sometimes I hate her for going into the forest, for not being safer, for making me feel so bad. Every night, I hope and dread to dream about her, but she never comes to me. It's stupid, I know. I never believed in ghosts before.

The day before the funeral, I drift through my house in a daze.

"You look exhausted," Dad says. "Take a nap, Gwenny."

Like a zombie, I shuffle upstairs. My bed holds no comfort for me.

The morning of the funeral, we climb into our sky blue sedan. The color looks too cheery. I huddle in the back and shut my eyes. A warm hand finds mine. I peek out and see Megan touching me without looking. I shut my eyes again and clasp her hand. We reach the church— not the white clapboard one in downtown Klikamuks, but a stone Victorian one, with Gothic arches and ivy, in the older part of town.

Inside the church, less than a dozen people sit in the pews. A soft Enya song comes from somewhere I can't see. Dad keeps tugging on the knot of his tie, his face pale as he sits in a pew. Mum and Megan follow, equally pale. I stand beside them. I feel numb and shivery all over, as if my whole body got a shot of novocaine.

Then I spot a familiar face: Tavian, strangely out of place. Why is he here?

Mum glances at me, then whispers, "You don't have to look if you don't want to."

But I do. I plod up to the open casket like I'm wading through a dream. Chloe lies there peacefully, as if she might wake up at any moment. She's wearing a white dress with a high collar. To hide her torn throat, I guess. I wonder if they stitched it up.

My numbness vanishes, and the icy reality sweeps over me.

I turn away from the casket and walk back down the

aisle. Mum is waiting for me in the pew, smiling through her tears, but I pass her.

"Gwen?" she calls.

I pick up speed, throw myself at the heavy doors, and burst outside like a breath held too long. I flee. My throat is on fire. Gasping, I run down the street, where everything is bright and noisy and alive. People stare and point.

"Gwen!" I hear the church doors thudding shut behind Tavian. "What's wrong?"

I clutch a stitch in my side and try to answer, but I can't breathe through my sobs. Am I hyperventilating?

Tavian runs to me. "Are you okay?" He hovers beside me but doesn't touch me. "Are you okay?" he repeats, louder.

He looks so scared I laugh.

"Gwen!" He tries to catch my eye. "Do you want me to get someone?"

I shake my head.

The world spins. I feel like I'm going to fall; I am falling. Tavian catches me and I cling to him, my eyes squeezed shut to block the spinning and the sights I will never be able to unsee. He holds me as if I will shatter.

"I'm sorry," I gasp.

"Why?" He sounds dumbfounded.

"I—can't—stop."

"What?"

"Crying."

He exhales and draws me closer. "It's okay."

I withdraw and wipe ineffectually at my face until he offers a crumpled tissue.

"Thanks," I whisper. I dab my face. "Why are you here?"

Tavian stares at me, his face tight. "I heard what happened, and ..."

"Were you not invited?" I try to frown, but I'm glad he's here. "Did you know her?"

"I ..." A shadow of an emotion crosses Tavian's face. "I knew her, but not as well as you."

"What do you mean?"

Tavian looks away. "It's hard to explain." He steps back from me. "I should go."

"Why?"

"I need to get back to work. Are you going to be okay?"

"Yeah." I heave a shuddering sigh. "Goodbye."

He slips away, and I linger near the church, unwilling to go back inside so soon. I wish I didn't have to look at Chloe again. Then worms of guilt wriggle in my gut. What am I thinking? She was my friend.

After staying outside as long as I can, I trudge back up the stone steps to face death. But they're carrying the casket out the door now. I don't recognize any of the pallbearers. Two of the men have green eyes like Chloe, but darker skin. Dryads? I never knew her family, though I suppose someone must have made the funeral arrangements.

Mum is standing to the side, a tissue pressed to her mouth. She sees me and hurries down the steps, her shoes rapping. "Gwen!"

"I'm sorry, Mum," I say.

"Don't be," she whispers.

I let her hug me, and then we follow the casket to the graveyard behind the church. I pass tombstones with faded, forgotten names. Stone angels stare at me with faces as peaceful and blank as Chloe's is now.

I watch them lower the casket into the ground. It seems fitting for someone who lived in the trees. She will be taken into their roots again—but it all looks too somber. Chloe liked laughter and sunshine, not a reverend droning prayers over her body. I want to rip the clouds like a scab from the sky.

Around me, people sniff and cry openly. I see a stranger lurking at the edge of the crowd. No, it isn't a stranger, but Randall in a suit—I didn't recognize him, all somber and clean. He meets my gaze, and I look away.

Something in his eyes makes me shiver.

I remember him brooding the day Chloe disappeared. I remember him tearing out floorboards with such savagery. Did he ever show love or tenderness toward her? Does he even care?

They begin to bury Chloe. I watch with dry eyes, as if I've spent all my tears. Megan clutches my hand.

I squeeze her hand. I want to say, it's okay. You're not Other. You're safe.

As we're walking out of the graveyard, I see Randall approach Chloe's grave. Something small and gold flashes in his hands. He kneels by her headstone, then stalks away, his hands empty. I slip away from my family and jog back.

Chloe's maple-blossom earrings lie by her headstone.

He had them before—I saw him. Why would he leave them by her grave?

Cold seeps through my veins.

That evening, everyone is hushed. Dad turns the TV on, but keeps the volume really low. On the news, a farmer in Montana bewails his bewitched cows. Megan laughs quietly. I can't remember how to laugh.

After the bewitched cows bit, the fakey blonde newswoman returns. "Yet more werewolf sightings in Klikamuks. They have been seen lurking at the outskirts of town, though there have been no reported attacks yet. Yesterday, a local man brought a pelt to the police, but it turned out to be from a Samoyed dog."

Disgusted, I go upstairs.

As I lie in bed, chewing on my lip until it bleeds, I wonder why Randall returned to Chloe's grave. Murderers are supposed to do that, from what I've heard. But how did he get her earrings? Maybe he kept them as a trophy. But Chloe wasn't bitten, she was … No, don't imagine what it looked like.

An ember of anger smolders inside me. If he killed her, someone should kill him.

The night grows old. I can't sleep—the air in my room feels hot and suffocating. I slide the window open to let a breeze shush inside, sweet with the perfume of night-blooming flowers. The curtains billow around my face.

A long, low howl keens in the distance, sharp with longing. Whether it's hunger, sadness, or loneliness, I can't tell. I shiver. The moon rises on the horizon, bright as a silver coin, only a sliver away from full.

Maybe it's the wildness of the howl calling to me, or everything I've bottled up starting to escape—I don't know—either way, my pooka side wakes up. It stretches languorously inside me, and I clamp down on it.

Not this again. My body can't just decide it needs to change when I don't want it to.

I feel a low, itching throb in all my muscles, even when I'm not moving, like ants gnawing on my nerves. I climb out of bed and try stretching. It feels better for only a minute or so. With a groan, I try clenching all my muscles instead. The throbbing persists. I grit my teeth and lie back down, perfectly still in bed.

I deserve this pain. It's nothing compared to what Chloe must have felt. I can't stop thinking that.

Feverish and cramped, I roll over and concentrate on breathing slowly. Inhale, exhale, inhale, exhale. I will not shapeshift. I will not. I grip my arms so hard my fingernails make deep marks in my skin. Tears burn in my eyes. Focus on something, anything, else.

Tavian. Somehow, he suspects the same thing I do—that a murderer's killing Others—and he suspects I'm Other, too. His shadow … did it really have a tail? I try to remember, and end up remembering the way his eyes narrow to black crescents when he smiles. Thinking of him calms my pooka side, for some reason.

Numbing sleep laps at the edges of my vision. Triumphantly exhausted, I finally drift away.

Shafts of sunlight pierce the forest canopy. Emerald leaves rustle around me, whispering like a hushed conversation that I strain to hear. I see a glow ahead, brighter than the sunlight. It drifts closer, slipping through trees, never wavering from its course directly toward me. Fear squeezes my heart like a cold fist.

I turn to run, but my legs won't move, I can't look away.

The glow stands in front of me. Chloe, shining as if illuminated by a heavenly light. Her hair blows in a wind I can't feel.

"Chloe," I say. "Chloe!"

She stretches out her hand and whispers, "Randall."

I gasp and lurch awake as if surfacing from deep water. For a minute, I just lie there, my clothes clinging to my sweaty skin.

Questions whirl in my head like a mobile set spinning. My brain is moving too slowly to grasp the answers, so I let myself fall back into a dreamless sleep.

When I wake late in the morning, my skin itches with restlessness. I still feel feverish.

"Randall," I whisper.

Did she love him? Was he the last person she saw before she died? I try to shove these thoughts from my mind, but I keep seeing things—fur and fangs and blood—and it makes dread coil like a snake in my stomach. I keep hearing Chloe tell me she could trust Randall, even though I knew she shouldn't.

Just be careful, okay?

I will if you will.

I don't want to do this. I don't want to be the one to face her killer.

twelve

At breakfast, I joggle my leg and chew through granola so fast I feel like a squirrel.

Mum raises her eyebrows. "Hungry again?"

"Yeah," I say, around a mouthful of granola.

Through the kitchen window, sunbeams crack the clouds. I squint in the light. My hands tremble as I reach for the box of granola, and I clench my fingers into a fist. Going without shapeshifting doesn't seem to agree with me.

Dad puts his bowl in the sink, and I say, "Can I help at the hardware store?"

He glances at me, eyebrows arched. "You want to?"

"I just said so."

Dad scrunches his face quizzically. "You must be feeling better, if your snarky is back."

A smile ghosts across my face. "Snarkiness," I correct.

I want something to do, something to distract me.

Otherwise I feel like I'll just wallow in angst and weepiness. A total waste of time. What good will that do for anyone? Least of all Chloe. It's too late to help her.

No. Don't think of that. I focus instead on finishing breakfast and getting ready. When I don my red apron at the hardware store, I feel purposeful. I sweep the floors, sort inventory, add price stickers on sale items, then sweep the floor again. Even if my life's a wreck, the hardware store can look nice. I notice there's still dirt on some of the windows and grime along the edges of the shelves. I get out the mop.

"Gwen." Dad puts his hand on my shoulder. "Did you eat lunch yet?"

"No."

"It's one thirty. Go take a break."

I mop harder. The muscles in my arms ache.

"Gwen . . . eat."

"This place really needs mopping."

"You can do it after lunch, okay?"

I sigh and let him take the mop away.

Dad stuffs some money into my hand and steers me to the doors. "Go. Pizza beckons."

I manage to laugh. But as soon as I'm out of the hardware store, my smile vanishes. I cross my arms tight and trudge down the sidewalk, my head bowed.

When someone calls my name, I glance up, startled.

"Gwen? Is that you?"

I turn. "Hey, Ben. What're you doing here?"

He shrugs, his hands in his pockets. "Looking for lunch."

"Yeah, I'm going to the Olivescent."

Ben smiles. "Mind if I walk with you?"

I shrug. "No."

His smile fades at my apathetic answer. I keep walking, and Ben shortens his loping stride to match mine.

"What's wrong?" he asks. "You seem depressed."

I shrug again.

He clears his throat. "Is it because of what happened?"

I chew on my lower lip. What did Zack tell him? I don't see anything beyond curiosity and concern in Ben's eyes.

"How much do you know?" I mutter.

Ben glances away. "Sorry. I'm not trying to be nosy. You must feel horrible after what you went through. I know I would."

I feel bitchy. "It's all right. I guessed Zack would tell you."

"Zack? Oh." Ben steps back, something changing in his eyes. "Yeah."

An unpleasant prickling passes over my skin. "I hope he didn't say too much."

"Nothing too personal." He rubs behind his ear. "But he does still talk about you."

"Oh?" My voice cracks, and I keep walking. "I'm ... I ..." I'm tempted to say that I'm over Zack, but I can't. "Really?"

"You two were together for a long time, right?"

"Yeah." It all seems like such a waste of time now, but I can't imagine how different the past year would have been without Zack.

I glance at him. "What kinds of things does he say about me?"

"Like I said, nothing too personal. Just little things. Like how you used to go to the park together, or that this was your favorite movie."

His words squeeze my heart. "Really?"

"Yes."

I laugh to mask my unease. "I should forget him."

"He hasn't forgotten you."

"Yeah, yeah, I know." My words sound more insolent than I intended, and I regret them. Ben's just trying to be nice.

"I apologize," Ben says. "I didn't mean to be nosy."

"Oh, no, it's okay."

Outside the Olivescent, he holds the door open for me. "After you."

"Thanks."

I turn to Ben, about to say more, but a familiar face snags my gaze. Tavian, walking through the door, gives me a crooked smirk. He looks sexy in a black army jacket—brass buttons and braids—over a white shirt.

I have to admit, he's got style. I can only hope it's not gay style.

Ben glances at Tavian. "A friend?"

"Yes," I say.

"Two's company, three's a crowd." Ben waves at me. "I'll catch you later."

"See you," I say, and we go our separate ways.

Tavian strolls over to me. "Hi, Gwen."

I can't stop thinking of how I cried so shamelessly in front of him, and how he held me.

"I'm really sorry about Chloe," Tavian says. "My condolences." He sounds so formal. As if we never saw each other at the funeral.

I stare at the floor. "Yeah. Thanks."

"What do you feel like eating?" Tavian says. "It's on me."

I blink, surprised by his segue. "Oh, I've got money."

"Please, I insist," he says, with his most charming smile. "You look like you could use something nice today."

"Do I?" I say, with a trace of my usual dryness.

"Definitely." Tavian arches an eyebrow. "Well?"

I tilt my head to one side. "Well, if you're paying, I'll have a slice of three-cheese pizza."

"That all?"

"I'm not really that hungry…"

Tavian shrugs and heads for the counter. There's no sign of Ben—he must have gotten his lunch to go. Tavian buys a slice of the pizza of the day, with artichokes, zucchini, and mozzarella. I raise an eyebrow.

"What?" he says.

"You're going to risk that? It looks weird."

"I like weird."

We sit opposite each other at a corner table. He slings a book bag off his shoulder and pulls out a sketchpad. A breeze from the door ruffles the pages, revealing a drawing of a winged girl. Tavian flips to a new page and starts sketching something. I try to peek, but he curls his arm around the paper. I drink some water and peer over the glass to study the way his glossy black hair falls over his eyes.

"So, are you good at art, or humble-secret-genius good?" I say.

He laughs without looking up. "If you have to ask..."

I love how normal it feels just to flirt with no strings attached, and joke with somebody who doesn't know too much about me.

Tavian bites his pizza and rotates the sketch pad in my direction. "There."

I lean over to see. He drew a fox dancing on its hind paws.

"What is it with you and foxes?" I ask.

"Why not?"

"I still don't get that drawing you posted on your blog, with the foxes in kimonos. Did you just make it up?"

His eyes linger on mine, dark and unreadable. "No. They're *kitsune*."

"Kit-what?"

Still looking at me, Tavian turns to a new page and keeps sketching. "A kitsune is a fox spirit from Japan."

"Like a werewolf? Werefox, I mean?"

"No, it's more complicated than that. They can be helpful or harmful. Either they're servants of the rice god Inari, or tricksters with allegiance to no one. They have one, five, or nine tails, depending on their age and power."

"Wow, you know a lot about them. What sort of powers do they have?"

The corner of his mouth twitches. "Shapeshifting. Invisibility. Illusions. The power to enter dreams. Foxfire, which is kind of like static electricity from their tails. You'd call it a will o' the wisp."

Very interesting. I decide to play dumb. "Are they real?"

Tavian narrows his eyes. "Are Others real?"

My face goes hot, then cold.

"What's wrong?" he says. "You just went pale."

"I think I'm getting sick. I've had a sore throat all morning."

"Oh. That sucks." He smiles sympathetically, but his gaze is still intense. "I'll do my very best to distract you."

I force a laugh and look anywhere but his eyes. My stare falls on his current sketch. Is it ... me? He's drawn me in a way I never see myself in the mirror. Pretty.

"Tell me you're not going to keep that," I say.

Tavian toys with the edge of the paper. "But I like it." He cocks his head. "You didn't answer my question."

"Which one?"

"Are Others real?"

"Isn't it a rhetorical question?"

"Is it?"

My heart's thumping so hard I'm sure he can hear it. I do feel sick, now.

"Tell me this," I say, sounding much bolder than I am. "Why are you so interested?"

Tavian doesn't bat an eye. "Why are you?"

"I'm tired of this guessing-game crap."

He says nothing, just stares at me. His eyes make my heart beat faster. I shove my chair from the table and wince at the screech.

Tavian catches my wrist. "Where are you going?"

I twist away. "I've got to get back to work. Sorry."

"But you didn't eat anything."

"I said I wasn't hungry."

People start to stare. Tavian follows me out of the Olivescent. My pooka side tenses, ready to emerge. I swallow hard.

"Gwen," he says. "I just want to talk."

I ignore him and keep walking.

"Gwen!"

I whirl on him. "What do you want from me?"

We're both breathing hard. I'm on the verge of tears or shapeshifting, maybe both.

Tavian lowers his voice. "You can talk to me."

"I barely know you."

"We have more in common than you want to admit."

"No, we don't. Leave me alone."

Tavian's eyes flash green-gold for a fraction of a second. I blink, and it's gone.

"I can wait," he says, and then he walks back into the Olivescent.

Damn. He's most likely Other, and he definitely knows

I am. I can't do this. Now's a very, very bad time to reveal myself. What if he's connected to the murders in some way? I shudder and hug myself.

I hurry back to the hardware store and clean hard, as if I can scrub my worries away.

As soon as I get home, I search for "kitsune" online. It takes me a few tries to spell it right. I find a lot of links to sites on folklore, stories, and role-playing games. I click on the most likely. My gaze speeds down the page.

"Shapeshifting spirits," I murmur. "Foxfire... illusions... tricksters..."

Either Tavian did his research, or he has some first-hand experience.

I open up a few more pages. They disagree with each other. Some say kitsune grow an additional tail every hundred years. Other sites say kitsune only get all nine tails after nine hundred years. A lot of stories have kitsune as fox-wives that seduce mortal men. One site says almost all kitsune are female, or at least they always change into women regardless of their fox gender. How much of this is true?

Huh. Supposedly kitsune crave sex. Let's just say I don't think Tavian's crazed by the sight of me. Oh, this website says sleeping with a kitsune can be more pleasurable than most humans can handle. Oookay.

So is Tavian a kitsune or not? The shadow of a tail... the flashing eyes...

I chew on my lower lip and lie on my bed to think. Assuming he's a kitsune, what does he want from me? They aren't supposed to be trustworthy. But he doesn't seem to be trying to seduce me or con me into anything. I can't be hypocritical—pookas are supposed to be supreme tricksters, according to human propaganda.

He's going to have to make the first move, because I'm not telling him anything.

That night, the not-too-distant crack of gunshots wakes me. I sit bolt upright in bed, then kick off the covers and slide open the window. I crawl out into the cool night air and crouch like a gargoyle on the roof.

A howl pierces the night, and another answers. A gunshot cuts the first howl short.

I stare into the darkness, my eyes rounder than the waxing moon. They're hunting the werewolves. What do they call it? Curhounding. I imagine silver wolf pelts stained red, and my pulse pounds in my ears. A twisting feeling fills my chest. I grip the windowsill, my sharpening fingernails biting the wood.

My own breathing sounds too loud. I swallow past the tightness in my throat.

A snarl rumbles through the night, faint and faraway, but it scares me as if it were right behind me. I grip the edge of the roof to keep myself from scrambling back into my bedroom. My heartbeat thuds against my ribs.

My pooka half rises slowly within me, leaning against my bones. It isn't eager to shapeshift and fight. It's ... defensive. Feeling my fear. My fear? It *is* me, of course. I can't talk about myself as if I have split personalities. I can't section off half of myself and pile all the recklessness and shame there.

My entire body throbs with pain. I clench my teeth, and a muffled groan escapes. I can't keep doing this. Shaking, I slide inside and grope through the darkness to the door. In the bathroom, I swig a glass of water so cold it makes my teeth ache, concentrating on swallowing and trying not to look at my shifting reflection.

My gut cramping, I double over and retch. Breathe, Gwen. Breathe. I get a grip on myself and return to my bedroom. Yet another gunshot shatters the night. I want to go out and look, to see who's winning, even though I know it's totally stupid. Fear and recklessness battle inside me. Guess which one wins.

I grab a notepad and scribble, *Heard howls. Went out as an owl to see. Don't worry!!! Love, Gwen.* I leave it on my pillow.

Face flushed with shame, I yank off my clothes before it's too late, climb onto the roof, and jump. My stomach lurches as I shapeshift. My owl wings strain upward, slowing my descent. I flap hard and gain altitude. The moon shines through a filigree of boughs, casting milky light upon the forest.

Danger draws me like a moth to a flame. I'm just waiting to get burned.

I knife through the darkness, soaring low over the trees. Dark shapes are loping below me, keeping out of the moonlight. The sight of them sends a thrill down my spine. They're so huge and wild and *real*. They don't pant, as if they're desperately trying to keep quiet. I sweep the air with my wings, to keep up without flying too fast.

Behind me, I hear a hissed curse. I swivel my head and see a figure with a gun. Owls must have better hearing than werewolves—I hoot in warning. One of the werewolves looks back and barks. They scatter into the shadows.

"Damn owl," someone whispers.

I tilt one wing down and bank toward the figure. It's a tall man all in camouflage, wearing night-vision goggles, holding a rifle with a laser rangefinder scope. Somebody spent a lot of money on high-tech hunting gear. Behind him, I spot four shorter guys in black ski masks. One of them holds a shotgun.

"Where'd they go?" says the guy with the shotgun.

I recognize the voice in a heartbeat. Chris. I know who the other three short guys must be.

"Shhh," says the tall man. I have no idea who he is.

He stalks forward, then hooks his fingers and beckons the others. I sail over their heads silently, then circle back and follow. The guys sneak into the darkness after the werewolves. Gunfire rattles nearby. My heart skips a beat.

The hunters move faster, running in a crouch. Ahead, I see more men with guns. They look familiar, Klikamuks townspeople I don't remember by name. They nod at the tall man with the night-vision goggles.

"We got one," a bearded man says.

"Good," the tall man says. His voice. Have I heard it before?

"It's wounded," the other man continues, "but it kept running."

"Let's get it," Chris says, his voice quivering with bloodlust.

I'm flying too close, too low. I flap and try to slow, but owls can't hover. The wind from my wings ruffles their hair.

They look up.

"There's that fucking owl again!" Chris says.

He raises his shotgun and takes aim. Holy shit—I don't want to die. I fold my wings and twist into a dive. *Bang.* Shot tatters my tail feathers and peppers the trees. I tumble, then flare my wings and swoop up.

"It knew," the tall man says softly.

I don't stay to hear what he says next. I beat my wings hard and get the hell out of there. My ragged tail makes flying wobbly. I reach my house in record time, diving through my open window and crash-landing on my bed. I sink my talons into my mattress and drag myself upright, shapeshifting.

A girl again, I hug myself and shiver. My ears are still ringing. I smell gunpowder.

On my pillow, I see my note. I grab it and try to imagine Mum reading it in the morning while I lay bleeding in the forest.

I crumple the note, slam my window shut, and climb into bed. I drag the covers up to my chin. The urge to hide beneath them grips me, and I laugh hysterically. I hate this. I don't want to be afraid of dying anymore.

I bury my face in my pillow and scream.

No one comes running, luckily, and I stare into the darkness until I succumb to sleep.

thirteen

When I wake at five the next morning, I'm exhausted, as if I didn't get any sleep at all. I yank open my curtains and squint at the dawn. Thin clouds ripple across the sky, the sun tinting them gold. When I was a little kid, I used to think there had to be clear skies for someone to die, so they could go to heaven.

Did werewolves die last night? I abandoned them to the hunters. But what could I have done?

I swallow hard. It's not worth pondering it—it's none of my business. Blinking my bleary eyes, I shuffle over to my computer. Checking my blog seems comfortingly mundane. No new comments, so I open my email next. My gaze snags on an old email from Chloe, just a short message about lunch. It hurts to read.

I scroll past it and select all the spam, my finger on the

delete button. Wait. Is that spam? A message from Fox-Fire88.

> Gwen,
>
> I didn't mean to pressure you yesterday. My apologies. I need someone to talk to, someone who understands what's really going on around here. Chloe, Mr. Quigley, that couple who supposedly drowned. They're all connected. We both know we're also in danger because of who we are. You don't have to reply, but consider that we might be able to help each other.
>
> Tavian

It feels like the bottom of my stomach has dropped out. Oh, man. He *is* an Other. A kitsune, a fox spirit. And he's sure I'm Other, too.

What do I say? Do I have to reply?

Tavian confuses me, to make the understatement of the century. And I think I've had enough of guys and their cryptic statements. I've had enough of letting my guard down and getting hurt.

I close my email and blow out my breath. The scent of bakestones trickles under my door. No matter how crummy I'm feeling, I can't resist bakestones—they're a kind of Welsh scone. Mum always adds golden raisins. I suspect this is part of Operation Cheer Gwen Up. Well, it's working. I hurry downstairs.

"Morning," I say, and cram a bakestone into my mouth.

Ah, heavenly. Ambrosia isn't Greek; it's Welsh. Guilt

needles me. It's only been a week since Chloe died. How can I be so happy? But an undercurrent of pain lurks beneath the surface. I dip into it, then pull myself out again.

"Mail," Dad calls, slapping it on the table.

Mum riffles through the mail. "There's something for you, Gwen." She hands me a cream-colored envelope.

"Oh?" I say, my mouth full of hot buttered bakestone.

"What is it?" Megan asks, leaning closer.

I grab the envelope. Zack's return address, written in impeccable cursive handwriting—not his. The bakestone suddenly tastes like cardboard. I swallow hard and rip open the envelope. Out falls a folded brochure and a note.

I read the note first. It's also written in the cursive handwriting.

Dear Gwen,

I hope this will provide some comfort in your troubled times. I know it has helped quite a few people find happiness.

God bless,
The Arrington Family

My chest tightens. I unfold the brochure. The first thing that catches my eye is a picture of two girls laughing. They have pointed ears—faeries, or elves. Beneath them it says, *Freedom is possible through the Lord!*

Oh, no. I don't want to keep reading, but I do anyway.

Are you struggling with your paranormality or "Otherness"? Do you feel distanced from your family and friends? At times it can seem impossible to escape sin's grip, but remember that God still loves the sinner. There's no need for suffering. If we trust Him to heal us, His unlimited power will help us. You can successfully manage paranormality and live a full and holy life. We know the journey isn't an easy one, but the American Association for Research and Treatment of Paranormality will stay by your side throughout the process. For more information, please visit our website or give us a call.

My hands clench involuntarily around the paper. I shove my chair from the table, stride to the garbage can, and tear the brochure into pieces. Mum, Dad, and Megan gape at me. I'm breathing hard, trying not to cry.

"What was it?" Megan asks, in a tiny voice.

"Shit. Total shit."

"Gwen!" Mum looks shocked.

I don't say any more, afraid my voice will crack. I just shake my head and go upstairs to my bedroom. I curl on my bed and hold my shark toy tight even though I know it's stupid and immature. It takes five minutes—I count—for the burning in my eyes to stop.

When I think I can talk again, I grab my cell phone and dial Zack's number.

"Hello? Gwen?" he says, his voice disbelieving.

"You told them?"

Silence.

"Don't play dumb. I got the brochure. Was it your idea?"

"No. Ben thought we—"

"Oh, great." I clench my jaw. "Your brother's just as preachy as the rest of you."

"It's not like that, we—"

"Why did you tell them?"

Zack exhales in a hiss. "I had to. What was I supposed to say?"

Something inside me snaps, and I'm yelling. "Nothing! You didn't have to tell anybody anything. I trusted you, Zack. Do you know how hard it was for me to tell you the truth? I thought you would understand."

"Gwen..."

"I thought you were different, not another one of those narrow-minded prejudiced Christians who thinks all Others are sinful and evil. But you're just like the rest of them. You'd rather believe other people over me."

No reply.

"Zack? Zack, are you listening?"

"I don't know what to say. What do you want me to say?"

"I...I...do you still love me?"

"I loved the Gwen I knew."

My heart folds and crumples. "Fine."

"Gwen...it's all been so sudden. I've barely had any time to think about it."

"Why am I even wasting my time on you?"

Zack's voice chills. "If that's what you think..."

It isn't, really, but I can't bring myself to say so. "I have to go. I'm sorry."

I hang up before he can hear me crying. But my tears stop much sooner than they usually do, as if I've used them up. My pulse throbbing in my temples, I sit at my computer and reopen my email. My fingers rattle the keys.

Hi Tavian,

All right. You want to talk? I'll be at the Boulder River Wilderness Area today, probably from now until noon. Look for a huge bigleaf maple about a mile from the Kliminawhit Campground. It's east of the Boulder River. Not too hard to find.

See you,
Gwen

My finger hovers over the send button. Should I? What the hell. I do.

I might as well just tell Tavian. He seems to know already. I'm sick and tired of dragging things out.

After refreshing the page every thirty seconds, I decide to test a novel I checked out from the library. It turns out to be a steamy romance involving a hunky alpha werewolf. Ugh. I've had enough of werewolves.

My email dings two minutes later. Apparently Tavian's also haunting his inbox.

I click on the message, my heart thumping.

Gwen,

I'll definitely be there. Looking forward to it.

Tavian

I get ready in a flash, stride across our backyard, and stalk into the forest.

The sun is lurking behind clouds, and a lukewarm breeze slides languidly through the trees. The quiet mismatches my thumping heart. I near the Kliminawhit Campground and veer around it. Ahead stands the maple—Chloe's maple.

"Tavian?" I call.

An ocean of leaves sighs around me. I glance at the maple's crown.

What was the last thing Chloe saw? Was she still alive when the murderer hung her? I suck in a slow breath and banish those thoughts from my mind. I don't feel at peace, but I feel numb, which is almost as good.

It's cold in the forest. Or maybe it's just me.

The wind nuzzles my neck and rakes its fingers through my hair. I shiver and cross my arms. You know, it's probably not particularly safe to be standing out here in the open, alone. I glance at the maple again.

I have an idea. Slightly crazy, but I feel slightly crazy today.

I kick off my shoes and curl my toes in the leaf litter, feeling the cool loam beneath. I flex my fingers. My nails blacken and curve into claws. Tan fur shadows my skin, but I hold the rest of the transformation back. Half-cougar, half-girl, I quiver on the brink of shapeshifting. I swipe at a tree and gash bark, wondering what flesh would feel like. Nobody better try to mess with me now. My muscles bunch, and I spring in one fluid motion. Claws biting the bark, I climb to a high limb.

With a triumphant sigh, I relax into girl form and shut my eyes. That felt *so* good. It's about time I shapeshift when and how I want to. My arms dangle beneath me. Bark presses its pattern into my skin.

"Gwen?" calls a faint, familiar voice.

I keep my eyes shut.

"Gwen?" Tavian calls, closer to me.

I open my eyes and watch him wander closer. He looks small beneath me.

My heartbeat thunders in my ears. He found me. He actually came. What should I say? How can I trust him?

Tavian glances around, then up. "Gwen!"

I say nothing, just stare at him with lowered eyelids.

He half-frowns, half-smiles. "How did you get up there?"

"I climbed." My voice sounds flat, contrary to the excitement jittering inside me.

Tavian squints. "That's a long way up."

"Yes, it is."

He stares at me for a moment. "Aren't you going to say hello?"

"Hello."

"Why don't you come down?"

"I don't want to." Actually, I doubt I can without changing back into a cougar.

Tavian frowns at me. "Okay. Fine." He rummages in the pocket of his jacket. "But I wanted to give you this."

I stare at the envelope in his hand. What's inside? A confession that he's Other?

"What is it?" I say.

He smirks. "You'll never know unless you come down."

"I already said I'm not."

Tavian waves the envelope at me. I don't budge. I'm obviously stalling for time. But I have an awful track record when it comes to telling the truth.

"Why did you *really* come?" I say.

He cocks his head. "Why did you?"

Growl. Enough of this. If he's Other, he can say it first.

I yawn, feigning laziness, and close my eyes again. I wait for him to say something or go away. Instead I hear scraping, a grunt. I look down. Tavian has jammed his foot in the fork of the trunk and is hauling himself up.

"You won't make it," I say.

"Oh yes I will," Tavian says.

He scrambles onto a higher branch. I watch him for a moment, then stare at the sky. If he wants me, he can come get me.

Leaves shudder around me. The wood creaks and groans. Tavian's breathing comes closer, then there's a loud crack.

"Oh, shit!"

My gaze snaps in his direction. A rotten branch has crumbled beneath his feet, and he's hanging from a higher branch, staring at the falling fragments. The envelope flutters down. His legs dangle at least twenty feet above the ground.

I grip bark as if I'm the one in danger, not him.

Tavian tries to lift himself onto the limb. He pulls himself halfway up and holds himself there, his muscles taut, then struggles to hook his leg over the branch. But after a minute his arms tremble, and he swings back down.

"Uh, Gwen? A little help?"

My heart thumps in my ears. How can I get to him without shapeshifting? I'll have to try it as a human first.

"Bollocks, Tavian!" I hiss as I crawl closer. "I told you not to come up."

"Actually," he says, grimacing, "you told me I wouldn't make it."

"Shut up, or I'll let you fall."

"You wouldn't." His smile is strained. "You like me, don't you?"

My face flushes. "No," I lie.

I climb down the tree, as close to him as I can. There's a big, swaying gap between me and the branch he's hanging from.

"Don't jump," he says, the humor gone from his voice. "It's too dangerous."

"You're a fine one to talk," I say.

I crouch and slowly stand, my arms outstretched like a tightrope walker. I wobble, then find my balance.

"Gwen. Find a safer way down. Go get help." His hands slip, and he struggles to hold on. "Don't do anything stupid."

"Damn it, Tavian! I'm not going to leave you hanging there. I'm not going to let you fall. You should have never come after me! You're going to get yourself killed, just like—" My throat constricts, and the word doesn't come out.

Tavian gapes at my eyes. I know they're glowing.

"Screw it," I say. "Don't look, okay?"

He continues gaping.

"Just don't look!" I tug my shirt off, and that finally makes him shut his eyes. "Okay, now hold on."

"I don't plan on letting go."

My clothes float to the ground. Somehow I think I'm too experienced at perching, naked, in trees. I leap from the branch, my arms spread. Tawny cougar fur sweeps over me. Claws scythe from my fingertips.

Tavian peeks. Great. "Gwen!" he shouts.

I try to tell him to shut his eyes, but a strangled cougar scream escapes.

Yelling, Tavian lets go of the branch, which is quite possibly the dumbest thing to do. I bite the back of his shirt like a cat does with a kitten's scruff. My momentum slams us both against the trunk, and I dig my claws into the bark and cling to the tree. Leopards make it look so easy, carrying gazelles up trees. Tavian keeps yelling, and it hurts my ears.

I growl around a mouthful of shirt: *Shut up!* He must get the message, because he does.

My claws slip, gashing the bark. I inch, backward, down the tree, then lose my footing and scrabble down the rest of the way. With an undignified thump, we both land in the leaves, bruised but alive.

I spit Tavian's shirt from my mouth. I have a sudden urge to groom myself, so I go ahead and start licking my front leg.

Tavian huddles on the ground, his eyes like saucers. "Oh. My. God."

I narrow my feline eyes. Bollocks, why can't pookas talk in animal form, like the stories say? I stalk toward my clothes, my head held low. Tavian continues goggling. I growl, a low rumble, and he retreats. When I nudge my clothes with my nose, he finally gets it and turns his back on me—reluctantly.

I shapeshift fast, quivering with the effort, and yank on my clothes.

"What are you?" Tavian says, his voice carefully calm, his back still to me.

"What did you expect?" I tug my hair through the neck of my shirt. "You knew I was Other, didn't you?"

"Yes."

I grab his shoulder and spin him around. "You can't tell anyone."

He stares into my eyes. "I knew you were Other since

the moment I met you. You smell like magic. And I haven't betrayed you."

"I smell like magic?"

A slight smile tugs at his mouth. He leans a little closer. "Now, especially."

I pull back, not ready to get touchy-feely, and pluck leaves from my hair with shaking hands. "What does it smell like?"

"Lightning," he says.

"Ozone?"

"Kind of. But sweeter." Tavian touches the back of his neck, and his fingers come away red with blood. "Ouch."

"Oh," I mutter. "I didn't mean to hurt you. Sorry."

My head spins. It's probably not the blood—I have a strong stomach—but shapeshifting so rapidly.

In the smallest voice that's still audible, Tavian says, "I am, too."

"What?"

Tavian draws a shaky breath. "I'm Other."

The strength goes from my legs as if relief cut the strings holding me up. I drop to my knees with a sigh.

"Gwen?" He sounds a different kind of scared. "Are you okay?"

"Yeah," I say.

That's not entirely true. The world whirls around me, and my stomach clenches on emptiness. The cougar thing drained me. Woozy, I lower my head. Triple bollocks. That's what I get for show-offy transformations.

"What kind of Other?" I say, trying to sound upbeat.

Through the hair curtaining my face, I see Tavian's worried expression.

"Kitsune," he says. "Japanese fox spirit."

"I know." Oh, man. I feel really, really dizzy. "I Googled it."

"I'm half human, actually," Tavian adds.

I fall sideways. It seems pointless to try and sit up straight.

"Gwen?" His voice sounds distant. "Are you going to faint?"

"Not if I can help it."

But then I do.

fourteen

When I open my eyes, I see Tavian kneeling near me. "Gwen! You okay?"

"Basically."

"I was going to get help, but then I thought I should stay with you, and then..."

I blink and sit up. I still feel lightheaded, but not in imminent danger of fainting now. Note to self: eat more.

Tavian's eyes never leave my face. "Are you sure you're okay?"

"Yes!" If I could die of embarrassment, I would keel over right now. I spot the envelope, half-covered by leaves, and pick it up and open it.

"Oh, that." Tavian rubs the back of his neck. "Yeah."

It turns out to be a card with a Japanese woodblock print of white lilies on the front. Inside, it says, "I share your sorrow." Tavian signed it with rather spiky handwriting that reminds me of crickets, for some reason.

"This better not be some Mr. Nice Guy ploy," I say gruffly, to hide how I really feel.

"My mom bought it for me," he says. "Didn't like anything I picked out."

I keep staring at it. My eyes sting, and I blink fast.

"My grandmother died two years ago," he goes on. "So I know how you feel. I mean, it's different for everybody, but anyway…"

"Yeah," I say hoarsely. I clear my throat. "Thanks."

"You're welcome."

We avoid each other's eyes.

My stomach growls. "I need to eat. It happens after I shapeshift too fast."

"Okay." Tavian scrambles to his feet. "I saw some blackberries over there. Stay here and let me get them for you."

I nearly say I'm not an invalid, but it's cute to see him so concerned.

"By the way," I say. "I'm half pooka. My dad's a Welsh shapeshifting spirit."

Tavian glances back, his face illuminated by a smile. "Cool. We're both halfies."

After a moment of sitting on the leaves, I get bored. I climb to my feet and follow him on still-watery legs. All right, so I stagger like a drunken sailor. When he spots me, he darts toward me as if I'll fall.

"I'm okay!" I say.

Tavian nods, but keeps glancing at me from the corner of his eye.

A thicket of blackberries grows in a jumble before us. I pick berries at a manic pace and cram them into my mouth. Sweetness bursts on my tongue. I moan, my hunger satisfied. Tavian looks sideways at me, and I blush.

"Here," he says.

I cup my hands, and he pours berries into them. I eat them like an animal.

Tavian raises his eyebrows, smiling slightly. "Feeling better?"

"Definitely. It's amazing how fast sugar enters your system."

I keep guzzling berries. Our fingers brush, sending a tingle through my skin.

"You say you're Other," I say. "Prove it."

He meets my gaze for a long moment, and panic stabs me. Did he lie?

"Okay," he says.

He shuts his eyes and sucks in air through his nose. He clenches his hands, then flings them outward. A wave of gold ripples from his feet and out through the leaves around him in a rattling cascade. He now stands on a carpet of coins.

Magic prickles my skin. It feels like cold fire.

"Wow," I whisper.

He opens his eyes. The sky darkens to a glorious violet and orange sunset.

"Turn it back," I say in a small voice.

Tavian blinks, and the real colors rush back into place. He stumbles forward and catches himself with his hand.

"Illusions," he says. "They take a lot of energy."

"What else can you do?"

Tavian smiles at me, and it makes him look very foxy. No, I don't mean *that* kind of foxy. Then his dark eyes shift to amber. His ears sharpen into furry fox-ears, white on the inside, black on the outside.

"And that's as far as I'm going," he says, flashing fangs as he talks.

I'm grinning despite myself. "What, your shapeshifting also involves a lack of clothes?"

He nods, then his ears change back to a boy's, so easily it makes me envious. Maybe he's had a lot more practice fine-tuning control.

"I'll bet you're a cute little fox," I tease.

Tavian gives me a cool look. "I prefer not to be called 'cute' or 'little,' thank you very much." He grins again. "I should get a T-shirt that says that."

"Sorry." I laugh. "I'll try not to mortally wound your ego."

"So," he says, "what were you doing in that tree?"

My grin turns into a grimace. "Nothing. Sometimes I like to be above everything."

Tavian turns back to the blackberries.

I hate this. I hate the gnawing inside me, the unspoken words. So I say them.

"It's where she died."

"Who?"

"Chloe."

He meets my gaze, his eyes sharp. "What happened? The news was so vague."

"What, you want details?"

He nods. "Unless you'd rather not."

"I found her hanging." I realize I'm gripping the brambles in my hands. Blood trickles between my knuckles. "Her throat was slashed."

"That must have been ... awful," he says.

I let go of the brambles and stare at my wounds.

Tavian eyes widen. "You hurt yourself!"

"It's not very bad." Part of me likes seeing the vivid red, proof that I'm alive.

Frowning, Tavian pulls a handkerchief from a pocket in his jeans. "Don't worry, it's clean." He tears it in half.

I hold out my hands, a mute patient, and let him bandage me. I don't wince.

He looks at me, his face pale. From my blood or my story, I can't tell. "Someone's killing Others," he says. "Even if the police don't believe it."

"I know! I can't believe how incompetent they are. It's such a relief to talk with somebody who knows what I mean."

"Yeah." Tavian flashes a smile, then sobers. "We're both in so much danger right now it's not even funny."

"I know." I set my jaw. "I'm going to find whoever killed Chloe."

He meets my gaze. "I'm with you."

"Really?"

"I owe you."

"Good," I say grimly. "I've already got a prime suspect."

He looks startled. "Who?"

"Randall."

"Who's he?"

"Chloe hired him to renovate her B&B a few weeks ago. He's most likely the last person who saw her before she died, and he told me they got into an argument right after she dumped him like I kept saying she should do. I saw him leave her favorite earrings at her grave. That's really suspicious. And he's a...he's *creepy*."

Tavian squints. "Creepy how?"

"He's..." I drop my voice. "He's a werewolf."

"Really!" Tavian raises his eyebrows. "Sounds like he's the killer."

I hesitate. "I'm not sure, yet. But he's a prime suspect."

"Any other suspects?"

I shrug. "No."

Tavian ruffles his spiky hair. "What do you propose we do?"

"Gather evidence. Make sure he doesn't skip town."

"What, stalk him?"

I smile grimly. "If necessary. You game?"

Tavian stares into my eyes. "I'm game."

Of course, real life gets in the way of detective work. Namely, Tavian's job at Slightly Foxed Books and mine at Dad's hardware store. I'm working less hours than Tavian, though, so I have time for a little snooping around, if not the guts to do it alone yet.

On a particularly summery, baking-hot day, I go downtown, allegedly to buy some new sandals. Actually, I'm thinking of checking out Bramble Cottage. I haven't been there since it happened. I'm afraid of what I might find.

Chloe's beautiful rosebushes are wilting, dry on the verge of dead, and I can see their spiny skeletons. Wind-loosened petals seesaw through the air and settle on the yellowing lawn. I frown. Nobody waters the garden?

I stride down the sidewalk and try to open the front door. Locked, of course. I jiggle the doorknob, then shade the glass of the door window and peer inside. Bramble Cottage looks so old and empty inside. It's sad. I spot a garden hose snaking through the grass, so I twist the faucet and start watering the roses. The dirt's so dry that water makes silvery pools on top of the dirt instead of soaking in. Poor roses.

The sun heats my skin, and my mind drifts. What was Chloe thinking the last time she went to the forest? She said she felt like she was being followed … but maybe she knew her killer. And trusted him.

I feel a tightening in the pit of my stomach, a stinging in my eyes. There has to be something in Bramble Cottage that will help me catch Chloe's killer. And I need to find it. I should call Tavian and see if his shift is over.

The water darkens the sidewalk. I turn off the faucet, then admire the reviving roses. My mouth feels as dry as dirt. I crouch and bring the hose to my lips. When I try to stand, my hair snarls on the thorns, like it knotted itself.

"Bollocks," I hiss. I drop the hose and fiddle with my hair. I really should brush it more often.

Footsteps crunch the dry lawn behind me.

"Excuse me?" says a low, husky voice. Randall.

Heart thumping, I jump back and only succeed in yanking my hair. "Ouch. Damn."

"Hold still."

I freeze as Randall untangles my hair from the thorns. Freed, I step away. His calloused fingers brush my cheek, and I shudder.

I face him. "Why are you here?"

Randall twists a rose from its stem with casual violence, then buries his nose in it and inhales deeply. The silver streak in his hair glints. "I came to get some of my stuff. I didn't get it all before…you know."

"I know."

His eyes smolder. "What are *you* doing here?"

"Watering the roses. Of course." He scares me, but I'm not going to show it. "Oh, that reminds me." I try to keep my voice bland as I lie. "Chloe said you had something of hers that she wanted back. She was going to give them to me."

Surprise flits across his face. "What?"

"Her maple-blossom earrings. Do you have them?"

"No. Sorry." Randall glances at the B&B. "I've got to

192

get moving." He digs a key from a pocket in his jeans and unlocks the back door.

Holy crap. He could have gotten inside at any time.

The back door of Bramble Cottage stands ajar now. Here's my chance. I slip inside and tiptoe through the rooms, looking for signs of a struggle or golden bloodstains. Dust specks dance in sunbeams. Floorboards creak under my feet.

My breathing sounds loud in my ears. I stay tense, ready to transform and fight. Then footsteps thump nearer, and I stiffen.

Randall collides with me on his way down the rickety Victorian stairs. "Sorry."

I notice that he's carrying an ugly maroon duffel bag. "What's in that?"

"Clothes," he says.

"What, you've left them here for more than a week after…?"

His eyes bore into mine. "Is this the first time you've been back?"

"Yes."

"Well, I don't know about you, but I didn't feel like coming until I had to."

I force myself to stare steadily back, trying to decipher his eyes. Did he lie low because of the police? Did guilt or grief keep him away?

"Excuse me," he says, edging past.

I follow him out of Bramble Cottage. He locks the door behind me.

"So, where will you go now?" I try to sound casual.

"Kliminawhit Campground. Not like I can afford a hotel."

Wow, he's essentially homeless. Wait, isn't the pack of werewolves around there? That means he lied to Chloe—he told her he wasn't with them.

Again, Randall stares at me, his eyes narrowed slightly.

"Well," I say quickly, "at least it's nice this time of year."

He shrugs. "See you."

"Yeah, bye," I say.

He shoulders the duffel bag and strides away. No car, apparently. I should totally follow him to Kliminawhit and see what he—along with the rest of the pack—is doing out there in the wilderness. But with Tavian as backup.

Fingers a bit unsteady, I unzip the Bean and find my cell phone. Brilliant. I totally forgot to swap numbers with Tavian. Guess I'll have to tell him in person.

My nerves settle down as I leave Bramble Cottage behind me. At a crosswalk, I recognize Justin's white van waiting for the light to change. I return his friendly wave, trying to keep my face normal though I'm sure I look somewhat pale. When I open the door to Slightly Foxed Books, the marmalade tabby leaps from a window seat and chirps. I try not to trip as it winds around my ankles like a furry serpent.

"Heathcliff likes you," Tavian says, emerging from behind a bookshelf.

"Yeah." My voice sounds froggy, and I clear my throat. "Guess who I just ran into."

"Who?"

I sit on the window seat, and Tavian sits beside me.

"A certain someone who's very suspicious," I say.

"You know you're being maddeningly vague," he says. "Tell me what happened."

So I do, in a condensed version.

"Wait." He snaps his fingers. "So he just left, like we thought he would?"

I nod. "I almost followed him, but—"

"Too dangerous." Tavian leans back against the side of the window seat. "He'd know it was you. Now we know where he lives—"

"Where he says he lives, at least."

"—and we should investigate another day."

"We need to check out Kliminawhit." I lower my voice. "I don't know about you, but I've heard howling and gunshots coming from the forest. You know as well as I do that the pack's hiding there, and they're being hunted."

Tavian sighs. "Do you really want to take on an entire werewolf pack all by yourself?"

I narrow my eyes. "I'm not *that* reckless. But if Randall actually is the murderer, I won't be able to sleep if I know he's running loose."

Tavian narrows his eyes right back. "I didn't say we should let him run loose."

"Well, what did you mean?"

"We should do this together. Right? That's what we agreed on."

"So what's your brilliant plan, then?"

"We go to Kliminawhit this weekend, and—"

"That's four days away. We should go tomorrow."

Tavian snorts. "Eager, aren't we?"

I cross my arms. "I want to get him before he gets us first. I'm tired of sitting around."

"Hey, at least you found out where Randall's living. At least you didn't spend the last three hours sorting trashy old romance novels."

A smile tugs at my mouth. "Actually, I was watering roses before Randall came."

"Even so, you weren't reading about Miss Rosabella Sluttington falling onto a bed of petals with her lover, Lord Studly Champion."

I laugh. "I see your point."

Tavian grins, and damn, he's cute. Flutters take flight in my stomach.

"So," I say, trying to sound blasé, "we head to Kliminawhit tomorrow?"

"Sure." He rummages inside the pocket of his jeans and pulls out his cell phone. "Here."

I hold his cell phone in the palm of my hand.

"Your number?" he says.

"Wow." My face heats. "That's blunt."

Tavian smirks. "I'll give you mine if you give me yours."

Good lord, I'm blushing now. "Sounds practical."

Trying to be casual, I enter it myself. He does the same with my cell phone. No big deal, right? Friends do that kind of thing. Friends who're working together to track down a killer. Nothing particularly odd about that.

Tavian glances at me, his black eyes sparkling. "If your

boyfriend asks why you've got my number, you can say we're blog buddies."

I laugh, then cough. "Actually, I'm single now."

He arches an eyebrow. "Oh?"

What's that supposed to mean? I'm tempted to ask, but I restrain myself.

"Call me," he says, handing me back my cell phone. "I'm free any time tomorrow."

His fingers linger on mine until I blink and pull away. "Will do."

fifteen

The next morning, I call Tavian, my stomach doing acrobatics. The plan: he'll drive to my place, and we'll walk to Kliminawhit from there. I wait for him at the bottom of our driveway, on the pretense of picking blackberries. I end up eating several handfuls despite the jittering in my stomach. When I hear a car nearing, the jittering multiplies. But it's only the USPS jeep, here to deliver mail. Oh well, I might as well get it.

I cross the street to our slightly rusty mailbox. Junk, junk, bills, junk. But at the bottom of the heap, I come across a white envelope marked *GWEN*. I open the envelope and pull out a paper, folded poorly in half, with childish handwriting in red crayon.

I KNOW YOU

Below these words is a crudely drawn four-legged animal. With hooves. A horse? A pooka...? Who sent this? How do they know what I am? Did they see me shapeshifting in the forest?

Icy shivers trickle over my skin. But maybe it's just Chris and Brock, trying to scare me. That makes sense. Morons.

Anger flares inside me, melting my fear, and I crumple the letter into a ball and stuff it into the pocket of my jeans.

A coppery orange Honda Element coasts down the street, slows, and pulls over. Tavian lowers the window and looks over his reflective sunglasses.

"Excuse me, ma'am. Does anyone named Gwen live around here?"

I laugh, the letter not so important now. "New car?"

"Yeah."

"Your parents buy it for you?" I try to sound teasing.

He shrugs, takes off his sunglasses, and slips them into a pocket on his jacket. "They're pretty well-off."

I wonder just how well-off. "You going to park there?"

"I guess. Does your family know I'm coming?"

"Not yet. Wait, do you want to meet them?"

Tavian arches an eyebrow, then kills the engine and hops out. "Why not?"

I scratch the back of my neck and shrug, then start walking up the driveway.

Foxgloves and nettles sway on either side of my driveway, beautiful and stinging. Steeplebush flowers—tight pink spikes of starburst blossoms—perfume the air with their nectarine scent. Bees hum and butterflies zigzag through the air, and I feel a whirring like their wings inside my chest.

"I'm lucky my parents adopted me," Tavian says, out of the blue.

I glance at him. "Oh?"

"My mother raised me until I was about six. My real kitsune mother, I mean. She had to leave one day, and she never came back."

"Oh. Sorry."

He shrugs. "You don't have to say that. It's weird when people apologize for something they had nothing to do with. After my mother left, I don't remember much. They found me eating beetles and snarling at humans."

I make a face. "Beetles?"

"Like a fox. An orphanage tamed me, and by the time I was seven, a Japanese-American couple adopted me. The Kimuras. My parents."

"They knew you were a kitsune?"

Tavian nods. "From day one."

"That was open-minded of them," I say, trying not to assume too much.

"Oh, definitely." Tavian squints wistfully at the sky. "What are your parents like?"

"Well, you're going to meet them in a few minutes."

"Cool. So your dad's the pooka, right?"

"Oh, I've never met my biological dad." I frown at the gravel, then laugh humorlessly. "Sorry. I don't usually talk about this."

"It's okay," Tavian says in a light tone. "I know what you mean."

I sigh. "My mum scarcely knew my biological dad, either. Back in Wales, she'd see a pooka following her around, sometimes as a horse, sometimes as a handsome man. Somehow they fancied each other, and…you know."

"Yeah."

We reach the top of my driveway. Someone tugs aside a curtain in an upper window—Megan, in her bedroom. Clouds clot in the sky behind my house, as if the roof is damming their flow. Birds fly low—rain's coming.

"I guess I'd better introduce you," I say.

"Announce my arrival," Tavian says, with a mild laugh.

I pretend to cuff him on the head, then reach for the front door. It whisks open just as I touch the doorknob, and Megan stands there, slightly out of breath. Jeez, she must have run downstairs when she saw us coming. She looks Tavian up and down, measuring him with her gaze.

"Who's this, Gwen?"

"Tavian," he says, shaking her hand.

"Megan," she purrs, with a blatantly flirty smile. Oh, horrors. She glances at me. "I didn't know you had a new boyfriend already."

Red alert! Red alert! It accurately describes my face, anyway.

"No," I say quickly. "We just—"

Mum steps out from behind Megan, patting down her frizzy hair. "Gwen! You didn't tell me you invited someone over."

"I'm Tavian Kimura," he says, "and you must be the mother of these lovely ladies."

Mum laughs, one of those polite I'm-so-flattered laughs.

"Mind if I borrow Gwen for a moment, Ms. . . . ?"

"Williams. Where are you going?"

"For a forest walk." He smiles, acing the suave act. "I'll return her in mint condition."

My blush reaches plasma hotness. Mum and Megan share a glance.

"That sounds lovely." Mum's eyes narrow a bit, but she keeps smiling. "Stay on the path, Gwen. Watch out for wildlife."

I sigh. "Mum, I live here."

She tilts her head, giving me a definite you-know-what-I-mean-young-lady look.

"I'll make sure your daughter's safe, Ms. Williams," Tavian says, piling on the charm.

Mum's smile becomes a little more genuine. "All right, then. Have a nice walk."

I grab Tavian's hand and march toward the forest before we're delayed any longer. As soon as we're in the trees, I let go.

"Great," I mutter. "Now they think you're my boy-friend."

"What's the problem with that?" Tavian says innocently.

Is he joking, or does he mean that for real? Not sure what to say, I just roll my eyes.

After a pause, he says, "I like your name. Gwen Williams."

"Actually, that's not my whole name."

"Oh? What is it?"

I sigh. "Gwenhwyfar Williams."

"Gwen-wee-what?"

I repeat it, slowly. "Gwen-*whee*-var."

"Gwenhwyfar," he says, mangling it only a little. "Now that I know your true name, do I have any power over you?"

I throw back my head and laugh, but I can't hide the flush in my cheeks. "You wish."

"Well, I like your name. It's pretty."

I snort. "You don't have to spell it."

We push farther into the forest. Clouds flow above us, mirrored by a tide of mist. The trees look like columns in a forbidden temple. The trail meanders along Boulder River, through trees in their pelts of moss and plumage of ferns. We hear the river's endless shushing, and glimpse it when the maples and thickets thin, then hear only our footsteps and the plip-plopping rain, just beginning to fall. At a curve in the path, Tavian stops at a bigleaf maple.

I caress its trunk. Chloe would have loved it. "So old," I murmur.

Tavian sniffs the air, then buries his nose in the moss.

"What?" I say.

"A werewolf brushed past this tree not too long ago."

I shudder. "We must be close to the Kliminawhit Campground."

"I wonder if they're stalking campers." Tavian curls his lip. "Morons."

"Yeah," I say half-heartedly.

Among skeletal, lichen-shrouded alders, I see a flicker of movement. A squirrel? Or just the swirling mist?

We walk closer, our shoulders bumping.

"I smell something," Tavian whispers. "Like old blood."

"Blood can't be good."

He grimaces. "Let's keep walking."

Under the pewter blanket of sky, Kliminawhit Campground looks abandoned this afternoon. Leafy bushes crowd the road, and brambles creep over paths. In a campsite with a sign saying *Campground Host*, a yellowed rectangle of grass marks the spot where there must have been a trailer some time ago. A crow lies near a hunk of meat, its head flung back, claws clenched, wings twitching.

"Poison," Tavian says, and I shudder.

We crisscross through the trees. A familiar baby blue pickup is parked by Campsite 15.

"That belongs to the werewolves," I say.

I stroll into the campsite, trying to look casual. A peek into their tattered tent reveals only a few blankets. Scattered bones, little ones, lie on the ground by the campfire. The ashes look fairly new.

"Where did they go?" I ponder aloud.

"I don't know," Tavian says. "They're probably still close."

We follow the road through the campsite loop. In a spot I thought was unoccupied, I see a rusty wheelbarrow hidden beneath the fresh boughs of Douglas fir. I tug aside a branch and find a battered cooler, a sack of kibble patched with duct tape, and an ugly maroon duffel bag.

"Randall," I mutter. I unzip the duffel bag and find a bunch of shirts and jeans. Nothing incriminating. I shift the clothes aside and discover a seriously grungy chew toy that appears to be a mangled hedgehog, many years old.

"Tavian?" I say. "What the heck is this?"

I glance over my shoulder and see him sink into a crouch, his teeth bared.

"What—?"

Something cold and wet touches the back of my hand, like a dog's nose.

Slowly, I look down, fully expecting to freak out. A wolf pup is sniffing my hand. Then he wags his stumpy tail.

I can't help smiling. "Hello," I say. "I didn't expect to see you."

Tavian's eyes gleam orange. "Gwen…"

"Calm down. It's just a werepuppy."

"There are two of them."

Another pup prances up on big clumsy paws. She bows, her forelegs flat on the ground and her butt in the air. They both have blue eyes.

I can't imagine who would be cruel enough to kill a werepuppy for the $150 bounty.

"You want me to play?" I ask.

The pup yips.

I pick up a twig and toss it. Both pups scamper after

it, pounce, and tumble into a tangle of snarling fuzz. They scuffle, and the girl pup emerges victorious. She struts away, the twig in her mouth, then starts gnawing on it.

"You're so cute," I say, still smiling.

"Cute?" Tavian stares at me. "You shouldn't play with them."

I sigh. "Tavian, just once, would you not look at me as if I'm insane?"

"We need to keep going," he says, even edgier than before. "We're here to look for evidence against Randall, right?"

"I know, I know…"

Of course I do. I'm just not sure I want to see what could be waiting for us.

The twig snaps. Both werepuppies trot over to me. I crouch and hold out my hand. The pups sniff it, making little whistling noises. One of the pups licks me with a slimy pink tongue. It tickles like crazy.

"Stop," I giggle. "Stop!"

The pup licks harder, then nips my finger with needle teeth.

"Ouch!" I yank back my hand. "Don't bite!"

Tavian's at my side in a flash. "Did it draw blood?" He grabs my hand and turns it over.

"No, luckily. Besides, I'm not sure werewolves can infect people who're already Other."

"You're half-human," Tavian reminds me.

The pup flattens his ears and whimpers. His fur shrinks back, revealing pink skin, and he turns into a chubby baby.

Tears well in his eyes. He takes a shuddering breath, then starts to bawl. The girl pup howls.

"Shhh," I say. "Be quiet!"

They bawl and howl louder.

"It's okay!" I try to use a singsongy voice. "Don't cry, little pups."

Tavian snarls. I glance at him, surprised. A thunderous growl rumbles behind me. I whirl around to see Randall. He has shadows beneath his eyes, and his hair looks even shaggier. Thin red slashes mark his cheek. From the fingernails of a victim? Blood spatters his flannel shirt, and a lot of blood crusts his left sleeve.

"Oh," I say, and my mouth stays in an O.

Randall advances on us. "What the hell are you doing here?"

Tavian snarls again. "Don't come any closer." He looks feral—bared fangs, orange eyes.

The werepuppy flees between Randall's legs, and the baby keeps bawling. Randall grabs the hedgehog chew toy from his bag and chucks it at the baby, who starts sucking on it. I try not to laugh at the absurdity.

Randall wrinkles his nose at Tavian. "You stink like a fox."

"That toy belong to you?" Tavian sneers. "Had it ever since you were a werepuppy?"

"Shut up," Randall says, his cheeks reddening. I bite back a smile as he turns to me. "And *you*...I don't even know what you are."

My eyes start stinging, glowing. "How long have you known I'm Other?"

"Since I met you." Randall sidesteps around Tavian, who moves to face him.

He's been keeping tabs on the Others in the area?

"What happened to your arm?" I say. "Somebody shoot you?"

Randall's hair bristles into silver fur. "You should get out of here. Now. Before the rest of the pack comes."

I stand my ground. "I want to know why you lied to me."

"About?"

"Chloe's earrings. I saw you leave them at her grave."

"So?"

Tavian flashes his fangs. "So, it looks very suspicious."

"Why should I fucking care what you think?" Randall says.

Tavian steps forward, and I grab his arm. Things could get really bad, really fast.

"Randall," I say, my heart beating a million miles an hour. "If you cared about Chloe, we have something in common."

Randall narrows his eyes, and I see a gleam of something—guilt? Sadness?

"Listen," Tavian says. "We're trying to figure out who's been killing Others. Either you're our friend or our enemy."

"I don't fucking have to be on anybody's fucking side," Randall says.

"We're wasting our time," Tavian says to me. "He's obviously guilty of something."

Randall laughs. "You going to try and kung fu my ass?"

"Kung fu is Chinese," Tavian sneers. "I'm Japanese."

"What, karate then?" Randall says. "Huh?"

Tavian's eyes glitter with rage.

"Come on," Randall says. "Or do you only fight guys your own size?"

Tavian bares his teeth. "I fight assholes of all sizes."

"Stop it!" I say. "We're not here to fight."

Both guys glare at me, then go back to glaring at each other.

High-pitched cries, somewhere in the forest nearby, make my chest tighten. It's horrible, almost like a human baby in pain.

"What's that?" Tavian says, his eyes still on the were-wolf.

"Oh, shit," Randall says. "Where are the pups?"

We all glance around. The baby sits nearby, still sucking on the hedgehog toy, his blue eyes huge. Jeez, the poor kid has probably heard so much foul language. I don't see any sign of the werepuppy, and the cries escalate.

Randall barks, "Get out of here!" and sprints toward the sound.

Tavian and I share a glance.

I say, "Should we—?"

"Yeah."

We run after Randall, keeping a safe distance. He kneels

with his back to us, bending over something. What's he doing?

I stalk closer, tense and ready to transform. Oh no.

The werepuppy yanks, writhes, and rolls, straining against the iron jaws of a wolf trap clamped on her tiny leg. Blood smears the leaves. A thick chain anchors the trap to a tree. Randall tries to calm her.

"It's okay!" he says, his voice raw. "It's going to be all right."

He strokes the werepuppy's head, and she snaps at his hand. He narrowly avoids being bitten, but continues to pet behind her ears. Her yelps die to quiet whimpers. Chin trembling, the werepuppy lies down by the trap.

My stomach churns. I walk numbly to them. "Randall?"

He whirls on us, his hair bristling into fur. It flattens only a little when he sees us. "I said get out of here!"

"We—we might be able to help."

The werepuppy's head wobbles, then lowers to the ground. This can't be happening. She can't be … dying.

Randall curses through clenched teeth. "Okay. We have to pry it open."

The trap looks grotesquely huge in comparison to the werepuppy. It's obviously meant for adult werewolves.

"How?" Tavian says, his face ashy.

Randall glances between us and jabs a finger at me. "You weigh more than the little guy. Come here. See the metal tabs on either side? They're connected to the springs. We need to push them down. A foot on each tab."

I nod, and part of me wonders how he knows this. I gingerly set my toes on one of the tabs.

Randall shakes his head. "You have to put all your weight on it." He stomps on the other tab. The werepuppy yelps shrilly, twisting in the trap.

"Do it quick," Randall says.

I put my foot on the tab and press all my weight onto it. The springs squeal, and the jaws of the trap open a fraction of an inch.

"More," Randall says. "Don't take your foot off."

The werepuppy's yelps escalate, but I ram my foot on the tab. The trap springs open. Randall swoops down and grabs the werepuppy by the scruff of her neck. The trap clangs shut, slick with blood.

"Is she okay?" I force myself to look away from the werepuppy's mangled leg.

The werepuppy's yelps become more like human whimpers. She changes into a black-haired baby girl. Randall cradles her awkwardly. Without fur to hide the baby's wound, I can see the odd angle of her leg, the broken bone. My stomach clenches.

"Let me call 911." Tavian fumbles with his cell phone.

"No!" Randall gets a panicky glint in his eyes, then shoves the baby into my arms. "Don't drop her, and don't move. I'll be right back."

"Whoa, wait!" Tavian says, but he's ignored as Randall sprints into the forest.

The baby's shrill cries hurt my ears. I clutch her close, trying to comfort her, and her wails become broken sobs.

She grips my hair with a pudgy little fist and buries her face against my chest. I try to keep her blood off my shirt.

Tavian chants curses under his breath. "We should call 911."

"I don't know." My voice sounds surprisingly calm, considering how much I'm shaking. "I don't think so."

"Are you okay?"

"Yeah. Is she...?"

Tavian cranes his neck to look at the baby. "She's still awake. I think." He touches the baby's head gingerly. She makes a stifled sob.

"Poor thing," I say, and I realize how close to tears I am.

"Are you sure you're okay?" Tavian says.

I nod, because I don't trust my voice. A tear rolls down my cheek, and I try to rub it on my sleeve, but I can't. "Damn it."

Tavian's face tightens. He reaches for me, and I turn away.

"I'm okay," I mutter. "I just hate getting all weepy."

He rubs away another of my tears with his thumb. "Gwen."

Once I look at his eyes, I can't look away. Then I hear the thundering of paws. Tavian's pupils narrow into fox-like slits.

A tawny-skinned woman with wild dark hair runs toward us, with three black wolves at her heels. She's wearing ragged jeans and an inside-out T-shirt—she probably just transformed. I recognize her from Safeway, of all places.

She advances on us with fury in her face. "What did you do?"

sixteen

The woman snatches the baby from my arms. "Oh, God." The baby starts to cry again.

"We rescued her from a wolf trap." I clench my sweaty hands. "Randall went to get you."

The black wolves slink closer to Tavian and me, fur bristling along their spines. I can't believe how huge they are. One of them meets my eyes and growls softly. Tavian hides a stick in his hand behind his back. Sunlight flashes along its length as he transforms it into a dagger, then points it at the werewolves. Can illusions kill?

"No," the woman says, her voice low and commanding.

The wolves stop moving, their ears pricked.

"Kurt," she says, "go back to the others and tell them to call off the hunt."

One of the wolves makes a huffing woof and trots off the way he'd come.

"Isabella, Jessie," the woman says, "keep an eye on the strangers. Don't let them go." She strides toward the campsite with the still-crying baby. "And put down that stick, boy," she calls, without looking back.

Tavian's eyes narrow. The black wolves snarl in unison, and he slowly lowers the dagger. When he drops it, it becomes a stick again.

I grab his arm. "Come on."

We follow the woman to the campsite, herded by the wolves. It all seems surreal.

"Who are you?" I say.

"Winema," she calls back.

"Where's the other pup—I mean, baby?"

"Safe," Winema says.

"And Randall?" Tavian says.

She says nothing. Maybe she just feels she doesn't have to answer. She yanks open the tent flap and ducks inside. She lays the baby on a ragged blanket, then vaults back out and into the rusty bed of the pickup truck. After rummaging around, she yanks out a chipped metal first aid kit.

"I have a phone," Tavian says, clearly uneasy. "I can call 911."

"I'm a doctor," Winema says. "Was. Before I was bitten."

"Oh."

The baby punches the air with both fists and wails, her face crimson.

"Shhh!" Winema rushes over. "It's okay, Ava."

"Ava," I repeat. "Is she...?"

"She's not mine." Winema opens the first aid kit. "Her mother abandoned her."

Tavian furrows his brow. "How ... ?"

Winema unscrews a canteen, pours water onto a rag, and cleans Ava's wound. "Her mother was bitten while she was pregnant."

I share a glance with Tavian. I barely know anything about lycanthropy and pregnancy.

"She didn't want an abortion," Winema continues, "so she left her baby by our pack."

Ava continues kicking and screaming. Winema struggles with her, sighs, and gets out a syringe. She jabs it in the crook of Ava's elbow. I wince. Tears leak from the baby's eyes, but she quiets down.

"Sedative," Winema says. "Had to."

"Are you sure you don't want us to call 911?" Tavian says.

"I already said no. What do you think they will do? Up in Canada, they told us to take our children to the vet."

Tavian and I share an equally appalled look.

"You both smell of magic," Winema says. "You're not human, are you?"

"Hell no," Tavian says. "We're Others. Fox spirit and pooka."

"Then I'm sure you know by now that the authorities can't be counted on."

"Yeah." I force a laugh. "The police around here have been pretty useless."

Winema lifts an eyebrow. "They can be more than use-less."

"How so?" Tavian asks.

"I've found it to be much more dangerous to Others once the police are involved." She stares at us as if expecting a response.

Tavian and I share a glance, and I shrug.

Winema finishes cleaning Ava's leg and inspects it more closely. "It might have been broken, but it's healing now."

"She's going to be okay?" I say.

Winema fixes me with a stare, her amber eyes sharp. "Physically, yes."

I blink and look away.

"What are you doing in our territory?" Winema says.

"*Your* territory?" Tavian says, but I cut him off.

"I've heard werewolves in the forest. And gunshots. I was worried..."

Winema's face becomes stony. "Hunters have been hounding us for weeks now. They left the wolf traps and the poison."

My stomach squirms. "What about two young guys? With a shotgun?"

"They won't return," Winema says in a matter-of-fact voice. "Hopefully."

Tavian stares at her. "What did you do to them?"

Winema begins bandaging Ava's leg. The wound's healing amazingly fast. "Humans are such clumsy creatures," she says. "The last town we stopped by, people set out poisoned steaks. What a waste of meat!"

I have to admit, it does sound dumb. But I don't like it when werewolves scoff at humans, as if they weren't humans to begin with.

"Why did you come to Klikamuks?" Tavian says.

"Yeah, why?" I say. "People here don't exactly roll out the welcome mat for Others."

Winema laughs bitterly. "We can see that. We've pissed on wolf traps before. The pups, though, are too young to know any better."

"Maybe you should go back to Canada," Tavian says.

Winema's eyes burn like coals. "Do you think they want us in Canada?"

"No, but…" He flings out his arms. "It's bigger!"

"You don't know what you're talking about, boy. They drove us out of Alaska, shooting at us from airplanes. They called this aerial hunting a sport. We stayed many winters in Canada, where we thought we were safe, but people from our pack started disappearing, one by one. We found them shot to death and left to rot in the forest. We can't go home." Winema bares her teeth. "And you can't tell us to go."

Tavian bristles. "All right then." He folds his arms. "Can I talk to your Alpha?"

"I *am* the Alpha," Winema says.

"Oh," he says.

"What are you going to do?" Winema says. "Turn us in? Betray fellow Others?"

"Fellow Others?" I glower at her. "You can't compare natural born and bloodborn."

Her eyebrows arch. "Aren't we treated the same? We're all gicks."

"But...that's not what I mean. We aren't the same."

"United we stand, divided we fall. It's already Others versus humans. Others versus Others, and we don't have a chance."

"That's ridiculous," I say. "I'm not...I mean, I'm Other, you're Other...but..."

"But?"

I don't know what to say. I feel sick.

"Speaking of Others," Tavian says, "what do you know about the murderer?" There's a glint in his eye. It seems he's decided to bait the werewolves.

Winema delicately bares her teeth. She has impressive fangs. "I will kill him."

"Him?" Tavian cocks his head. "You know it's a he?"

"Why do you doubt me? Serial killers are male, ninety-nine percent of the time."

"Which is also a stereotype," Tavian mutters.

"We know this one is a man," Winema says. "And we believe he is one of those who took the lives of so many werewolves in Canada. Friends of the pack have told us that the killer went south, and now we are hunting the hunter."

I frown. This doesn't quite sound like the same killer to me. "Do you know anything about the victims who weren't werewolves?"

"Ask Randall," Winema says. "He loved one of them, the poor girl."

Some alibi. I'm getting really tired of not hearing the truth about Randall.

"Where is he?" I say. "Can I talk to him?"

Winema glances out at the black wolves. I'd almost forgotten them. They lie like sentinels on either side of the tent.

"Isabella," she says, "tell Randall he can come now."

One of the wolves trots off, her head held low. Soon she—Isabella—returns, Randall following. He's wearing his dirty old clothes again and carrying the second baby in his arms. The baby squirms, then shifts back into pup form. Randall sets him down. The werepuppy piddles and romps off.

Randall won't meet Winema's gaze. Werewolf etiquette, I guess. "Ma'am."

Winema sighs, her face tired and serious. "You did what you could."

"Yes, ma'am."

"This girl wants to talk to you."

Randall's shoulders stiffen. "About?"

"One of the victims. What was her name?"

"Chloe," I say.

Randall's gaze snaps to mine, as if magnetized. "Fine."

"You can go." Winema waves me away, but beckons Tavian closer. "As for you…"

Tavian's eyes widen. "Me? What?"

Winema's face remains impassive. "I have some questions for you."

"Uh, okay."

Tavian and I look at each other, then nod. Randall stalks off, and I follow.

Randall stops at the edge of the campsite and folds his arms. He looks at me sideways. "So, Gwen, what *are* you?"

"Half pooka. Shapeshifter."

He nods. "What about that twitchy little guy?"

"Fox spirit."

He snorts. "Figures. What do you want to know?"

"Where's all that blood from?"

"Huh?" Randall glances at his arm. "Oh. That. I don't have a whole wardrobe of clothes, okay?"

I tilt my head to one side, my eyes narrow. "How did it happen?"

He rolls up his sleeve, peeling the bloody fabric from his skin. He furrows his brow, and I grimace with sympathetic pain. Tooth marks puncture his forearm. They look deep, though older than I expected. He licks his wounds.

"Oh, gross. You shouldn't do that."

Randall bares his arm for me to see. "Cleaned it up a bit."

"So what happened?"

His face looks like a closed door. "Winema bit me."

"Why?"

"To stop me from giving those fucking guys with their fucking guns what they deserved." Randall slams his fist against a nearby tree, then leans against the trunk. "God, people can be such bastards!"

I flinch, startled by his violence. He must be talking about those hunters.

"So they're not…?"

"Dead? No, unfortunately."

"Okay." I exhale shakily. "Will you tell me why you had Chloe's earrings?"

Randall leans his forehead against the bark. "I kept them. After we…broke up."

"Why?"

"Why do you think?"

I take a deep breath. "Were you the last person who saw her at the B&B?"

Claws slide out of Randall's fingertips, then back in. "What is this, a fucking investigation? I don't have to answer you."

I glare at him to mask my shakiness. "Who do *you* think killed Chloe?"

"I have a pretty damn good idea." His eyes glitter with intensity. "There was this guy, see? He came to the B&B once. He asked her for directions, then started talking about the weather—how it's so cloudy and rainy here all the time, but he doesn't mind. Bullshit like that. After that, I kept glimpsing him around her. He was just…watching her. I tried to tell her." His voice roughens. "And then she died."

I'm caught up in the flow of his story until I catch myself. "And his name?"

Randall shakes his head and doesn't answer.

"You don't know or you won't say?"

He snorts. "Yeah."

"Okay …"

"He's been stalking people," he says. "So I've been stalking him."

"But that doesn't equal murderer." I step back under the force of Randall's glare. "I mean, you don't have any evidence." And your alibi is a piece of crap, too. But of course I don't tell him that.

"I'm going to get some evidence," he says in a low, intense voice. "Wait and see."

I retreat, unsettled by his vehemence. "Okay. Thanks for answering my questions."

"You're welcome," Randall deadpans. "Is that all?"

What a dick. I have no idea why Chloe went for him. I hope the police nail his ass.

"You can go," I say.

He lowers his eyelids and smooths his hair, masking his emotion with calm. "Good."

I hurry back to the tent and find Winema sitting on a cooler, cradling a sleeping Ava. Tavian's kneeling on the ground at her feet.

"Gwen." He stands up. "You ready to go?"

I nod, fold my arms tight, and rub the goose bumps on my arms—it isn't even cold.

Winema meets Tavian's eyes. "Remember what I said, and stay safe."

He nods. "You too."

I raise my eyebrows at him, but he just grabs my hand and leads me away.

When we're out of the werewolves' sight, he whispers, "What did Randall tell you?"

"That he's innocent, of course." I repeat what Randall said, in condensed form. "His alibi has more holes than a colander."

"Hmm," says Tavian. "Do you think he made up the stranger who talked to Chloe?"

I stare at the ground, the patterns of pine needles crisp and much easier to focus on than the confusion in my head. "Probably."

"But what if we're wrong? What if it's not Randall, or the werewolves?"

"I don't know. I'm not sure of anything anymore." I grab fistfuls of my hair. "What do you think? Am I crazy?"

His mouth twitches. "Now that you mention it…"

"Tavian!"

"Gwen, I'm frustrated, too. But we won't get anywhere by yanking out hair."

"I still feel so stupid. I just can't figure it out. And crap, I'm crying now."

Irritated by my own weepiness, I sit on a mossy log and rummage for a tissue in my pocket. I find only a crumpled shred. Scowling, I rub the tears off my cheeks. Tavian hesitates, then sits next to me.

"You okay?" he asks.

"Yeah. I'm fine. Even if I am a disgusting, sniveling mess."

"Hey, don't be so hard on yourself." Tavian tries to

smile. "You need to take some time off from being a badass super ninja pooka."

I manage to laugh. "I wish I could."

"You totally can."

"Not with some crazy murderer running around."

"Gwen, none of this is your fault. You don't have to catch the bad guy."

I stare at him. "If I don't, who will? The police? Like they care."

"The werewolves care. You heard what they said about the killer in Canada."

I chew on my lower lip, then remember what Chloe said. "Don't you think this sounds like the White Knights? You know, those people who burned crosses and lynched Others. Everybody thinks they're gone, but what if they aren't?"

Tavian shakes his head. "I don't know. We would have to find out more."

"Yeah." I heave a shuddering sigh. "I don't want to think about that right now."

"Hey," he says, his tone lighter. "So was Randall actually babysitting the werepuppies?"

I smile weakly. "Apparently." I glance sideways at him. "Do you actually know karate?"

"Hell no. Wish I did," he says wistfully.

"It was kind of funny."

"Yeah."

Splinters of sun pierce the thick canopy, and the earth exhales dancing tendrils of mist.

Tavian's fingers curl around my hand, and it's friendly enough for comfort. He's silent all the way back, until we reach his car.

"Let's do something that doesn't involve drama or danger," he says. "Something fun. Got to balance out all the negativity with a bit of positivity."

"Like?"

"How about the Evergreen State Fair? It just started."

A smile creeps over my face. "Seriously?"

"Why not?"

"'Cause it's crazy. Considering the circumstances."

"Then why are you still smiling?"

I laugh. "Because I like the idea."

"Excellent," Tavian says. "State fair, Saturday afternoon?"

"If you insist."

He squeezes my hand, then lets go.

"Well," I say. "I guess this is goodbye."

An uncertainty, a possibility, wavers through the air between us. I blink, and it's gone.

"See you Saturday," he says, and he walks away.

I watch him go, already missing him—as silly as that sounds.

seventeen

A few days later, I find an envelope waiting for me on my desk. Written on the front, in red crayon: *GWEN*. Not another one of these. Do Chris and Brock really find it so amusing to send me lame-ass attempts at hate mail?

I tear open the envelope. It takes me a while to decipher the crudely written words.

> *Gwen I now you are lik me. The Bad Man nows you*
> *too. The Bad Man is scary. Write to me and put your*
> *letter by the river.*
>
> *Your freind,*
> *Maris*

What the hell? Who is Maris? Or the Bad Man, for that matter? I knead my forehead with my knuckles. Could

Maris be some sort of nearly illiterate Other hiding in Klikamuks, who saw me shapeshifting and wants to talk?

Maybe Maris saw the killer...maybe that's the Bad Man.

I log onto the Internet and type an email to Tavian. I copy down the letter and ask what he thinks of it, then hit *send*.

The Bad Man. Well, at least that narrows down the suspects to men. But who? Randall? Another werewolf? Even Chris or Brock?

Time to learn more about the suspects.

"Brock Koeman," I mutter, my fingers clacking the keys.

There's not much about Brock online. Just a trashy MySpace page with a photo of him drinking, and the Klikamuks High football team's page. There's no mention of him being bitten by werewolves, though I suppose they wouldn't release his name since he's a minor. I don't find much more about his brother, Chris.

Oh well. They seem too stupid and klutzy to be killing Others anyway.

What's Randall's surname again? I wrack my brain. Ah, Randall Lowell. Not much information on him, either. Wait, what's this? An online newspaper clipping. *Randall Lowell, 27, found guilty of petty theft. Sentenced to 30 hours community service.* He has a criminal record, then. Did Chloe know that when she hired him? Surely she Googled prospective employees. Maybe she dismissed the theft.

This doesn't tell me much about Randall's possible murderous tendencies, though. I wonder whether he's always been a member of that Canadian pack or if he joined recently. So I search for "werewolf pack Canada Randall Lowell." No hits. I change the search to "werewolf pack Canada" and get a ton of sites. Got to narrow the search. I add "Winema." Bingo: *... current Alpha of the Bitterroot Pack, Winema Crawford, took control in...* The link leads to me to a page called *Werewolf Packs of the Western United States and Canada.* Wow—why didn't I look before? I guess I assumed they weren't online.

There's a list of all the packs in the area. Bitterroot Pack is near the top.

BITTERROOT PACK

A large, secretive pack originating in Alaska and western Canada, the Bitterroot Pack has long had an unstable relationship with humans. In some areas, particularly British Columbia, this pack has earned an infamous reputation. Although members of this pack have been convicted for crimes ranging from theft to assault, there is no conclusive evidence that a Bitterroot werewolf has ever committed rape or murder. The current Alpha of the Bitterroot Pack, Winema Crawford, took control in 1997 after the previous Alpha, John Skerry, died of exposure in Yukon Territory, Canada. Winema seeks to improve the pack's reputation and welcome lone werewolves into the community. Under her leadership, the Bitterroot Pack has left their traditional hunting grounds and now appears to be traveling south. Where they plan to settle is unknown.

I read this once more, then lean back in my chair and frown, trying to imagine them trekking through wintry Canada in search of food and shelter. How did they manage with the tiny werepuppies? I guess Randall joined them recently, since Winema wants to welcome lone werewolves. Most importantly, they've never been convicted of murder—though that could just mean they've never been caught.

I don't know. It doesn't make any sense. If the Bitterroot Pack has already suffered such persecution, they don't seem the type to go after fellow Others. Why would they be killing in such a calculating, methodical way? When I think of werewolves, I think bloody kills and carcasses that get eaten. Unless they're eliminating competitors or trespassers on their territory—but that seems too bloodthirsty and far-fetched.

Then who is the killer?

I love the smell of the Evergreen State Fair. Onion rings and corn dogs, cotton candy and Belgian waffles, elephant ears and bad popcorn with fake butter. Ah, the joys of fair food. Add the animal smells of manure and alfalfa and you have Eau de Fair. And it's always so loud—live bands dueling with endless calliope music, the hiss of balloons being inflated, the babble of conversation punctuated by wailing babies.

My cell phone rings, and I extract it from my purse. Tavian's number.

"Hello?" I say. "Where are you?"

"I spy a gorgeous redhead," he says.

I blush. "Oh really."

He laughs. "You're supposed to spy a handsome guy standing by the cotton candy."

"Tavian. There's tons of cotton candy."

"Turn around."

I do, and see Tavian waving at me. I sigh and wave back as he strolls over.

"Where are we going, anyway?" I ask.

"No particular destination," he says. "So long as it's fun. Hungry?"

"Kind of."

After buying us each an elephant ear and a snow cone, Tavian slips his hand in mine. Startled, I glance at him, and a smile ghosts across his face. I twine my fingers with his, a warm glow in my chest. We thread through the crowd, hand-in-hand. I see moms pushing strollers, old guys with big cameras, kids running loose while blowing bubbles, college students with blond dreadlocks, and high-school punks in ripped black finery. We pass one of the many stages. A troupe of goth-slash-tribal belly dancers shimmies and clangs finger cymbals. A banner proclaims *Mordika's Fledglings*. I snort—Vampire wannabes. Cool clothes, though. Some people dressed as Klingons and assorted other aliens strut past.

"Look at them," I say. "Sometimes I think ordinary humans are weirder than Others."

Tavian laughs. "True." He slicks back his hair.

Beneath his fingers, it fades to corn-silk blond from the roots to the tips. I stare at him. He grins and does it again, his hair turning cotton candy pink, then rainbow, then flame colored.

"Tavian!" I whisper. "Are you insane?"

He arches an eyebrow. "You don't like it?"

"Wow," says a little boy. Ice cream slides from the cone in his hand. "Is that magic?"

Tavian winks. "Why, of course."

"Cool!" says the boy.

I steer Tavian away. "Turn it back," I say, "before somebody else notices."

He shakes his head and flings the illusion away. We keep walking.

A tall, light-haired guy waves at me. Not Zack—Justin. What if he's with Zack's family? I glance around, but he seems to be alone. Probably just enjoying his vacation. Then, as quickly as he appeared, Justin melts into the crowd again.

I spot a table of oddly shaped glass bottles full of rainbow sand. Some of them have dyed chicken feathers stuck in the sand.

"Ugh," I say, "who would even buy that crap?"

Tavian shrugs. "Who knows."

"Aficionados of fine sand products," a guy says near my ear.

I snap my head in the direction of the voice. "Ben! Don't scare me like that."

"Sorry." Smiling, Ben nods at Tavian. "Hello, stranger."

"Hey," Tavian says, looking more than a little bemused.

Then I glower, remembering the Christian pamphlet I got in the mail. I don't trust Ben's current Mr. Nice act, and obviously he's going to tell Zack about Tavian and me. Whatever. They're going to judge me, anyway.

"I'm Benjamin Arrington," he says with a big smile. "Also known as Ben. And you?"

"Tavian."

"Let me guess," Ben says. "Your parents invented it, or they named you something longer and more embarrassing. Correct?"

Tavian laughs. "The second, actually. Octavian Kimura."

"Cool." Ben nods, grinning. "Thought so."

I narrow my eyes, annoyed by his perpetual goofiness. "I saw Justin just a few minutes ago. You should catch up with him."

"Justin?" Ben cocks his head. "Where is he?"

"He went that way." I point randomly into the crowd. "See you later, Ben." I grab Tavian's arm and march him away.

"Who was that?" Tavian asks me.

"Brother of my ex."

"Your ex?" He gives me a look.

"Yeah, I know, it's weird. Let's just forget about him."

Over the hubbub, a dog barks. Tavian stops walking,

and I glance at him. His eyes narrow. A big dog bounds through the people toward us.

Bollocks! It's Blackjack.

The pit bull zeroes in on Tavian, who stiffens. The fur along Blackjack's spine bristles. He sniffs and slobbers on Tavian's snow cone. Tavian clenches his fingers into a fist, as if afraid of getting them bit off.

I glance around for something to distract Blackjack, and then see Chris and Brock marching through the crowd.

"Come on." I grab Tavian's wrist.

I drag him, or vice versa. Hard to tell. We zigzag through the people and duck behind a booth selling jewelry. Panting, we crouch in the shadows. Barking approaches, and Blackjack galumphs past.

"Hey! Get back here, you stupid dog!" Chris bellows.

I stifle a nervous laugh. The Koeman brothers run past us in pursuit of the pit bull.

"Those guys are total assholes," I say. "I've run into them before."

Tavian sucks in air through his nostrils and exhales slowly.

"You don't like dogs, do you?" I say.

He shakes his head. "They don't like me."

"A kitsune thing?"

Tavian nods, his gaze on the ground, then rolls up his right sleeve. Two crescents of scars mark his upper arm— pale permanent tooth marks. I run my finger along them. He flinches away as if they still hurt.

"Sorry," I say.

"Ah, no, it's nothing." He manages a lopsided smile. "Stupid, really."

Before I can say something else, he straightens and walks out from behind the booth. He tosses his drooled-on snow cone into a trash can. I jog after him, frowning. How the heck can I tell what he's thinking?

I catch up with him. "Tavian, wait." I squeeze his hand; I want to see him smile again. "Let's ride the Ferris wheel."

His face brightens. "Okay."

Final rays of sunlight gild the fair, and the kicked-up dust becomes a golden haze. As we buy tickets for the Ferris wheel and stand in line, the sun slides beneath the horizon in a blaze of tangerine clouds.

"Pretty," Tavian says, looking at me.

When am I going to stop blushing around him?

We climb into a seat on the Ferris wheel. I slide closer to him. We stay silent until it climbs high above the crowd.

"Did you get my email?" I ask. "About the letter from 'Maris'?"

Tavian nods. "I'm not sure what to make of it. Maybe it's a prank. Or maybe it really is an Other who wants to talk."

"Who do you think the Bad Man is?"

He rubs the bridge of his nose. "Well, maybe the killer. Or maybe just made up."

"Do you think it's worth writing back and leaving a letter by the river?"

"I don't know. If you really think it's worthwhile."

"What if—"

"Gwen." He raises his eyebrows. "We're at the fair. It's time for fun and frolicking, not serious detective mode."

I sigh. "Sorry."

"It's cool."

We look away from each other. My gaze drifts over flashing lights, flags snapping in the wind, and crowds eddying through paths.

"So, can you change into any animal?" he asks. "Or is it mostly a black horse?"

I smile. "Any animal. Did you Google 'pooka' like I Googled 'kitsune'?"

He laughs. "Yes."

"Is it true that kitsune have nine tails when they get older?"

"I have no idea. Probably I'd have to be really, really old. I only vaguely remember my kitsune mother, but I'm sure she had only one tail." A smile shadows his lips. "I can remember her stroking her tail to make *kitsune-bi*. It would light our way at night." He laughs again. "And confuse travelers."

"Kitsune what?" I say.

"Kitsune-bi is the Japanese word for foxfire." Tavian stares out over the fair, his gaze distant. "She liked to play tricks on people. She would make plums roll in front of passersby, but when they picked them up, the plums vanished. And I remember her making a flower grow out of the snow for me. It melted."

"Sounds lovely."

I want to ask what happened to her, but I don't want to make him sad.

Evening ripens into a blackberry sky seeded with stars. The moon peeks above the horizon, fat and nearing full, dripping silver juice. Tavian lowers his face, his eyelashes dark crescents on his cheeks. Shadows sharpen his high cheekbones. We hover at the apex of the Ferris wheel. He leans closer, until I can feel the warmth of him and smell the wild spice of his scent. His hand settles on my shoulder.

After a heartbeat, I say, "Tavian," and he takes his hand away.

The Ferris wheel spins around once, twice, before he speaks. "Sorry."

"It's okay. I just want to take things slow."

He nods. "Makes sense."

"Yeah," I say, though my heart falls down a notch or two.

As the Ferris wheel swings toward the ground, I see a familiar shaggy-haired guy at the edge of the crowd. He's by himself, staring skyward.

Tavian says, "Is that—?"

"Randall. Why's he here? Is he stalking me?"

Tavian looks grim. "He'd better not be."

We share a glance.

"Let's see what he's up to," I say.

But the Ferris wheel swings upward again.

"Damn," Tavian says. "How long is this ride going to last?"

I clench my hands around the safety bar at my waist. "Maybe I should shapeshift into a bird and go after him."

"Okay, so I can't change my hair color, but now you're shapeshifting in public?"

I grimace. "Good point."

Tavian drums his fingers on the side of the seat. "Come on." Then he tilts his head to one side and squints. "What is that...?"

"What's what?"

"Shhh. Listen."

I shut my eyes and strain to hear. The wind is blowing voices down from one of the gondolas above ours on the Ferris wheel.

"...Don't let them get too close. That would be a disaster."

It's a male voice, soft and hard to pinpoint. I crane my neck, but I can't see who's above us.

"Yeah, we know," says another, louder male voice.

Tavian glances at me. "Is that...?"

"Chris." My eyes widen.

"Fucking werewolves," says a third voice, clearly Brock.

"Don't wait..." The wind gusts harder, whistling in my ears. "...Eliminated."

Tavian growls under his breath. "I can't hear anything."

The Ferris wheel circles down and stops, and the operator waves for us to get off. As soon as we hop down, I spin around and stare. Another gondola is emptying right now, but the sea of people engulfs me and two girls drag an armada of balloons in front of my eyes, completely blocking my view.

"Bollocks," I say. "Where are they?"

Tavian peers through the crowd. "There's Randall." He grabs my wrist, his eyes glowing like a fox's in the deepening dark. "Let's go. He's on the move."

"Wait—go after him?"

"Yes. He's up to something."

I hesitate. This could be dangerous. Really, really dangerous.

But I say "Okay," and jog ahead.

Wind whirls through the fairgrounds and tosses my hair. I rake it from my eyes. The fattening moon floats higher in the sky. A shaggy-haired guy is stalking through the casual strollers. He glances sideways, and I hide my face. Yes. It's him. Then Randall lopes faster, swinging his head like a bloodhound following a scent. We're nearing the House of Horrors. The ticket guy outside chats with a big-boobed lady, distracted.

Randall sidesteps through the dark doorway. What's he doing?

Tavian grabs my arm. "Gwen."

"We're going to lose him!"

He glares at me, his eyes orange. "Do you really—"

"Hey! Get back here!"

I whirl around and see Chris, Brock, and Blackjack on our heels. What happened to the third man in their gondola? Who was he?

Chris jabs a finger at us, his face red, and bellows, "They stole my wallet!"

I yank Tavian into the House of Horrors before the big-boobed lady ceases to fascinate. Inside the dimly lit House of Horrors, cheesy "spooky" organ music plays, punctuated by ghoulish laughter. Wooden vampires and other unrealistic Others spring up as we pass. I just hope we don't run into a very realistic werewolf.

Strobe lights flash, disorienting me. I stumble into a hanging ghost and bat it away, then walk through a narrow hallway flanked by two snarling beasts.

Three beasts. Randall is crouching in the shadows, his eyes glowing.

I whirl on him, and a growl rumbles from his throat. Tavian drags me back. Cornering a werewolf is definitely not smart. Randall barrels past us and leaps out of the House of Horrors. We stumble out in time to see Randall weaving through the crowd, people shouting in his wake. As we dash after him, I clutch a cramp in my side. Randall sprints past cages of chickens. They squawk, flutter, and beat against the bars.

"Hey!" yells a policeman. "What's going on here?"

"Nothing, officer!" I say. I don't want the police bungling things.

Ahead, Randall widens the gap between us. He vaults over a low fence and hits the ground running. We follow him into a field of high grass that comes up to our waists. I nearly trip over an abandoned hubcap.

Trees bristle ahead. We're going to lose him.

"Randall!" I shout. "Wait!"

He whirls on us, his hair silvering, his teeth feral. "Get the fuck out of here. You're leading them right to me."

I take a step back. "What are you doing?"

"Trying to keep the pack safe," he slurs around a mouthful of fangs. "And trying to keep you from getting killed."

Tavian narrows his eyes. "Is that why you were watching us?"

"Not you. Them." Randall crouches low. "Oh, shit."

I glance back and see a ropy brown tail wagging above the grass. Blackjack.

Tavian grabs my hand and drags me toward the trees. We duck behind a clump of ferns. Our breathing sounds so loud I'm tempted to hold my breath. Randall crouches in the field, clenching and unclenching his hands, flashing hooked claws. I can hear grass hissing past Blackjack as he picks up speed, his paws thudding closer.

"He's going to fight him," Tavian whispers, with a low whistle.

I squeeze his hand. "Shhh."

He squeezes my hand back, and we lie on our bellies on the fallen leaves. The harsh fairground lights seep through the black trees and cast crazy shadows. Tavian's eyes gleam, and I edge into owl form to help me see.

Blackjack emerges from the grass, panting, sniffing, and stops not more than two yards from Randall. The pit bull lifts his blocky, muscular head and growls. Randall growls back, deep and wolfish, as his silvering hair sweeps over his skin and cloaks him in fur. Then he doubles over as his spine curves, crunching along every bone. He fumbles with his belt buckle, yanks down his jeans, and falls to his hands and knees.

I try not to stare. I've never seen a werewolf transform before, not in real life.

The change is shuddering through Randall, both violent and beautiful. A metamorphosis and a deformation. He lifts his head, now a huge silver wolf. As if finally recognizing the nature of his enemy, Blackjack starts barking, spittle flying from his mouth. Randall flattens his ears against his skull and bares vicious fangs.

Tavian swears under his breath. "This is going to get ugly."

eighteen

Blackjack marches closer, stiff-legged and snarling. Randall slinks sideways, circling his opponent. The pit bull lunges, the werewolf dodges, and Blackjack swerves just as Randall jumps high. Randall twists to avoid the dog's jaws, then sinks his teeth into Blackjack's shoulder. Blackjack yelps shrilly and shakes Randall off.

My heart thuds in my ribs. I don't realize I'm shaking until Tavian holds my shoulders.

Blood is trickling down Blackjack's side, and he skitters back, disoriented. Randall growls thunderously, and Blackjack charges. Randall rolls nimbly out of the way and, as Blackjack skids to a stop, Randall pounces. He bites the back of Blackjack's neck and brings him down. As a wolf, he must weigh twice as much as the dog.

"Blackjack!" Brock calls, not too far away.

The pit bull tries to struggle to his feet, but Randall pins him to the ground.

"Blackjack? Come here, boy!"

Brock bursts through the tall grass. Winded and red-faced, he gapes at the fight. His older brother catches up to him.

"Fuck…" The color drains from Chris's face. "Fuck!"

Brock glances wildly at his brother. "He's killing him. He's killing Blackjack!"

Chris pulls a gun from his jacket. I dig my hands into the dirt, coldness seeping through my skin. I can feel Tavian tense beside me.

Brock grabs Chris's arm. "Don't shoot! You'll hit Blackjack."

"I don't have a choice," Chris says, his face grim. "The cur is going to kill us next."

Randall's yellow eyes roll toward them, but he keeps his muzzle clamped on Blackjack. The pit bull whimpers, and Brock's face twists. Chris cocks the gun. His hand trembles ever so slightly. I marvel at how quickly their bravado can crumble. Did they think they were invincible with their pit bull and their daddy's guns?

"Chris, wait," Brock says. "Just wait a minute."

Has Brock ever killed anything, or anyone, before? Is he having second thoughts?

The gun lowers, and Chris gives his brother a cold look. "What?"

Before Brock can answer, Randall releases Blackjack

and lunges. He flings himself on Chris, knocking him flat on his back. The gun goes off, and my hands flinch to my ears. A snarl tears from Randall's throat. He bites Chris's arm and shakes it, the gun skidding into the grass. Then Randall pins Chris, his full weight on his chest and his teeth locked on his shoulder. Chris screams. Brock stands by his wounded dog—his hands clenched by his sides, his face colorless, his eyes clearly saying he can't believe he's so helpless.

Chris kicks Randall in the belly, and the werewolf growls louder. When Chris punches Randall in the muzzle, Randall bites his wrist with a sickening crunch, then closes his jaws on Chris's neck. Not hard enough to choke him or puncture his jugular, but enough to make him freeze, and for blood to trickle beneath teeth.

My imagination spins out of control. Blood-slick muzzles, guts spilling on the ground.

"Tavian," I hiss. "We can't just hide here. We can't."

He looks at me, his eyes black and unreadable. "They brought this on themselves."

"Even these guys don't deserve this. You're going to let them die?"

Tavian stares at me a moment more, then stands. "Randall!" he shouts.

Brock's head whips around. "Help! You've got to . . ." When I get to my feet, recognition dawns on his face. "You gicks. This was a trap!"

Randall's head twists in our direction. His teeth dig deeper into Chris, who groans.

I shake my head, then take a step toward Randall. "You know if you kill them, you're dead. They're going to hunt you down and kill you." I try to sound as if Randall and I are on the same side, as if I'm not afraid he's going to kill me, too.

The werewolf growls. My heart skips a beat.

Tears streak down Brock's face, but his expression hardens. "Fuck this."

Tavian's gaze snaps to the gun on the ground, and he's halfway to it before Brock snatches it up and aims it at Tavian's head.

"Don't move." The gun doesn't shake in Brock's hand. "Or I'll blow your face off."

I raise my hands above my head. "Brock, we don't want to fight you."

"Shut up." Brock's face is a mask of rage. "Shut the fuck up, you gick bitch."

"Put down the gun." At gunpoint, Tavian remains remarkably calm. "Nobody has to die."

"Shut the *fuck* up." The gun swings toward Randall. "Get off my brother!"

Randall slowly opens his jaws and crawls off Chris, who gasps and clutches his neck. Blood dribbles from Randall's mouth and he licks it clean. I shudder and try not to let revulsion show on my face. Brock takes three steps forward, the barrel of the gun and the waiting bullet aimed right between Randall's yellow eyes.

"Brock," Chris rasps. "Don't let—" He coughs and clutches his throat.

The gun wavers in Brock's hand and he steps away, toward his brother. Blackjack struggles to his feet with a cross between a whine and a growl, blood glistening on his brindled coat. Randall bares his teeth at the pit bull.

I share a glance with Tavian, wondering what we can possibly do to end this madness.

"Chris, what do I do?" Brock says, his voice high and tight.

"Shoot—the—gicks."

Damn it. Am I going to have to shapeshift? Can I possibly do it fast enough? My pooka side paces within me, anxious to emerge.

Tavian glances at me. "Gwen—"

In a silver blur, Randall lunges at Brock and knocks him down.

"Get the gun!" I shout.

Tavian and I both leap for it, even as my instincts scream to get the hell out of there. Randall bites Brock's arm and shakes it hard. The gun falls, and I claw at the metal, my fingers shaky with adrenaline. I grab it and back away.

I can feel the weight of the gun's power in my hands. I'm afraid to be holding it.

"Randall," I say. "Let Brock go."

The werewolf's golden eyes burn, and he growls low in his throat, his teeth still deep in Brock's arm. But under my gaze, he opens his jaws and leaps away. Brock staggers to his feet, his face pale, and touches the bite on his arm.

Tavian slips his cell phone from his pocket and dials a number.

"What are you doing?" I say.

"911."

"The police?" I suck in my breath. "But—"

"We're not going to stay here," Tavian says, his face emotionless. "We're going to leave and let the police do their job."

I face Brock, the gun still mine. "You can't tell the police what really happened."

He just stares at me, then at the bite on his arm.

Chris is breathing unevenly now. Blackjack limps over to him and nudges him with his nose.

"Brock," Chris rasps. "Did he get you?"

"Yeah." Brock's voice breaks. "He got me."

Randall stands with his head and tail held low, the fire in his eyes fading. He exhales deeply, almost a sigh, then turns and lopes into the forest.

Tavian and I run. We have to.

We sprint through the trees, the gun growing heavier and heavier in my hands, until I stop and fling it into the ferns.

"Gwen." Tavian takes my elbow. "We can't do that. We have to hide it."

A burning in my throat keeps me from replying right away. "Yeah."

We find the gun again and bury it deep in the forest. Part of me feels guilty for hiding evidence, but part of me doesn't want the police to ever know. When we're done, I kneel on the leaves, my head bowed, my bones like lead.

"Gwen?" Tavian brushes my hair from my eyes, smudging dirt on my face. "You okay?"

"Of course not. I never want to do this detective shit again."

A tiny smile touches his eyes. "At least your snarkiness is still intact." He holds out his hand. "Come on. You're getting muddy."

I let him help me to my feet as I heave a shuddering sigh. "I want to go home."

"Me too."

We stride together through the night. The moon ladles silver light over the forest. It drips down the trees and pools on the ground.

"Randall scares me," I say, my voice small.

Tavian nods. "Though he had to do what he did. He was protecting his pack."

"You think he's not a murderer?"

He looks at me, a sheen of moonlight in his eyes. "He didn't kill them."

"Only because we stopped him."

Tavian shrugs.

"Do you think...?" I clench my jaw. "Those guys...?"

"Those guys what?"

"Do you think they're infected with lycanthropy now? It seems like the ultimate revenge. To hunt a werewolf only to become one."

"They did get bitten." Tavian glances away, his face shadowed. "What are the chances?"

"Of dying, or of becoming infected?"

"Both."

"I don't know. It depends on how tough you are. I think it's a fifty-fifty chance if you're healthy. But Chris was bitten badly."

Tavian twines his fingers with mine. We slow to a walk at the edge of the forest, the lights of Klikamuks like jewels in the darkness.

"Our date," he says, "was a disaster."

I start to laugh, but the laughter snags in my throat, and then I can't look at Tavian because of the tears escaping my eyes.

"Gwen." He says it so softly, I almost don't hear him. "Gwen."

"I just want to quit," I say. "I don't want to be a part of this anymore."

Tavian rests his hand on my arm. He seems hesitant, as if he isn't sure what to do or say.

"I've lived in Klikamuks all my life, but I've never really felt unsafe before." I rub my face dry on my sleeve. "I feel like I can't even try to be happy anymore."

"Hey," he says. "This is going to pass. This isn't going to last forever."

"You think?" I laugh bleakly. "How many people are going to die first?"

Tavian grabs my shoulders. "Don't think about that, okay?"

My words tumble out. "Did you find your best friend dead? Is there a pack of werewolves running wild in your backyard? Did you get dumped by someone right after you gave them your virginity and told them you're Other?" Instantly I regret what I've said. I press my knuckles to my mouth and turn away.

Tavian is silent for a long, long moment.

I'm too pissed at myself to cry more. "I have a pretty screwed up life at the moment. I'm not sure you should want to be part of it."

He grabs my shoulders and turns me around. "Gwen," he says, his eyes intense. "I've wanted to be part of your life ever since you first walked into the bookstore. I can't get you out of my head. But you can't keep up this self-loathing thing, okay? I'd never forgive myself if I let you throw your life away."

I try and fail to scoff. "I've never thought of suicide."

"You've been so reckless, it's like you're trying to run at death head-on!"

I'm trembling now. "It's better than running away from it."

"No, it's not. You shouldn't keep thinking of death. If you need help, get help."

Part of me wants to argue, to tell him he can't tell me what to do, but more of me knows he's right. I should stop doing this. I stare at the ground, my hair curtaining my face. "Okay."

"Come here." Tavian sounds gruff, and I wonder if he's trying not to get emotional. He drags me into a hug and holds me tight.

I sniff and bury my face in his shoulder.

"I'm here for you," he says. "If you need to talk, you can talk to me."

"Okay," I say again. "Sometimes none of this seems worth it."

"I know what you mean. But then I think of things worth living for."

I stare at his face, my arms still linked around him, and question him with my eyes.

He laughs, a tired little laugh. "All the sappy-sounding stuff. Beauty. Hope. Love."

I might be falling in love with him, but I'm still too afraid to admit it.

He lowers his voice. "Your ex dumped you after you slept with him? For the first time?"

"Yes."

"What an asshole. I would never have done that to you."

I wait for him to speak again, to admit that he's feeling the same sweet ache in his chest.

"Though my first time sucked, too," he says. "Junior prom. Empty classroom."

"Ugh. Really?"

"Yeah." He twists his lips wryly. "Everybody was really horny. Peer pressure, too."

I don't want to think about him with some other girl. "I'm glad I'm homeschooled."

"Guess we have to make up for crappy first times," he says. "Thank God it gets better."

My face hot, I say, "Well, I wouldn't know. There's only been one time for me." I laugh at myself. "Just warning you." Admitting all this to him makes me feel lighter, as if I've tossed aside a burden.

"I believe in second chances," Tavian murmurs. "They can be just as special."

At first I can't look him, but then our eyes meet. His are glimmering like obsidian.

"I'll make it better," he says, "I'll make you happy. Okay?"

My eyes sting, and I blink.

"We'll go on another date," he says. "A real one. A good one."

"Okay," I say, just to see him smile.

I can't fall asleep that night, until I put on headphones and blast hard rock so I can't hear myself think. What a lullaby. Sleep seems impossible, but exhaustion drags me into unconsciousness.

I see Chloe again and again, swinging from the tree like a pendulum, the branch screeching. Her eyes are still moving. I know she's alive, but I can't reach her. Hands slide around my throat and choke me.

I twist around and stare into icy blue eyes. Not Zack. Justin.

I fall out of the dream and out of my bed, sheets tangled around my neck. I struggle free. Breathing hard, I crouch on my hands and knees.

This is crazy. My own mind is betraying me.

I squeeze my eyes shut and force myself to think nothing, to be nothing. I imagine my thoughts swirling down a drain, my skull emptying. Only then can I climb back into bed. Only then can I sleep—but I don't dream.

It's on the news, of course:

"Late last night, two teenaged boys, aged seventeen and nineteen, were hospitalized after being attacked by werewolves on the outskirts of the Evergreen State Fair. Police report that the boys were unarmed and attempting to confront the werewolves. One of the boys was treated for minor injuries and released. The other remains in the hospital in critical condition. Both victims are receiving anti-lycanthropic treatment. Police advise that everyone in the area avoid werewolves for their own safety."

Werewolves. Plural. Chris and Brock must have lied to the police.

Megan stands in the doorway to the kitchen. "What's anti-lycanthropic treatment?"

"It's a drug," I say in a monotone. "It's supposed to keep people from turning into werewolves after they've been bitten."

Mum stares at me. "What time were you at the fair?"

"Not sure. Late." I can't look at her.

Mum cocks her head, her eyes narrowing. "Did you see anything?"

My face flushes. "No."

"Gwen, I want you to be more careful. I don't want you going places alone, is that clear?"

"I wasn't alone," I say. "Tavian went with me."

"For heaven's sake," Mum mutters. She starts chopping carrots again, faster. "Our own backyard isn't safe anymore."

"What do you mean?"

"What do you mean, what do I mean? Werewolves!"

I think of Randall, but then I think of Winema and the werepuppies.

"That's like me saying, 'Humans!' You can't make generalizations like that."

Mum gives me an eagle-eyed stare. "I don't want you associating with those kind of people just because they're Others. They're not like you."

"But we—"

"We?" Mum stops chopping carrots. "Since when was it 'we'?"

"Never mind."

I slip away before she can extract the truth from me. I'm not hungry anymore, especially since it feels like I swallowed a block of ice.

In my bedroom, my cell phone beeps. Voicemail. I lie on my bed and listen.

"Hey, Gwen! It's me, Tavian. I was wondering if you might be interested in hanging out with me sometime. And by hanging out, I mean the wonderfully witty pleasures of my company, enhanced by the deliciousness of a picnic."

I laugh, and a wave of warmth thaws the coldness inside me.

"Anyway, I was thinking Wilding Park, tomorrow. Call me back if you're interested. I totally owe you a good time. Talk to you later!"

I replay the message, then close my eyes with a sigh. I curl on my bed and let thoughts pool in my mind. All I want to do is go out with Tavian, take a walk, sit together, talk, maybe do more than talk... Why don't I? It's not like I'm going to get picked off by the murderer as soon as I go on a date. That's just paranoid. Right?

What the hell. I'm calling him back to tell the truth: I'd love to go.

nineteen

Tomorrow turns out to be a beautiful, sun-drenched day sweet with the smell of clover and alfalfa fields. The ascending warble of Swainson's thrushes embroiders the air. I'm wearing a loose cotton dress in cornflower blue. The fabric clings to my sweaty back, but I like how it ripples around my ankles in the wind.

Wilding Park makes me remember the times that Zack and I spent there. I shut those thoughts from my mind as I sit on a bench overlooking the Stillaguamish River.

"Hey Gwen!"

I twist around and see Tavian strolling toward me. "Where were you?"

"Sorry I'm late. Got held up at the bookstore." He stops behind me and puts his hands on my shoulders. "Hey, what's that?"

I frown up at him. "What's what?"

He's looking at the back of my neck. "I didn't know you had a tattoo. Cool."

"Yeah. I got it on my sixteenth birthday, when my parents finally relented."

Tavian grazes the clover with his fingertips, and I remember how Zack always used to kiss it. I lean away from him.

"What?"

"It tickles."

"Really?" He gives me a crooked smile. "Just how ticklish are you?"

I'm sure my smile looks fake, so I give up. "My ex liked that tattoo."

"Oh." Tavian sobers. "Bad memories?"

"Well, not necessarily *bad* memories..." I see his face and switch in mid-sentence. "But I definitely want to forget them."

"Now's a good time to forget," he says, his eyes mysterious.

My heart thumps like crazy, but he walks to his car and pops open the back door. He brings over a picnic basket and pulls out two bowls, balancing them like scales. "Do you want the *abura-age* or the *kitsune udon*?"

"The what or the what-what?"

"Abura-age is deep-fried tofu." Tavian makes a salivating noise. "Kitsune udon is a soup of abura-age with udon noodles. It's got kitsune in the name because foxes love it." He winks. "Myself included."

"Well then," I say, "who am I to stand in the way of a fox and kitsune udon?"

He laughs, then sits and hands me the bowl of abura-age. The fried tofu, golden and crispy, tastes delicious. I lie on the lawn, feeling so decadent just savoring the sunshine, the good food, and the sweetness of clovers. Wind sizzles through the dry rushes by the river, and swallows dart and chirp high in the turquoise sky.

My mind wanders back to yesterday. "Did you see the news last night?"

"No."

"Chris and Brock are in the hospital, being treated for lycanthropy."

"Ah." Tavian stares at the grass. "So the police found them, then."

I braid and unbraid my hair, my fingers restless. "I can't help feeling bad," I say. "Even though they deserved it, probably."

"Gwen," Tavian says, "you're too sensitive."

"What's that supposed to mean?"

"I mean you don't have to care about every asshole in the universe."

"I don't!"

His hand closes around mine, stopping my fidgety braiding. "I just hate seeing you get all worked up over things that aren't your fault."

I sigh and lay back in the grass, staring at the clouds.

"It's a nice day, remember? You're supposed to be *enjoy-*

ing yourself." He pretends to be exasperated, a teasing smile on his face.

"I know," I say, and it comes out more mournful than I intended.

"All right." Tavian climbs to his knees. "You asked for it. I'm going to make this day *so* nice you won't be able to resist."

I hide my laughter behind my hand, my face hot.

He plucks a silver rose from thin air and offers it in a grand gesture. "Remember?"

"Uh, no …"

"*Der Rosenkavalier*? The part where Octavian presents the silver rose?"

"Oh! Right." Blushing, I bring the flower to my nose. I catch a whiff of an ethereal fragrance—what starlight might smell like—before the rose vanishes.

"How sweet," I say.

"You want sweet?" he says. "I'll show you sweet." He gives me a cherubic smile, then grabs my hand and plants a dramatic kiss on it. I clap my other hand over my eyes. Tavian leans into my face to sing part of a horrible sappy song with lyrics that say, "You're my one and only."

I burst out laughing. "Dear Lord," I say, "please save me from this lunatic."

"Trust me, this is not Lunatic Tavian. He's somewhere in a straitjacket."

I laugh until my sides hurt, then realize Tavian's still holding my hand and looking intently at me. My laughter fades. He brushes a curl from my face. The tenderness in his eyes makes me feel soft and shaky. I want to kiss him so bad, but I'm not sure if it's—finally—the right moment. Is it?

We drift closer, slowly, like two leaves in a pond. For an instant I expect a passionate, breathtaking movie kiss. It's not—but it's real. Tavian's lips clumsily brush my cheek, then meet my mouth. He strokes my neck, his fingers leaving tingling in their wake. A sweet ache blossoms in my stomach.

When he withdraws, I catch my breath and try to imprint this feeling into my memory.

"I've wanted to do that for so long," he murmurs.

"You could have done it sooner," I say, trying to sound teasing.

He smiles. "Alas."

My happiness deflates a little, and I wonder why. Then I remember—that sounds so much like what Zack would say.

"What is it?" Tavian says.

"Got to use the bathroom." I force myself to smile. "Excuse me."

I walk briskly to the toilets. Two girls are chatting and washing their hands. I stand by a mirror and pretend to fiddle with my hair. The girls leave, and I knead my forehead. I thought I was done with Zack. Shouldn't Tavian be enough to take his place? No, not take his place. Our relationship is definitely different. Better, even.

Am I falling in love with Tavian? Am I holding myself back?

I argue with my reflection. Admit it—you're scared of getting involved with another guy who might hurt you. But this is different, since Tavian knows I'm Other. Even better, he's Other too. Then why don't we talk about it more? Because you're scared to show anyone your Otherness. To be that intimate.

"Bollocks, bollocks, triple bollocks," I mutter.

A silver-haired woman steps inside just then. Her eyes get big, and I blush.

Okay. I'm going back out there, and I'm not going to let my past define my present.

When I return, Tavian's lying on his stomach, propped up on his elbows, a butterfly fluttering idly by his head. He's reading a manga, one of those comics, in Japanese. I creep up behind him, my hands bent like talons.

"I can see your shadow," he says calmly.

"Gah," I say.

He rolls over and stares up at me, squinting in the sun. "What were you going to do?"

"Do?" I smile wickedly. "Well, I was going to scare you, but I might change my mind."

He laughs, low in his throat.

I drop to my knees and crawl around him. "As the lioness stalks her prey," I say in a fake British accent, "she smells a hint of fear."

He smiles at me and crosses his hands behind his head. "This should be interesting."

I growl and narrow my eyes, then pounce on him. I pretend to sink my teeth into his shoulder. My hands press his wrists down. I growl again and nibble his ear, then lick his cheek. "Tasty."

"This won't actually involve eating, will it?" Tavian asks.

"Be quiet. The lioness is getting impatient."

"Oh, right," Tavian says, smirking. "Mustn't piss off the lioness."

"Silence, prey." I whack him on the shoulder for being so cheeky.

He laughs and pretends to fend off my blows. We play-fight for a minute, and then we're kissing again. It isn't as hesitant as before, but long and sweet and lingering. I relax into his arms, leaning against him. He smells musky and male—very sexy. My nails sharpen into claws that dig into the lawn on either side of him. I feel fox-fangs graze my lower lip. I moan and press closer. He moves his face toward the hollow of my neck, inhales my scent, then nips my shoulder, just hard enough to make me gasp.

"Wait, wait," I say. "Slow down."

We break apart. Tavian pushes himself up on his elbows and stares at me with foxy, marmalade eyes. I'm sure mine are glowing.

"Sorry," he mutters. "Got carried away."

"No, it's okay." I rake my fingers through my tangled hair. "It's half my fault."

I glance around Wilding Park to see if anyone's staring. Nobody meets my eyes, but I'm sure they saw us. My face feels hot.

"Do I look…normal?" I ask in a low voice.

Tavian arches an eyebrow. "Normal?"

Embarrassed by his direct stare, I blink and look away. "You know what I mean."

"I don't see how what you are—what we are—isn't normal."

I shake my head. "You're so comfortable with your Otherness. I'm not like that."

He frowns, as if he doesn't even understand what I'm saying.

"This is way too public," I say.

Tavian smiles. "Let's go somewhere private. Somewhere we can be ourselves."

A flock of fluttering whirls inside my stomach. "What do you mean?"

He tilts his head down and arches an eyebrow. "I think you know, Gwen."

"Okay." Before my confidence can fail me, I stand. "Let's go."

We leave the mowed lawn of Wilding Park behind and wade hand-in-hand through a sea of grass higher than our heads.

"I like this," I say.

"Perfect for hide-and-seek," Tavian says, and I'm not sure if he's joking or not.

We swim deeper into the grass, startled birds peeping in our wake. Through the greenery, I glimpse slivers of the water. The poplars ruffle stiffly in the breeze. I drink in the cool liquor of river-scented air, then stumble and drag us both down.

"Sorry!" I say.

He laughs. "Klutz."

We sink into the grass, tangled together. I test the feel of his body against mine. My skin heats as he stares into my eyes. Tavian looks … beautiful. The blue-black sheen of his hair, the line of his jaw, the way his eyelashes shadow his cheeks. His hands cradle my hips. Our lips meet again. We kiss for a long, long time. My pooka side paces inside me, but I'm not sure it's eager to emerge.

Sweat trickles down my nose and lands on his face, and I grimace. "It's so hot."

He smiles. I love how it makes him look foxy. "There's one solution …"

"What?"

He pulls away from me and starts unbuttoning his shirt. "Care to join me?"

"Uh …"

He laughs, flashing sharp teeth. "Shapeshifting?"

I shiver with delight, with fear. "Oh. Okay." I don't know why I'm stammering. "Sure."

Tavian turns his back on me. "I won't look if you don't want me to."

"Thanks."

I can't help glancing at him as he tosses aside his shirt. My gaze lingers on his golden skin, the muscles in his back and shoulders. When he starts to unzip his jeans, I wade deeper into the grass, aware that he's hearing me leaving just now.

With shaky fingers, I tug off my blouse and step out

of my skirt. I bunch my underwear and hide it inside the skirt, hoping it's not too ugly—and hoping he won't even come across it in the first place. Talk about awkward.

Okay. Hurry up and shapeshift. I concentrate on *fox*, an animal I can't remember becoming before. My pooka side remains restless but unwilling. I clench my fists and thighs to urge it on. Nothing happens.

"You okay?" Tavian calls.

A mental image of him naked in the grass nearby flashes through my mind. "Yeah!"

Do it, Gwen. I shut my eyes and try to visualize a fox. I keep thinking of Tavian, already transformed. My heartbeat races and I force myself to breathe. The muggy air feels like wet wool in my throat, and sweat rolls down my back.

"I'm going to wait for you," Tavian says. "Tell me when you're ready."

"I won't be able to talk," I say.

"Same here. Just yip or something."

"Okay."

Why isn't this working? What am I doing wrong? My stomach cramps, but nothing happens. I drop to my knees and bow my head.

"Tavian," I gasp. "I can't do it."

"Gwen? Are you okay?"

"Yes." My throat tightens. I can't breathe. I suck in air. "I just can't."

"Wait. I'm coming."

I shake my head, but of course he can't see me.

Grass rustles nearby and Tavian jogs up to me, zipping his jeans. His eyes glimmer orange, and his ears have already sharpened into foxy points. I huddle on the ground, crossing my arms to cover my nakedness.

"This is ridiculous," I say, not looking at him. "Most of the time I have to force my pooka side to quiet down, not the other way around."

"Gwen. Relax." He drops to his knees beside me. "Just let it happen."

"I am!"

"You can't force it."

"It's not working. Especially not with you watching. I don't want you to see."

"Why?"

"It's ugly, I'm sure."

"Gwen." He kisses my cheek. "I know you can do it."

I nearly start grumbling about the futility of pep talks, but he leaves me then. Part of me wishes he had some magic trick to make it happen, but of course it's all within my own power. I exhale and make myself unclench my muscles. Tingling builds in my chest, and then a wave of transformation sweeps over me.

I suck in my breath, my vision blacking. Warmth spreads through my body. My eyesight returns slowly, and I find myself staring at two paws—my paws. Dizzy, I sit up and wrap my bottlebrush tail primly around my legs.

I did it! I yip with excitement.

A red fox inches up to me, his head low, sniffing. Tavian can deny it all he wants, but he's seriously cute.

We touch noses, and he streaks away in a blur of orange. I race after him, then lose him in the grass. I circle, snuffling the ground. A chirp—I whirl in time to see Tavian pounce. We tumble, growling and nipping playfully. I fling him off. He rolls onto his back, his white belly bared, and paws the air.

I yip with laughter. Tavian cranes his neck to look at me, upside-down. He bares his sharp teeth—grinning, I hope. He leaps to his feet and lunges. We play-fight on our hind legs, our forepaws on each other's shoulders.

He buries his muzzle in the fur of my neck. I growl and nip at his ear. He grabs my ruff between his jaws. His teeth prick too hard, and I whimper. He loosens his hold a little, then drags me down and pins me. I squirm and growl.

He holds me there, his breath hot in my fur. I narrow my eyes and bite his paw. Not too hard, I think, but he yelps and withdraws. Then he lowers his ears and creeps up to me, his eyes apologetic, and nudges my chin with his head.

My bristling fur flattens. He licks my muzzle—a fox-kiss. How sweet.

Tavian changes back into a boy. The transformation ripples over him like a wave through water, or wind through a field of grass. Amazing. He crouches, unashamed of his nakedness, and dusts off his hands.

Laughing, breathless, he says, "I haven't played that way in a long time."

I lie there, panting, and stare up at him—focusing on his face.

Tavian cocks his head, a smile in his eyes. "Stuck?"

Of course not. I shove myself into girl form a bit too hard and gasp at the effort. On hands and knees, I try to steady my breathing. Is he looking at me? I peek at him. Nope. I look away just as he steals a glance at me. We laugh and let each other look, trying to be nonchalant but blushing.

"No comments," I say, holding up a hand. "Please."

"Why?" he says in a husky voice. "You're beautiful."

I smirk to mask my desire. "Oh, you only say that *after* I'm naked?"

He laughs, but his eyes stay serious.

My sense of smell remains heightened. He smells of crushed grass and musk. My gaze lingers on the feathery hair between his ear and cheek. I want to touch it, but instead I steal glances at his still-foxy, marmalade eyes.

He flicks his eyebrows upward. "You make a good vixen."

I scoff, flustered, still acutely aware there's nothing but a few feet between us, and we're obviously stark naked. Let's not get that serious, that fast.

"Where are my clothes?" I say, trying to ignore the heat in my face.

"Back there," Tavian says.

I make an impatient huff. "Back where?" The fine hairs on the back of my neck prickle. I fold my arms tight, unease twisting in my stomach.

He cocks his head. "What's wrong?"

"I ... do you feel like somebody's watching us?"

Tavian glances around in sharp, swift movements.

"Do you see anything?" I whisper.

He shakes his head. "You?"

"No. But this was a bad idea. There's still a murderer on the loose, looking for Others."

His eyes darken to black, and his teeth shrink to human bluntness. "Gwen..."

"What?"

"I really don't think he's going to take us out downtown, in broad daylight."

I'm still embarrassed, and can't look at him. "Okay. So you think I'm paranoid."

"I didn't say that. You just don't need to be so defensive."

"I have good reason to be defensive, okay?"

I stalk away from him and find my clothes in the grass. As I yank them on, he gets dressed more slowly, his eyes reluctant.

"Hey." He lays his hand against my cheek. "Gwen."

The way he looks at me makes me melt. I don't even have to ask—I know he cares about me, and I care about him. Why am I shoving him away? I lean in for a kiss. When our lips meet, I sigh, the knot in my chest unraveling.

Electronic beeps interrupt us, and he checks his watch.

I exhale slowly. "Lunch break's over?"

"Yeah," Tavian says. "I have to get back to work."

I nod and kiss him again, letting it fill me with enough warmth to last through cold stretches of loneliness.

"Walk back with me?" he asks.

"Sure."

Tavian and I walk hand-in-hand down Main Street. I see a guy with a blond ponytail looking into an antique-shop window... Zack.

twenty

"Oh, bollocks," I whisper. My face heats, though my hands feel cold.

"What is it?" Tavian says.

"Just keep walking." I quicken my pace.

Zack turns around. "Gwen!"

I pretend not to hear, but furtively try to wriggle out of Tavian's grasp. He won't let go.

Zack jogs over. "Hey." Emotions tangle in his eyes. He presses his lips together, frowns, then tries a hopeful smile.

I grit my teeth. "Hey."

"Who's this?" Zack says to Tavian.

"Tavian," I say quickly. "Goodbye."

I try to drag Tavian along, but he won't budge. Jeez, he's strong for five foot four.

"Is this your ex?" Tavian says, excessively loud.

"Yeah, I am." Zack sizes up Tavian, who's so much shorter it's not even funny. "You?"

"Her boyfriend," Tavian says.

Part of me gets a thrill from hearing him say that so possessively. The other part of me wants to smack him, for the same reason.

Zack's eyes betray a deep hurt.

"Zack…" I say. "I…"

He smiles thinly. "I never expected this from you, Gwen."

"What's that supposed to mean?"

Zack can't keep up his smile. "That you would move on so fast."

"Hey," Tavian says, stepping between us. "We don't need your drama. Go audition for a soap opera or something."

"Drama?" Zack's eyes lock on mine. "What did you tell him?"

"What happened," I say, dread weighting my stomach.

"Everything?"

I shrug. "Define everything."

"For your information," Tavian says to Zack, "Gwen's going through a lot right now. She doesn't need you making her feel worse."

"I can speak for myself," I say, irritated at being referred to in the third person.

Tavian steps aside with a wave of his arm, as if ushering me to take the stage.

"Zack," I say. "I thought it was over between us. Nothing left."

"I needed time to think." Zack looks away, straightening his sleeves and the collar of his shirt. "You didn't even give me another chance."

Tavian rolls his eyes. "Lame."

"Shut up," Zack says.

Tavian laughs. "Make me."

"Screw you."

Jealousy crackles between them.

Zack stares over Tavian's head. "Gwen, I keep thinking about you."

I fortress my feelings with snarkiness. "Really? Then why didn't you do anything?"

"That's not—"

I slice the air with my hand to shush him. "I don't want to keep talking about this. It's too late, Zack. You should have been here sooner."

From the look on his face, my words have hit him like barbs. But he says nothing.

"I'm sorry." I clench my jaw and force myself to stay calm. "Goodbye."

Tavian clasps my hand, but I slip away and stride down the street alone. He jogs after me and catches up easily. "You're not totally over him, are you?"

Now he's angry, too. Wonderful.

"You still care about him?" Tavian asks. "Even after everything he's done to you?"

"For heaven's sake," I say. "We dated for over a year. He was my first boyfriend."

Tavian presses his lips into a thin line. Outside Slightly

Foxed Books he tries to kiss me goodbye, but I turn away and he bumps my cheek.

"Sorry," I mutter. "I'm just not in the mood anymore."

"Okay." Tavian sighs. "Bye." He lets the door to the bookstore slam behind him.

I grimace, a headache thumping against my skull. When I get home, I slam the front door so hard it makes even me wince. I prowl into the kitchen, swipe an apple, and retreat to my bedroom lair. Why do guys have to be so infuriating? I wish they came with instruction manuals. Or maybe I need an instruction manual for myself.

Later that day, I get an email from Zack.

Oh, *now* he wants to talk, after he sees me with Tavian? I'm tempted to delete the email, but I read it anyway.

> Dear Gwen,
>
> I started reading about pookas, but I don't know what to believe any more. Tell me if any of this is true. Pookas are malicious or mischievous shapeshifting spirits. They vandalize crops and homes. They become black horses and carry riders into ditches and bogs, even over cliffs. Or pookas drown riders, tear them to pieces. I didn't read anything about female pookas, or pookas that seduce humans. I hope you will reply.
>
> Best,
> Zack

P.S. My condolences. I didn't know Chloe as well as you, but she will be missed.

His email sounds so formal that I clench my jaw. My fingers rattle the keyboard.

Dear Zack,

Pookas do NOT kill people. Don't think that for a minute. You're mixing us up with kelpies. Also, I'm only half pooka. I have no idea what my pooka dad did in Wales, but I have never dumped anyone in a ditch or a bog. Pookas aren't supposed to seduce people, if you believe the stories. My mum and dad had a fling. People do that. I'm laughing if you think I seduce guys. You know me better than that.

Gwen

P.S. Thanks for the condolences.

All too soon, I have a reply. I almost don't want to open it.

Dear Gwen,

Thank you for answering my questions. I wasn't sure I could believe most of the things I read about pookas. The Internet is full of misinformation. I asked my parents, but they don't know anything. The Bible certainly doesn't mention pookas, either.

Confused,
Zack

P.S. I can't say that I love you because I don't want to lie to you. You deserve honesty. But I hate seeing you with another guy. Even if you're Other, even if it's impossible between us, it drives me crazy.

Tears sting my eyes. He thinks *he's* confused? Why does he say he doesn't love me if he hates seeing me with another guy? If he keeps thinking of me every day? I shouldn't have replied. Before I do something else stupid, I turn off my computer and curl on my bed. Emotions tumble over each other inside me. It's so hard to forget the guy who gave you your first kiss, and who you gave your virginity to.

I feel like a horrible traitor to Tavian for thinking of Zack, and to Zack for dating Tavian.

"Gwen!" Mum calls. "Come see the news!"

I jog downstairs.

On the TV, it's Ms. Fakey Blonde yet again. "...On suspicion of murder. This follows investigations into the deaths of Chloe Amabilis, Orrin Quigley, and several other victims. Police made the arrest based on circumstantial evidence, including eyewitness testimony that Lowell was seen at the crime scenes."

"What?" I say. "Lowell?" My brain isn't working fast enough.

Ms. Fakey Blonde adds, "It has also been verified that Lowell suffers from lycanthropy, better known as the were-wolf disease."

They show police leading a man, handcuffed and in an orange jumpsuit, down a sterile white hall. He shuffles past, his shaggy head bowed, then glances up at the camera. Feral rage simmers in his eyes.

I gasp. "Randall!"

My heart's torn between sinking and soaring. Is Chloe's killer really behind bars?

"Whoa," Dad says. "He's got that killer look."

Randall does look like a criminal, unshaved and unsettling.

"*And* he's a werewolf," Megan says, sounding smugly knowledgeable.

"So?" I say.

"What do you mean, so?"

I frown at her. "'Werewolf' doesn't automatically equal 'evil incarnate.'"

Megan cocks her head. "Why are you suddenly on their side? I thought you hated them."

"I'm not on anybody's side," I say. "There *are* no sides. Do you think we're all members of Team Other or something? No. Everybody keeps fighting with everybody else, and it's up to the prejudiced, incompetent police to catch the murderer."

"Gwen!" Mum startles me, standing right behind me. "Keep your voice down."

I open my mouth to reply, but decide it's not even worth it. I skulk upstairs and sit on my computer chair, swiveling around, then notice an IM window is open on my screen.

FoxFire88: Hey, Gwen.
FoxFire88: You there?
FoxFire88: Guess you're busy...

I quickly type a reply.

r3dgw3n: Sorry, I was away. Still there?
FoxFire88: Yes.

r3dgw3n: Did you see the news? Randall got arrested!!!

FoxFire88: Yeah! Crazy.

FoxFire88: You know how you thought someone was watching us at Wilding Park? Maybe it was your ex, but I've been having that feeling more and more lately.

r3dgw3n: Really? Like what?

FoxFire88: Like someone's keeping an eye on me, maybe following me.

r3dgw3n: Be careful!!

r3dgw3n: My friend Chloe also thought somebody was watching her, and then…

FoxFire88: Maybe I'm just being paranoid.

r3dgw3n: That's what Chloe said.

r3dgw3n: You think it really was Randall?

FoxFire88: I hope so. Then all of this will be over.

r3dgw3n: Yeah.

r3dgw3n: Okay. Switching topics.

FoxFire88: Go for it.

r3dgw3n: I'm sorry about this afternoon. I really didn't expect my ex to show up.

FoxFire88: It's cool.

r3dgw3n: I hadn't heard anything from Zack for a while, so when he just popped up and said he still thinks of me, I was totally thrown off.

FoxFire88: I understand.

FoxFire88: Is he still bothering you?

r3dgw3n: He emailed.

FoxFire88: What did he say?

r3dgw3n: Just asked some questions about pookas. Said he was confused.

FoxFire88: He sounds like he has major issues. You should avoid him.

r3dgw3n: Agreed.

r3dgw3n: Don't worry, you're a lot higher on my list than him right now.

FoxFire88: You have a list!?

r3dgw3n: lol
FoxFire88: I hope I'm number one. ^_^
r3dgw3n: lol, yes.
r3dgw3n: Well, it's getting late. I should go to bed.
FoxFire88: Sweet dreams, Gwen. ---,--'---@
r3dgw3n: Let me guess. A silver rose?
FoxFire88: ^_^
FoxFire88: Most certainly.
r3dgw3n: <3
r3dgw3n: Night!
r3dgw3n went away.

When I get another letter from Maris, I stare at it for a full minute.

> *Gwen pleas write to me. The Bad Man is very very*
> *close and I cant hide very much more. He nows*
> *where you are too. He wants to hurt you. Next morn-*
> *ing I will wait by the river and the big black tree.*
> *Pleas come and help me.*
>
> *Your freind,*
> *Maris*

I really can't believe this is from Chris or Brock. And Randall is in prison now.

I grab my cell phone and call Tavian. "I got another one. Another letter from Maris. It's the third one, come to think of it."

"Read it to me."

When I do, he doesn't say anything.

"What should we do?" I ask. "We can't ignore this one."

"Do you mean you want to go to Boulder River and meet Maris?"

"Yes. She knows who the Bad Man is."

"Gwen, did it occur to you that this might be a trap?"

"I…" I frown. "Well, even if it is a trap, we'll find out who the murderer really is."

"Hello, Mr. Murderer, my name is Tavian. Would you like to try and kill me?"

I laugh, without humor. "I'm not saying we rush over there recklessly. We're going to have to do this sneakily."

"Sneakily." Tavian sighs. "You're hell-bent on finding him, aren't you?"

"Yes."

"All right. I'm coming, if only to keep you from getting killed. And no, I don't think you're a damsel-in-distress. Crazy, yes."

I snort. "Why, thank you."

I skip breakfast the next morning, my stomach preoccupied by butterflies. I'm halfway out the door when Mum asks me where I'm going. I tell her Tavian and I have a date, and she frowns. My chest tightens at this lie. What if I never get the chance to tell her the truth, because this is the last time I talk to her? No, don't even think like that.

Tavian waits for me at the bottom of my driveway. I climb into his car silently.

"You look tired," he says, and kisses me on the cheek.

"I didn't sleep much last night."

"Me neither."

We say nothing as we drive to Boulder River. The clouds lie flat in the sky, tinged with a pallid yellow. My stomach feels heavy.

"There," I say, pointing through the windshield. "See that tree?"

A charred cedar, struck by lighting, stands crookedly by the riverside, its veiny black boughs stretching across the sky.

"Well," Tavian says. "It's certainly a big black tree."

He pulls over and kills the engine. The dead grass sizzles in the breeze, and mosquitoes whine fitfully through the muggy soup of air.

Tavian locks his car and glances at me. "Ready?"

"Yeah." I wipe my sweaty hands on my jeans.

He takes my hand, and we swish through the grass toward the blackened cedar. The wind gusts harder and I tense, wishing it didn't mask other sounds—like the sound of a killer stalking us, ready to strike—

"Gwen?" Tavian touches my arm. "Are you okay?"

I exhale in a shaky sigh. "Not really. I keep thinking we're going to get ambushed."

He narrows his eyes, his irises flashing orange, and tilts his nose into the air. "I don't smell anyone else here…wait…"

"Wait?" I whisper. "What is it?"

"Come on."

Tavian follows his nose, and I follow him. We reach the base of the cedar. The charred wood gleams dully in the overcast light. The slow, lazy snake of the river, glittering like scales, slithers through trees and muddy banks.

"Something smells weird," Tavian says. "Like … fish? No, not quite."

"Well, we are by a river," I say with a nervous laugh.

"Over here."

He tugs me down the slope to the riverside—me half following, half resisting. This scene seems too familiar to me. When I see a backwater pool glinting beyond the cattails, I freeze. I don't want to go any farther.

"Gwen?"

I shake my head. "No."

Tavian sucks in air, then grimaces. "The smell is close."

"Go ahead of me. Please?"

He hesitates, then nods and lets my hand go. I fold my arms tight, my hands tucked by my sides, and try to breathe only through my mouth. I don't want to smell what Tavian is smelling, because I think I know what it is. I watch him walk toward the cattails, his head held low, then turn my back on the river.

My hand flies to my mouth.

There, against an overhanging tangle of roots, sits a little girl. Her skin looks pale as porcelain, and she's staring at me with forget-me-not blue eyes. Dark curls, speckled with duckweed, hang around her angelically calm face.

"Hey," I say, my voice high, trembling. "You scared me. Are you … Maris?"

The little girl stares at me, unblinking, sightless. I step toward her, then stop.

Oh, shit.

"Tavian?" I call. "Tavian!"

He jogs back to me and covers his mouth with his hand. "That's it. The smell."

"I think it's Maris."

My feet move by themselves, bringing me closer to her body. She's holding a chunky red crayon in one hand. In the other, a folded paper.

"Look at her neck," Tavian murmurs.

I do, though I don't want to. Ugly bruises mark her pale skin. She was strangled.

"What kind of Other is she?" he asks.

I stare at her blue eyes. They look familiar, and so does the silvery sheen to her pale skin.

"Water sprite," I say. "That couple who died … they must have had a daughter."

"Ah." Tavian's face twists. "She's what, five? Six?"

I realize what the paper in her hand must be. "The letter. What does the letter say?"

"Gwen, we should get out of here."

"I want to read the letter."

"Let's go." Tavian tugs on my arm, but I don't budge. "Gwen."

I bend over the girl, over Maris, and grasp the corner of the paper, but it won't come free. I pry apart her icy webbed fingers and unfold the paper. Rather than Maris's childish handwriting, it's chillingly precise.

I read it out loud:

Gwen: You are Other, are you not?

Tavian seizes my arm and drags me away from Maris. I stumble after him, the letter clenched in my hand, my heart thumping a million miles an hour. We zigzag through the grass, my throat burning, my lungs crying for air.

"Slow down!" I gasp.

"He's here," Tavian says. "I smell him."

Terror electrifies my muscles and my feet fly over the ground. They hit pavement, and I see Tavian's car ahead. Yes. We're going to make it. He yanks open the passenger door and pushes me inside. I shut the door as he hurries around the car. I sink low in my seat, clutching my seat belt.

Tavian opens his door, and I ask him—

A gunshot. The world slows down. Another.

Tavian staggers forward, his eyes wide. A scream leaps to my throat, and I barely hold it in. Blood streams from a wound between his lower left ribs.

He's been shot.

twenty-one

"Oh, no," I say, my voice rising uncontrollably. "Oh, no. Tavian, get in the car!"

"I don't think I can drive." He winces and clutches his side. "Ah."

I wrench open my door and leap out of the car. Every muscle in my back tightens, waiting for another bullet. Every second feels like an eternity, and yet what happens next happens in a blur.

I help Tavian into the passenger seat and climb into the driver's side. I slam the door.

Please, no. Please don't let there be another shot.

After three tries, I start the engine and speed onto the road, the gas pedal to the floor. The car rattles over the washboard pavement.

"Gwen," Tavian says. "Slow down."

I glance at him. Blood soaks his shirt—so much blood.

Tavian tilts his head back and clenches his jaw, his face tight. "Oh, man. I didn't think getting shot would hurt this much."

"Put pressure on the wound," I say. "Stop the bleeding."

He nods and clamps a jacket over the wound. I realize the bullet was meant for his heart, but I don't say this out loud.

When he shuts his eyes, my heart just about stops. "Tavian! Say something."

He opens his eyes. "It hurts to talk."

"Then don't talk!"

He half-laughs, then moans. "You just said to."

"Shhh!"

"It's better if I breathe shallowly," he says. "Oh, hell, blood all over the seat."

"Wait." I grab my cell phone. "No service." I grab his. Same problem. "Shit!"

A widening circle of red is soaking through the jacket that he's holding over the wound. I look away. When we reach the main road, I stop and pull out my cell phone again, but it's still not getting any signal. I curse and toss it aside.

Tavian groans. Blood is dribbling from the corner of his mouth. "Damn." He coughs, bringing up more red into the palm of his hand. "Must have gotten me in the lungs," he says, sounding oddly detached.

"Are you okay?"

He smiles weakly. "Yes."

I know he's lying.

"No talking," I say.

Tavian twists his lips in what might be an attempt at a smile. "Yes ma'am."

I try to smile back, but I'm scared as hell. I keep glancing at him as I drive. His teeth are beginning to chatter. His lips look bluish.

"Are you going into shock?" I say, my voice shrill.

Tavian says nothing, his eyes closed. Is he breathing?

"Talk to me!" I cry.

He opens his eyes a crack and rasps, "You said not to."

"Don't *do* that to me." I hit the steering wheel. Maybe if I keep him talking, he'll stay awake and alive. "Did you see who shot you?"

"No."

"How close was he?"

"I don't know." His voice is barely above a whisper. "Gwen."

I glower at the road. "You don't have any idea?"

"Gwen! There's a guy out mowing."

I slam on the brakes. A stout man with a John Deere baseball cap is driving a lawn mower outside his farmhouse.

I wrench open my door. "Hey!" I shout. "Help!"

The man stares straight forward, oblivious.

"Help!" I scream, waving my arms.

The man glances at me, frowns, and shuts down his lawn mower. He pulls off his earmuffs and walks toward me.

"Help," I gasp. "Call 911. He's been shot."

"Who?" says the man.

I run toward the car and yank open the passenger door.

Tavian slumps in his seat, his eyes closed. His sodden, blood-soaked jacket lies on his lap. I check his neck for a pulse—it's there, but fast and erratic.

"Please don't die," I whisper.

The strange man calls 911 on his kitchen telephone, and I kneel by Tavian as he lies bleeding and silent on a couch. Soon an ambulance wails to a stop outside and the paramedics move Tavian into the back. I sit beside him and hold his cool hand. I realize I don't know the man's name, but it's too late.

They wheel Tavian into the ER, his hand slipping limply out of mine. I stand alone at the doors until a woman in purple scrubs asks me if I'm okay; do I need to sit down? I nod my head. She guides me inside to a waiting room where I sit, mute and numb. I blink at the too-bright lights and wrinkle my nose at the smell of disinfectant and death. The woman stops trying to ask questions and leaves.

He could be dying right now. I might never see him again.

I'm shaking uncontrollably, ice in my veins. I fold my arms tight and cross my legs, but it doesn't help. The woman in purple scrubs returns and drapes a hospital blanket over me. I throw it off and march down the hallway where I saw them take Tavian. She holds me back while I fight to free myself.

"I have to see him!" My voice sounds rusty. "He needs me."

She says she's sorry, I can't go in there right now. I sink onto a chair again. She murmurs soothing words I don't listen to.

The hospital doors slide open and an Asian couple comes running inside—a balding man with a trim goatee and a petite woman with steel-gray hair. The woman in scrubs leads them down to Tavian—their son, I realize—and leaves me alone.

The doors slide open again and three police surround me. Officer Sharpe is one of them.

"Hello again, Ms. Williams," she says. "You and trouble seem to go hand-in-hand."

I stare blankly at her, too numb to be afraid.

"We'd like to ask you a few questions. Where were you and Octavian Kimura when he was shot?" Sharpe says, her pen poised over a notepad.

"By Boulder River," I say. "On the side opposite the forest."

"What time, approximately?"

"I don't know. Morning. I don't know when, exactly."

"Did you see who shot him?"

"No."

Sharpe scribbles something. "What were you doing at Boulder River?"

I cross my ankles, stare at the bottoms of my sandals. "We were on a date."

"Anything in particular?"

I meet her gaze. "What do you mean?"

"Did you have anything in particular planned?"

My face heats. "No. Just a date." What does she want? Graphic detail?

Officer Sharpe raises her eyebrows and scribbles something else down. "Did you see any unusual activity in the area?"

I remember Maris, her face so doll-like and calm. How can I leave her there to rot?

"Yes."

"Can you be more specific?"

What should I tell her? How much more can I say before she thinks that I'm a part of these killings? That I'm guilty?

I shake my head. "You need to go there. You need to investigate."

Sharpe's eyebrows descend.

"Gwen!" Mum's voice tugs me to my feet. "Oh, Gwen, are you all right?"

My family hurries through the doors, and I run to meet them. Mum catches me in a hug and squeezes me tight. Dad wraps his arm around my shoulders. Megan hovers nearby, and I glimpse her scared face.

"What happened?" Dad asks.

"Tavian got shot," I say. "I'm okay."

"Shot?" Mum gasps. "By who?"

"I don't know." I glance at the police. "Nobody knows."

"We're working on it," Officer Sharpe says, her tone almost exasperated.

Megan touches my arm. "Is Tavian okay?"

I shake my head. "I don't know."

As if she heard our question, the woman in purple scrubs returns. I read her nametag: Gloria Rivera. Her face is blank—what does that mean?

"You can visit him now," she says to me.

I glance at Mum, and she nods. I follow the woman down a hallway.

Tavian is lying on a bed, hooked up to IVs and a cardiac monitor. There's a tube stuck down his throat to help him breathe. He looks so pale and vulnerable that I want to cry. His mother and father are sitting on either side of him.

Gloria clears her throat. "Ma'am. Sir."

The Kimuras glance at me. Mr. Kimura stands and shakes my hand. "They say that without you, he might not have made it."

Mrs. Kimura's dark eyes glimmer. "What happened?"

"He got shot," I say. "We didn't see who did it."

"Our son has told us a lot about you," Mrs. Kimura says. "Do you love him?"

I blink, startled. "What?"

"Do you?"

I'm not sure what this has to do with anything, but I say, "Yes." I do love him.

Mrs. Kimura gives me a wavering smile. "Good. He needs someone like you. You make him very happy, I can tell."

I hear Dad clearing his throat in the doorway, and Mr.

Kimura walks over to shake his hand, then Mum's and Megan's. They murmur introductions.

Mrs. Kimura keeps looking at me. "He said you were like him. Other."

"I am."

Mrs. Kimura smiles again. "He was so happy when he first told us about you."

I slip to Tavian's side and look down at him. Gingerly, I touch his hand, as if I might wake him. It's still cool.

"He lost a lot of blood," Mrs. Kimura says.

"I know," I say. "I saw."

Mrs. Kimura presses her lips together. "The bullet just missed his heart."

I swallow hard.

Megan creeps up beside me. "What … what was it like?" she says in a timid voice.

"Horrible," I say.

Gloria steps inside. "I'm sorry, but he needs his rest. You can visit again later."

We all shuffle out of the hospital room and down the hallway. I still feel numb. Why am I not crying? Why am I not relieved, or terrified?

I eat dinner mechanically. Input nutrition. Brush teeth. Try to sleep.

Who tried to kill Tavian? It can't be Randall, unless he broke out of jail. And not Brock or Chris either, unless one of them was trying to avenge being bitten by a werewolf in some twisted way. Besides, Chris must still be in the hospital. That leaves…who?

It's hopeless. Any happiness in my life has been shot down. When will it be my turn to die?

I shut my eyes and let sleep carry me away.

I'm an owl flying over a nighttime forest. Werewolves run beneath me, fleeing hunters. Dread fills me, but I'm powerless to change anything. A tall man dressed in camouflage, wearing night-vision goggles, holds a rifle with a laser rangefinder scope. Everything shatters, reforms, and I see a werepuppy in a wolf trap, writhing and yelping. The wolf trap clanks at the end of a thick chain anchored to a tree.

I'm at the hardware store. "I'm looking for some chain," Justin says. "I want extra strong." He takes five yards of chain to the checkout, along with a camouflage poncho, three pairs of thick gloves, a shovel, and an ax.

As I scan the items, I say, "What's all this for, anyway?"

"Speaking of hunting," he says, "is it true that you folks have a werewolf problem?"

Randall looms behind Justin, his eyes burning. "He was just…watching her. I tried to tell her. And then she died."

I'm in the grass by Boulder River. A gunshot—a bullet from a hunting rifle.

I lurch awake, gasping as if surfacing from a deep dive. Realization drenches me like a bucketful of ice water.

Randall wasn't lying about the stranger in the B&B. How could I have been so blind?

Justin's here to exterminate Others.

Stunned, I stare at the ceiling. It can't be true. Would Justin really exterminate people as if they're vermin? I remember his white van with the grotesque cartoon of a dead rat. What did the motto say? I strain to remember; it seems important. *We Get What the Others Leave Behind.* The Others. A cruel pun?

But why would he do this? Zack's words echo in my mind. *"He loved this woman a year or so ago, even brought her to meet his family, but it turned out she was a vampire. I'm still not sure he's over her."*

Of course. Revenge. After being seduced and nearly bitten by an Other, Justin could have decided all Others were evil. The truth—if it is the truth—feels like a weight on my chest. I struggle to breathe. What does Zack know?

I leap from my bed, grab my cell phone, and dial Zack's number. One ring. Two. Three.

On the fourth ring, he picks up. "Hello?" He sounds startled.

"Zack." My voice shakes. "Why is Justin really here?"

He says nothing. I can hear him breathing.

"I saw Justin buying weird things at the hardware store a while ago," I say. "Stuff I don't think an exterminator would need. Also, does he own a pair of night-vision goggles? I thought I saw him wearing some."

"Yes," Zack says. "Justin owns night-vision goggles."

"Really?"

"He bought them from a friend in the Army. He uses them for hunting deer at night."

"Is that what he told you?"

"Yes."

I need to know if I can trust Zack. If he's just pretending to be clueless…

"What haven't you told me?" I say.

"Gwen." Zack sighs. "Can we meet at Wilding Park, tomorrow morning?"

My fear and curiosity battle with each other. "Okay."

Zack and I arrive at opposite ends of Wilding Park, the overcast sky a low gray blanket above us. We're the only ones here today. I squint, trying to see his face. Worries burrow into my heart like worms in an acorn.

He crosses the gap between us. "Gwen."

I lick my dry lips, then find I can't talk. Unsaid words clog my throat.

"Let's find somewhere to sit," he says, so stiffly polite.

I nod and follow him to a bench, but I don't sit or speak. My throat's still too tight. I'm afraid my voice will betray me.

"I have to think how to say this." He runs his fingers through his hair. "Wait."

I breathe slowly through my nose until the ache in my throat doesn't hurt so bad. "Zack." I say it as fast as possible.

"Things are totally screwed up between us, but I just want to say that I'm sorry and I need your help."

He fixes me with a glacial stare. "You don't want my help."

"Why not? And why did you want to meet here?"

He touches his hand to his temple, his fingers shaking a little. "You have no idea how bad this could be."

"I would if you told me."

"I'm not sure I should. Stay out of this, for your own good. Don't try to be a hero."

"You think I'm *trying* to be a hero?" I glare at him, my eyes blazing, as if I can melt away his cold. "You think I'm chasing after a serial killer?"

He grimaces at my words, but I plow on.

"I can't just stop being Other as soon as somebody starts killing them. Don't you think sometimes I wish I wasn't? That I was normal?"

His hard exterior starts to crack. "So you're thinking about…treatment?"

"It's not a disease!"

"You just said you wanted to be normal. God, I'll never understand you."

"Don't you care about me anymore?" My voice shakes.

"Of course I do."

I grit my teeth as a tear slides down my cheek. "Why do you keep saying you still care about me, but you don't love me?"

"Because I can't!" The words explode from him. "I can't love you anymore."

I try very hard not to scream. "Why not?"

The muscles in Zack's jaw tighten. "Are you sure you want to know?"

I'm not sure, but I nod and dry my face with a flick of my hand.

"Promise you won't hate me?" he says.

"How bad is it?"

"Promise?"

"Yes, I promise. Just tell me!"

twenty-two

Zack lowers his voice to barely above a whisper. "The Arringtons have a long history of involvement with the White Knights. I don't know what's still going on—I've never asked. That's why we can't be together."

I stare into his frosty eyes. "The White Knights ... still exist?"

"As far as I know, yes."

Oh, damn. Chloe was right. "Justin ..." I say. "Is he?"

Zack could have been chiseled from granite if it weren't for his glittering eyes.

"Is Justin a White Knight?" I repeat, slower.

"I can't say," Zack says. "I don't know."

I suck in my breath. "Are *you*?"

"No!"

"Justin bought extra-strong chain from the hardware store," I say. "I know that chain ended up on a wolf trap.

And I saw Justin hunting werewolves one night, but I didn't realize it was him until just now. He had night-vision goggles, camouflage, a rifle. And yesterday somebody with a hunting rifle nearly killed Tavian."

Zack recoils. "That guy you were with? He got shot?"

I nod, my throat burning again. "He's Other."

"You shouldn't be seen with Others," he says. "For your own safety."

"Zack!" I cry. "It won't make any difference whether I hide in a closet or wear a big sign that says *Shoot Me, I'm Other.*"

His nostrils flare. "I wasn't joking."

"You have no idea what's going on, do you?"

"Of course I do. We both saw those drowned people. They were Others, weren't they?"

"Yes!" I nearly break into a smile—crazy, I know—at his agreement. "Justin must—"

"No," Zack says. "There's no proof it's him."

"Is he a White Knight?"

"Stop saying that! I don't know, Gwen. You think he told me?"

I'm silent for a moment. "What did you tell him about me?"

"Nothing, I swear." Zack hesitates. "He wasn't around when I told my parents..."

"Are you sure?"

"Are you?" he says, forcefully. "Do you have proof?"

"No, but if you—"

"Gwen." Zack grabs my hand, and his touch surprises me into silence. "Stop."

"Do you really think I'm going to do nothing? Are *you* going to do nothing while your cousin murders Others?"

He says nothing, just watches me get up from the bench.

"It's obviously hopeless," I say. "I'm not going to keep wasting my time on you."

As I walk away, leaving him there, somehow I feel so relieved. I should have severed ties with him much sooner.

"Wait," Zack calls.

I don't stop for him. Why should I?

His footsteps pursue me. "Don't do anything reckless. Please."

"Why do you care?"

"Gwen!" He tugs me to face him. "We can't just go after anyone without proof that they're the murderer. We need evidence."

"We?"

"If it is Justin—and God, I hope not—then let me look. It'll seem much more suspicious if you suddenly start investigating."

Hope sparks to life inside me. "So you're going to help me?"

"I never said I wouldn't."

I exhale in a long sigh. I'm not sure whether I should laugh or cry. Maybe I should hug him—is that off limits now?

"Gwen, I'm sorry." Zack's eyes have softened into pools

of blue. "I can't give you what you deserve, not anymore. Our lives are just so different. Incompatible. Real life isn't some crazy Romeo and Juliet story. They both died, anyway." He closes his eyes. "I don't think I could live with myself if that happened to you."

My heart, clenched tight as a fist, starts opening like a flower. "I think I understand."

We embrace. Not as a couple, but simply as something like friends.

I drive the family car over to the hospital. I go alone, since Mum and Dad are both working, and mull over my thoughts. Rain is pattering on the windshield, and the wipers swish and thump. I pull into the parking garage by the hospital and spiral up to the second level. I park and get onto the elevator, clutching my purse in two hands, staring at the ceiling. I wonder how Tavian's doing. They haven't called today. I hope he's better.

I get lost looking for Tavian's room, but I find it by following the beeping cardiac monitor. He's still sleeping. He looks so peaceful, if I ignore his pallid skin and the dark shadows beneath his eyes. It seems odd to think that he was awake and animated just a day ago. I drag a chair to his bedside and hold his hand.

"Tavian," I murmur, barely above a whisper. "I know you probably can't hear me, but I'm going to talk anyway."

I rub the back of his hand with my thumb. The cardiac monitor is slow and steady.

"I know who must have shot you," I say. "It's all clear to me now."

I keep talking, drawing the words out like poison from a wound. When I'm done, I squeeze his hand. For a moment I hold my breath and hope he'll respond, but he remains silent, sleeping, his hand lifeless.

No. Not lifeless. He's okay, and he'll get better.

I rest my head on the pillow beside him. "I hope you know I love you," I whisper.

I watch the glowing green lines on the monitor moving in zigzagging jumps. My own heartbeat slows to match them. I sigh and lean back in my chair. Now that I've sat down, I don't want to get up. I'm so tired.

I rest my chin on my chest and let my eyelids lower.

After a long time—or maybe a little while, I'm not sure—Tavian walks through the door. Another Tavian, since I'm still holding hands with the one on the bed. I'm stunned into silence. Does he have an identical twin?

This duplicate looks at the Tavian on the bed. "Wow. I look awful."

"Who are you?" I say, my voice shaky.

"It's me, Gwen," he says. "You're dreaming."

"Oh!"

I leap from the chair and run to him, but stop short, afraid I'll shatter the dream if I touch him. He hugs me first, and it feels so real.

"Are you okay?" I say.

Tavian shrugs, his gaze on his body on the bed.

"Are you okay?" I repeat.

He still doesn't answer. In the back of my mind, I'm afraid he's come to say goodbye, or else he's dying and too confused to know it.

"Tavian!" I clutch his arm as if I can keep him from leaving me.

"Sorry," he says. "It's not too often you get to see yourself. Out of body experience." He wiggles his fingers. "Spooky."

I laugh—I'm close to tears.

He looks at me. "I heard what you said."

"You did? Everything?"

He smiles and brushes a curl from my face. "Yes."

Even the part where I said I loved him? I'm a little—no, a lot—scared to ask. Suddenly I wish I hadn't said it. Now that I did, maybe it jinxed things, or maybe he can die peacefully like in the movies.

"Why are you crying?" he asks.

"I was just so scared," I say. "I'm so worried about you. I—"

He stops me with a kiss, before I can tell him again that I love him. I melt in his arms. Maybe nothing needs to be said. It's deeper than words.

Then Tavian pulls back, a crease between his eyebrows, and clutches his chest.

"What is it?"

He shakes his head and opens his mouth to speak...and then I jolt awake, to the sound of the cardiac monitor beeping like crazy.

"No," I chant, "no, no, no. Tavian, don't do this to me."
Terror chills my blood. Nurses and doctors come rushing
into the room. They swarm over him, saying *he needs to go
into surgery, stat.* One of the nurses leads me out. She says
not to worry, the doctors will help him.

"Can I stay?" I ask.

"It might be a while."

"Hours?"

The nurse shrugs.

I can't handle waiting that long, waiting for him to live
or die. I'm crying hard now. Tears blur my eyes, and I trail
my hand down the wall as I leave. I feel listless, adrift. In
the elevator, I force myself to stop crying.

He's going to be okay. They're going to fix whatever's
wrong. He's not going to die.

Maybe if I tell myself that enough times, I'll believe it.

It's raining, gloomy outside. I gulp the exhaust-laden
air as I walk across the parking garage, then cough and
wipe my nose. The screech of distant tires makes me flinch
as I rummage in my purse for the key.

I can't find them. I want to give up.

When I grab a handful of tissues, I find the keys beneath
them. I know that my laugh makes me sound like a mad-
woman. Is this what hysteria feels like? I get into the driver's
seat and jab the key at the ignition. My hand's shaking. I
finally get it in and turn it, again and again, but the engine
won't start. What am I doing wrong?

"Need some help?" says a voice I know.

I look up into dark eyes. "Ben." I exhale. "My car is dead."

Ben wrinkles his forehead. "Do you need a ride home?"

"Yes, please."

I let him guide me out of my car and into a forest-green sedan. I buckle up and dab my eyes with a wad of tissues, trying to look a little less weepy. Ben glances at me out of the corner of his eye, but he doesn't say anything. A slightly sickening mint-gum-and-rotten-banana smell fills his car. I try not to wrinkle my nose.

"Thanks," I mumble.

"Don't worry about it," he says, starting the engine.

Ben backs out of the parking space and drives down the winding spiral ramp of the parking garage. I lean against the cool glass of the window and close my eyes with a shuddering sigh. My tears join the rain trickling down the window. Stop crying, I tell myself. Worrying about Tavian won't change anything. It's up to the doctors now ... there's nothing I can do to save him. I swallow another sob.

"Is it Tavian?" Ben says.

I nod, my throat aching. "How did you know?"

"Zack mentioned it."

Oh. I told him, didn't I ...

"Is it bad?" Ben asks.

"Yeah," I whisper hoarsely.

"Is he ... ?"

I shake my head, glaring at the idea of this. I don't know what I would do if it were true.

"He must be in pain," Ben says, very quietly. He accelerates up a ramp onto a southbound highway. "I'll pray for him."

I'm not sure Tavian would want to be prayed for, but I don't say this to him.

"Wait…" I say. "We're going the wrong way. We need to be going north."

"Oh?"

"Yeah. Klikamuks is the other way."

"Right."

"Take that exit." I point through the windshield. "We can turn around there."

Ben nods.

"Why were you at the hospital, anyway?" I frown. "And whose car is this?"

"I borrowed the car," he says. "Wait a minute, I need to watch traffic."

We take the exit, slow, and stop at an intersection. I try to catch Ben's eye, but he continues to stare straight forward, his face pale and tight. Did something happen to one of the Arringtons? The light goes green.

"What happened?" I say. I don't ask what I'm thinking: *Is someone else in the hospital?*

Ben clenches his jaw and accelerates through the intersection. He doesn't say anything as he drives through the suburbs and enters the trees. The rain thickens into a pelting downpour, and he switches the windshield wipers to a higher speed.

"Tell me." My voice sounds tiny.

Ben turns onto a dirt road and pulls over. Before I can ask what we're doing, he says, "Check the glove compartment for a map."

My heart clenches—it must be bad news if he won't even tell me. I open the glove compartment with sweaty hands, and Ben grabs a black bag from the back seat. He rummages inside it while I shuffle through the papers in the glove compartment.

"I don't see a map," I say.

"Gwen."

I twist in my seat so I can see his face, ready to hear what he says.

Pain stabs my jugular. I gasp and grab my neck, my fingers meeting his and the syringe in his hand. I see hardness in his face, glittering in his eyes.

"Ben?" A scream builds inside me. "What did you do?"

"Shhh." He empties the syringe and lets it clatter on the floor. "Don't fight it."

For an eternity of a moment, I stare at Ben.

And then I realize who he is, and what he is trying to do to me.

I scrabble to unlock the door, my fingers numb. He clamps his hand over my mouth and grabs my arm, surprisingly strong. I try to fight, but my muscles feel sluggish. Darkness edges my vision. What was in that syringe?

"Gwen," he says. "Don't try to move. It will only hurt more."

I bite his hand. He yanks it back, and I shove the door

open, tumbling onto the roadside. Numbness seeps from my neck through my veins. I want to shapeshift, but I can't focus on any one animal. I drag myself to my hands and knees. My limbs buckle and I collapse. A boot nudges me onto my back.

Ben stares down at me, and his dark eyes are the last thing I see.

I'm in a twilight place between waking and sleeping. Everything's soft and shadowy. Blackness cocoons me and I curl inside it, warm and peaceful. If this is death, it isn't nearly as bad as I thought it would be.

"Wake up."

I don't want to. I ignore the voice.

"Gwen." It's Tavian. "You have to wake up."

I try to see him through the blackness, but I'm blind. "Are you okay?" I ask.

"Don't worry about me. Worry about yourself."

I struggle to tear the blackness from my eyes. It tangles around me, suffocating me. I nearly panic, thrashing in it.

"Don't fight it," Tavian says. "Focus."

I remember what it means to be awake, to be alive, to feel sun on my skin. I see a murky red glow—light, filtering through my eyelids. Someone carries me in strong arms. I hear the swish of grass on legs. My eyelids feel leaden, but I manage to pry them open. I see my hair dangling to one side of my face, swinging as he walks—because I know it's a he. Him. Ben.

I make a soft muffled sound of fear.

"Shhh," he whispers. "Don't you worry. It'll all be better soon."

My heart beats against my ribs like a caged bird. I can't move. We're walking in a field. I know what will happen next, but I can't stop it—I'm a paralyzed prophet. Can't do anything.

He lays me on the grass, gently, supporting my head. Maybe he won't kill me—not right away.

Hair has caught on my open lips. Ben brushes it away, his touch almost fatherly. He picks something up. It jingles like it has metal parts, and I smell leather. He fits it around my head and cinches it tight. A bit digs into my mouth, the taste of iron sharp on my tongue. He's bridled me. He knows what I am.

"You won't have to suffer any longer," Ben murmurs.

This is it. I'm going to die. Game over, and there's no reset button. I stare at a dandelion blossoming beside my head, seeing for the first time the beautiful symmetry in its petals. This flower of a weed will outlive me. It seems like such a simple fact—nothing to fear. Calm settles over me like a blanket.

Ben climbs to his feet and stares at me as if admiring his handiwork. "Don't waste time trying to shapeshift," he says. "I injected you with enough anti-transformational drug to paralyze a pack of werewolves."

I watch, floating in a sea of numbness, as he slings a bag off his shoulder. I wonder what could be inside it. The wind rustles grass against grass. With my ear to the ground, I can hear distant footsteps pounding closer. Ben unzips his bag and sorts through it with the calm of a surgeon. He doesn't know someone's coming.

twenty-three

"Gwen!" Birds whirr into the air, startled by the shout. "Gwen! Where are you?"

Zack comes crashing through the grass and stumbles to a halt, breathing hard.

Ben glances at him, then zips his bag and stands up. "Zack."

"What happened?"

Ben pauses. "I found her like this. She—"

"Oh my God." Zack falls to his knees beside me. "Are you okay?"

A tear slides down my nose. I want to tell him what happened, to warn him, but I still can't move. My pooka side also remains paralyzed.

"Zack." Ben touches his brother's shoulder. "Zachary. I know this girl hurt you."

"We need to get help," Zack says. "We..." He glances up at Ben. "What did you say?"

Ben nudges me with his boot. "Gwen is Other."

"I know." Zack frowns. "I told you."

I blink, more tears leaking from my eyes.

Ben crouches beside his brother and slides his arm around Zack's shoulders. "Remember what happened to Justin. This is no different."

"The vampire? But Gwen isn't one of them—"

"They're all the same." Ben looks down at me, his face etched with pity. "Think of all the suffering caused by these unholy creatures."

Zack stares at him as if seeing him for the first time. "What the hell do you mean?"

"Think carefully, Zachary. What I've been doing is God's work."

"What you've—oh God, no. You've been killing them, haven't you? Innocent people?"

"Innocent?" Ben has a mad-dog glint in his eyes. "They're as innocent as thieves, whores, and murderers. But still, we must be merciful."

My heart beats harder, spreading warmth through my veins. I wiggle my fingers and toes.

"Murderers..." Zack's lips move soundlessly. "You're a murderer." He flings his brother's arm off his shoulders.

"Zack. Listen to me. I know this must come as a shock to you—"

"Are you one of them? A White Knight?"

"No. There are no true White Knights anymore." Ben

sighs. "Some, however, still pass on their wisdom. When I went to school up north, I found one of these teachers. He taught me many things, and he can teach you, too."

I fidget on the ground, testing my muscles, stirring my pooka side. It's slow, sluggish, more distant than ever. *Come on. Wake up.*

Zack gapes at his brother. "I don't believe you. You're insane."

Ben flinches as if his words are a splash of boiling water. "Please try to understand."

"Okay." Zack exhales, his face ashy. "I don't understand why you're killing Others."

"Their bodies are corrupt, their souls caged inside. And it's my duty to set them free." Ben's voice quivers with pride. "Justin understands. After his encounter with the vampire bitch, he was glad to help me with my work."

"No." Zack's mouth is a grim line. "You can't do this, Benjamin."

Ben glances heavenward. "Someone has to."

How fast can I shapeshift? Am I strong enough? I moan softly.

"Gwen," Zack says, his voice tight, "hold on. I'm going to get you out of here. It's over."

Ben looks truly pained. "You would betray your own brother?"

"You're not my brother. He would never do this."

"Zachary." Ben tries to touch his arm.

"Get away from me!"

"Fine," Ben says, in an icy smooth tone. "But do you

313

think the police will listen to you? Do you think they give a damn about Others?"

I remember Chloe hanging lifeless from the tree, Maris sitting doll-like and dead, Tavian bleeding in the car. I wrench my body from human to animal—it doesn't matter what kind, so long as it can do serious damage.

Pain rips through me as if I'm shredding muscles, but I can't stop, don't want to. My tattered clothes fall like leaves around me. I black out for a second or two. My vision returns, and I'm now on all fours. A horse, damn it—I wanted a predator. But a horse is the most innate pooka form, and my fury can more than make up for a lack of claws and fangs.

The bit digs into my mouth, tighter but unbroken. Coppery-tasting blood spills onto my tongue.

Zack's eyes widen. Ben also sees and whirls around, pulling a pistol from the bag. I charge him, running straight toward the barrel of his gun. I rear with a fierce whinny and strike out with my hooves. The gun flies from his hand and he crumples, his arms raised in front of his face, almost cowering.

I try to trample him, but he rolls away. I spin and kick with my hind legs. Missed.

Springing to his feet, Ben lunges and grabs my bridle. The bit cuts deep into my tongue and I squeal. Zack wavers, then runs at Ben and punches him. Ben's head snaps to one side. He stumbles, his grip loosening on the bridle. I yank free and swing my head, knocking him to the ground. I bring both front hooves down on him.

Ben cries out as he curls into a ball. "Zack! You have to help me. She's dangerous!"

Stop whining. I'm going to shut you up, you asshole. I'm going to make you wish you never came here. The fierce pleasure of vengeance intoxicates me. I trample him, bite him, pummel him with my hooves.

"Gwen!" Zack shouts.

I flatten my ears, irritated. Ben isn't moving, but I don't want to stop.

Zack grabs my bridle, the bit deepening the wound in my mouth. I rear, yanking him forward then knocking him down. He stares up at me, his eyes wide and bright. I lower my head to his level, my sides quivering, breathing hard, and stick my face in his. I can smell his fear, and I snort—cowardly human.

"It's me," he says softly, his voice level. "Zack."

I shake my head, flatten my ears, and pace back. Why won't he run? It isn't amusing if he won't run. Zack climbs to his feet and slowly approaches me, his hand outstretched. I flare my nostrils and huff in warning.

He seems unwilling to touch me, most likely terrified, but he brings his fingers to my face and strokes between my eyes. My pooka side recoils from this tenderness, leaving my humanity at the front of my mind. With a convulsive shudder, I shapeshift into a girl and fall into his arms. I'm trembling, gasping. My naked skin feels raw.

Zack unbuckles the bridle from my head. I spit out the blood and bring my hand to my mouth.

"It's okay, Gwen," he murmurs. "You're going to be okay now."

"Zack?" It's agonizing to talk, but I do anyway. "Did I hurt you?"

"No," he says. "It's okay."

"I lost it." I shut my eyes and lean against his chest. "I lost control." I see myself as he must see me—a bloodthirsty, demonic Other.

"You did what you had to do."

"I'm sorry," I say. "I'm so sorry."

"Shhh." Zack takes off his coat and drapes it around me. "Are you okay?"

I shake my head. Blood keeps trickling from my mouth. "Benjamin ... ?"

Zack kneels by his brother and checks for a pulse. I can't look directly at Ben's darkening bruises and bloodied face.

"He's alive," Zack says. "He's unconscious." His voice cracks. "My brother ... he's ... how am I going to tell our parents?"

I step toward him, and pain shoots through all of my muscles. I crumple to my knees.

Zack catches me and holds me against him. "Where are you hurt?" he says, an undertone of panic in his voice.

"Everywhere."

"What happened?"

"Shapeshifting—was really hard—and now it all hurts."

Zack strokes my hair with one hand, flips open his cell phone and dials 911 with the other.

"I'm—passing out," I say.

"Hold on, okay?"

I slide from his grasp and lie on the grass. Raindrops dot my face. I shut my eyes.

The paramedics whisk me away in one ambulance, Ben in another. They follow "special paranormal procedures" even though both Zack and I say my Otherness isn't contagious. The worst part—worse than all the needles and stitches— is when my family runs into the hospital and makes me cry. Zack stands at the threshold of my room until I wave him closer. I want him by my side. His eyes glimmer, and he clears his throat a few times as he tells my parents and sister what happened.

"Tavian," I slur, my mouth numbed by painkillers.

"Tavian?" Mum says. "Why ... ? Oh." She glances at Dad, her face tight.

"I heard he's doing okay," Dad says. "He came out of surgery a short while ago."

I shut my eyes for a moment and sigh.

Later, when Zack and I are alone, I scribble on a notepad, *How did you know to come?*

Zack exhales slowly. "I ran into Ben as he was borrowing my parents' car. When I asked him where he was headed, he said he was just going to the grocery store. But he had this really strange look in his eye. So I followed him. When I saw him go to the hospital, and then I saw you get into his car, I knew something was wrong."

I write, *Thank you.*

He takes my hand, then swallows hard. "Tavian. You love him, don't you?"

I nod, even though it saddens me to tell him.

He's silent for a bit. "I hope you're happy," he says, his tone genuine, not spiteful.

I smile and get teary-eyed. I scribble on the notepad, *Find a girl. Make her happy.*

Zack nods, swallows, and looks away.

When the police search Ben's belongings, they find a photo album. They let me look at it because they want me to verify something. On the first page, I find a photo of a woman sitting at the corner of a bar. Beneath her black cowboy hat, she has a pale face with an expression of haughty elegance. In the next photo, she's obviously dead, blood trickling from her open mouth. Fangs glimmer where her canines should be.

I slide the photo from its plastic sleeve. On the back, written in tiny, precise handwriting, I find: *Alexandra Langley. V.* At first I think "V" is the Roman numeral for "five," but a second later I realize it means "vampire."

The vampire Justin fell in love with, no doubt. Was she Ben's first killing?

I swallow hard and turn the page again. It's a strange photo. A man and a girl who look Mexican sit on dusty dirt, coyotes romping around them. On the facing page, there's a row of dead coyotes. Werecoyotes. Justin lives in Texas ... it looks like after Ben killed Alexandra Langley, he went after more Others there.

I flip faster through the pages. Many, many faces I don't recognize. Maybe a dozen pages of werewolves, probably from the Bitterroot Pack. The photos of bullet-shattered skulls and wolf traps make bile rise in my throat. I can only imagine what Winema went through. Then I find the water sprites … Maris … Mr. Quigley … Chloe.

Something squeezes my throat and burdens my chest. I can't breathe right anymore.

On the left page, a photo of Chloe planting seedlings outside her B&B, her lips curved in a smile. On the right page, Chloe lying in the forest with fresh golden blood oozing from her throat, her eyes unseeing.

It doesn't seem real. I can't keep looking at it.

Slowly, I turn the page. I see a photo of Tavian with nothing beside it. I yank it from its sleeve. On the back it says, *Octavian Kimura. ~~Werefox.~~ Kitsune.* My fingers clumsy, I replace the photo and turn the page again.

Me.

I stare at myself. I'm walking through downtown Klikamuks, near Main Street, my eyes distant. I look at the back of the photo. *Gwenhwyfar Williams. ~~Changeling. Half fey.~~ Half pooka.* He even knew how to spell my name. A faint ringing fills my ears, as if an explosion just went off, but I feel utterly numb.

It didn't seem real until now. A serial killer was stalking me all this time.

"Did you or do you know any of these people?" Officer Sharpe asks me.

"Yes," I say. "Tavian. Chloe."

"Octavian Kimura and Chloe Amabilis?"

"Yes. Oh, and Mr. Quigley."

Officer Sharpe nods curtly and takes the album back. "Thank you for your cooperation."

The police finally believe everything I've been saying all along. Sheriff Royle himself struts into the hospital to arrest Ben, though Ben has to stay until he's well enough to travel. He has three broken ribs, a broken nose, and internal bleeding. I cringe when I hear this, but Zack says he deserves it. I'm not sure anybody deserves anything horrible. I don't say this, though, because my mouth hurts too much.

Zack doesn't really tell me what happened when his parents found out about Ben. I know that Mr. Arrington refuses to visit Ben in the hospital, and the last time I saw Mrs. Arrington, she couldn't stop crying. Apparently Justin is now under investigation from the police for aiding a murderer, though it's not clear if he killed anyone.

I try not to think of all the victims, but their faces drift through my dreams.

Megan brings a huge bouquet of wildflowers for me in the morning. She keeps saying how brave I must have been, until I actually feel somewhat proud for what I did. A nurse pops in to say that Tavian's awake.

"Really?" I say, my heart swelling.

"You can visit him," the nurse says. "Would you like to?"

"You didn't need to ask." I smile, then wince.

Megan grabs a handful of poppies from my bouquet. "Come on. Let's bring these."

Tavian's lying in bed, propped up by pillows and flipping through TV channels. When he sees me, he mutes the TV and tosses aside the remote.

"Tavian," I say, and run to hug him. Even though it still hurts to move.

He exhales into my hair. "Gwen."

"I'm so glad you're all right."

When I pull back, he sees Megan in the doorway with the poppies. He smiles. "For me?"

Megan nods and rather timidly approaches his bedside. She crams the poppies into one of the vases already cluttering a table.

"Thank you," Tavian says.

Megan nods and smiles.

"What happened to you, Gwen?" he asks. "I've only heard bits and pieces."

I sigh and sit in a chair. "Megan, help me. I can't talk much."

Megan eagerly takes over the job of telling the story. She makes it sound exciting and heroic, which is what I want Tavian to hear. I don't want him to know how terrified I was, or the thrill I got from attacking Ben.

Finally, she peters out, and we're all quiet.

"Look!" Megan unmutes the TV.

On the local news, it's Randall, being freed from prison. He's even shaggier and more stubbly, but he has a dazzling smile. I bite the inside of my cheek. *I'm sorry, Chloe. You were right, and I shouldn't have doubted you.*

"He's really quite brave," Megan muses. I detect a crush coming on.

I roll my eyes. "Didn't you just think he was a serial killer?"

"I was wrong," Megan says blithely.

Tavian turns off the TV and glances at me. I glance at my sister, who gets the hint.

"I'm going to go look for a vending machine," she says. "See you." She leaves the room. You know, Megan's growing on me as she grows up. I hope.

Tavian meets my gaze, his eyes sharp. "Gwen, not everybody could have done what you did. That took real balls."

"Pfff." I toss my hand. "I don't need balls. Wasn't born with them."

He laughs, then clutches his ribs. "Don't make me laugh."

"Don't make me smile," I say. "It hurts just as bad."

"We're hopeless," he teases. "Two invalids."

I sigh, shake my head, and lean on the pillow next to him.

"Gwen?"

"What?"

Tavian blushes, a rare occurrence. "This is going to sound really cheesy."

I smile despite myself. "What? Say it."

"I hope you know," he whispers, "that I love you, too."

I'll admit, I'm scared of shapeshifting again. Months after leaving the hospital, I still haven't tried it. I lie on my bed one afternoon and watch the last flame-colored leaves drop from the trees. My pooka side remains silent.

A fox hops onto the bed and curls beside me. Tavian.

"Hey," I joke. "No animals on the bed."

He smirks at me in a way only foxes can.

"I'm going to pet you," I say. "You look so cuddly."

Tavian bares his teeth, and I grin. He shapeshifts into a boy and pins me to the bed.

"Take it back," he says, trying not to laugh. "I'm not cuddly."

"Of course not," I say.

I'm very aware of him being naked on my bed, even though it's not the first time. We lie close, our bodies fitting together like puzzle pieces, and I revel in the warmth and safety of his touch. I run my hands over his chest and touch the scar below his heart. He curls his fingers around my hand—he doesn't like me lingering over his scars.

"Why don't you join me?" he murmurs. "We can both be animals on the bed."

I blush red-hot—yes, I still do, even after all this time. "Maybe."

He cocks his head. "You still don't want to shape-shift?"

"I don't know."

I've already told him how I lost control, how I'm afraid of doing it again.

"Gwen," he says, "you were angry. Everybody loses it once in a while."

I sigh. He's told me that before, too.

"I'll tell you when I feel like it," I say.

He shapeshifts back into a fox and rests his head on his paws.

I get out of bed and walk to the bookcase. I glimpse my reflection in the mirror above it—calm, a bit tired, with faint scars at the corners of my lips. My eyes look hazel. Normal. They don't glow like they used to.

"What if that drug Ben gave me ruined me? What if I'll never be the same?"

Tavian's behind me, human again. He curves his hands around my shoulders. "Gwen."

I have nothing more to say. I look down at the folio of botanical prints on the top of the bookcase—the one Chloe bought at Slightly Foxed Books, a long yet short time ago. A quiver of sadness touches me, but I'm okay.

I leaf through the book, Tavian standing by my shoulder.

"We should go outside," he says.

"Yes," I murmur. "I want to visit Chloe."

We both bundle up and head for the car. I drive silently to the old church in Klikamuks. We head for Chloe's tombstone. I planted a little tree here, a vine maple seedling. Its reddening leaves shiver in the wind.

"Chloe Amabilis," I whisper. "Dryad."

That's what it says on her tombstone now. I'm not sure who asked to have it added.

"I wonder what happens to kitsune when they die, anyway," Tavian muses. "Reincarnation? Or kitsune heaven?"

"A land of tofu and soymilk," I say.

"Oh yeah!" He laughs. "And vixens."

A couple carrying a picnic basket glances at us as if we shouldn't be laughing in a graveyard. I think people who picnic in graveyards are the creepy ones. I take Tavian's hand and meander away. The couple stops at Chloe's headstone.

"Dryad?" the man says. "I thought they died out."

"This one's dead," the woman says, and she laughs quietly, nervously.

"If she really was Other. I thought dryads are immortal."

I frown, turn around, and walk up to them. They glance at me, surprised.

"Yes," I say. "She was Other. I am, too."

I feel no shame in telling them this. They look more than a little sheepish now, though not afraid. Before they can say anything to ruin the moment, I walk back to Tavian. He raises his eyebrows but makes no comment.

I hold my hand sideways so it slices the wind. "It's a perfect day," I say, "for flying."

Tavian's lips curve into a smile.

We race each other to the forest. He wins, as usual. Laughing, panting, I tug off my clothes and hand them to him.

"Your eyes," he says. "They're glowing again."

"Good. I want them to. I want this."

Clouds flee in the face of the sun, and blue sky reveals itself, bright as hope. With a deep breath, I stretch my arms skyward. As I exhale, they change into wings. I love the sweet ache in my muscles, the swift plunge into the shape of a crow. I love Tavian watching me with wonder on his face. I pump my wings and swing my legs, not sure I'm going to escape gravity's grip, but then I break away and catch a wind under my wings. I flap hard, ascending into the sky, and watch how small everything beneath me becomes.

I feel powerful. Free.

With a caw, I swoop among curlicuing leaves, while Tavian runs beneath me and smiles.